# Save Him

# Save Him

**By William M. Hayes**

Published by William M. Hayes

Edited by Kate Schomaker

Cover by Graphic Design by Pam
www.graphicdesignbypam.com

ISBN: 978-1-0879-8635-7

# Early Praise for Save Him

"...Hayes blends a lethal fusion of science fiction and faith in this gritty, military, science fiction novel."

~ V. Dublado, Readers' Favorite

"…an original story…I thoroughly enjoyed reading…a thriller packed with action, packed with discovery and one that has a nail-biting finale."

~A. Reynolds, Readers' Favorite

"…author very creatively depicted many unimaginable events…made me wonder what he was going to think up next in what I believe is an amazing book… the ending was extremely exciting."

~Team Golfwell Book Reviews

# Acknowledgements

Tom Balderrama and Bob Springett, thank you for your insight. Both of you went above and beyond.

A huge thanks to my editor Kate Schomaker for all the work you had to put into this book—doing it in such a professional manner and with an awesome sense of humor.

Matt DeMazza at *Reedsy*, thank you for the proofread.

Pam Cunningham at *Graphic Design by Pam*, the front and back cover are everything I envisioned.

And Beth Werner from *Author Connections*…I really enjoyed our conversations on how to reach readers with this book. You made the business part of selling a book enjoyable.

# Table of Contents

# Church

The married couple entered the empty church and, hand in hand, walked past the cherrywood pews. Ahead of them, red votive candles burned at either side of the altar.

The man took his time walking ahead. The black T-shirt, black cargo pants, black boots, athletic build, and strong, clean-shaven jawline screamed *military man*. He dropped to his knees in front of the altar, as did his wife, both facing Christ on the cross. The two bowed their heads and prayed. The woman—in her late thirties, curvy, with black hair and light-olive skin—turned toward her husband, touched his wedding band, and slid her index finger back and forth over the ring. She then gently touched the gold crucifix hanging from the chain around his neck.

"He's always looked after you. He will again. I'll be outside." She made the sign of the cross, rose to her feet, and left the church.

The sound of the doors closing behind him made the man lift his head. He stared at the cross once more. Before every mission, he took this time alone to be with Jesus Christ, eyeing each wound carefully. Always the same feeling of sorrow, tinged with anger, surfaced at each nail driven into his Savior. Ray Catlin stood, made the sign of the cross, and walked away.

He was ready.

—

Two hours later, Ray was in the back of a black civilian Humvee driven by a young officer who neither looked at nor spoke to him the entire hour it took to reach the military base. Outside of the twenty-foot chain-link fence around the base, the Humvee and its occupants were searched and their IDs verified before entering. At a helicopter hangar, the Humvee pulled up alongside a pair of wide double doors that were slightly parted. Ray stepped out of the Humvee and slipped through the narrow space the doors provided. Inside the surrounding walls of gray, the hangar was empty of any flying machine owned or operated by the military. In front of Ray, only his boys and girls stood waiting: ten operators clothed in black cargo pants and diverse black combat shirts.

For three years, in some of the most hellish circumstances, Ray had kept them safe. If it came down to their lives or his, he would die for any one of them, just like any good father would.

With the window of opportunity slowly closing on having children with his wife, Kate, Ray felt the members of his unit were his children to protect. It was a feeling formed on their very first mission together. Personality-wise, while they were all different, they were, at their core, connected. Everything different about each individual operator seemed to draw them together, the familial bond growing stronger over the years. And Ray was the proud father.

Ray walked closer and addressed his team.

"We're being flown out tonight to the Genesis lab. We'll prep there for our next mission. We leave in an hour."

# The Genesis Lab

The ten members of Ray's Unit were led by a man dressed entirely in white down a dark tunnel toward a white door. The members of the unit glanced at one another as they moved deeper into the tunnel, the looks they shared illuminated by the only light available—a narrow strip of fluorescent light overhead.

All of them had heard of the lab, as being in this elite unit allowed them access to privileged information. Due to the team's status and responsibility, each member was entitled to information withheld from other select groups in the military.

They were known simply as the Unit, or Unit 10. Their unit did not have a prestigious name like Delta Force or Navy SEALs, although most members came from those parts of the military. The members assembled when missions had to be completed overseas and kept American civilians safe from threats most people weren't even aware existed. Civilians did not want to know about some of these dangers— unless they never wanted to sleep peacefully again.

And now here they were, hidden in the woods of upstate New York. The military lab's rumored projects ranged from a better military boot to body armor that transformed soldiers into walking tanks. There were even whispers of invisibility.

Campfire stories. Military lore told by out-of-the-loop military men and women with a few fragments of real knowledge about the place.

Each member in the Unit had no idea which of the rumored projects actually existed. Yet they had all benefited. The Unit got the new stuff to try out first, though some could argue that they were all just military test dummies.

After being led into a large room, the members of the Unit sat silently on benches attached to long tables, like the ones in high school cafeterias. Everything was sparkling white.

A door opened, and a man walked in, coming to a stop in front of the tables. He was solid, with broad shoulders his black suit could not conceal. Since being reassigned to supervise the Genesis lab, the high-ranking officer was told not to dress in uniform. His blond hair was trimmed short on top and razor-close around the ears and neck. Formidable. But his eyes were inviting, understanding, warm.

As Colonel John Adams looked over the operators in front of him, another man in his early thirties, dressed in a white shirt and khakis, walked into the room followed by Ray, who stood and waited near the door. The man in the white shirt and khakis joined the colonel in front of the tables. Will Stevens, with his hair neatly parted to the side and clothes pressed to perfection, glanced slowly over the Unit in front of him, but not in the same way that the colonel had looked over the group. Will was the man in charge of the Genesis lab and could not hide the look of displeasure on his face.

These were the ones chosen from the best the military had to offer? He was angry to begin with that these operators had special access to information and projects at the lab without his approval. He did not see the men and women gathered in front of him as being close to his intelligence, and they were therefore not worthy of what he had to offer. They were grunts.

How fast things can change. All because of a few projects and their potential. Just a year before, there was only an occasional visit by military hierarchy, mainly to tell him what a great job he was doing here with the scientists he supervised.

He was no longer fully in charge of the facility. He did have his say, although not like before. Once the colonel—who had just the slightest background in science—arrived, the way the lab had been run previously was over. Admittedly, though, they still very much needed him with the new projects. The colonel himself told him to keep pushing the scientists like he always did to achieve their best. He would always be needed to run the facility and oversee the scientists.

It could never fully become the colonel's lab; the man was just not smart enough. Maybe one day there would be an accident at the lab. Maybe one day, the colonel would—

Colonel Adams placed a hand on Will's shoulder.

"You okay there, Will?"

Caught up in his thoughts, Will shook his head as if he had not heard the colonel when he very well had.

"Sorry, sir, what did you say?"

"Are you okay? You look like you're upset or something."

"I am sorry to appear that way. I hope my normal appearance has not offended the talented men and women before me now in any way."

The colonel nodded at Will to follow him, and the two walked out of earshot of the Unit. Colonel Adams was close to ripping into the little prick for his retort with undertones of feeling judged by his physical appearance, when it was Will who had been looking over the Unit as if they were some sort of biological waste. The colonel decided to let it go for now. The two would have a more in-depth conversation later.

"Do me a favor, Will. Try to present yourself in a more positive way than you are doing right now. Okay?"

Colonel Adams got a glimpse of the flat-out contempt in Will's eyes—just a flash—and then it was gone.

"Of course, sir."

The colonel turned and walked away.

That's when Will saw the man from the corner of his eye; he had forgotten about the leader of this elite-of-the-elite special forces unit. Will turned his head slightly and could see the man was not as far behind him as he had thought. Ray Catlin was his name. He knew that much about him—and not much more.

Ray Catlin was looking at Will with a slight smirk that said, I saw how you looked at them, asshole.

Will's stomach let out a sound he hoped only he could hear. A churning in his stomach, his breakfast wanting to be released through one end or the other. Will turned away from Catlin's glare and was able to somewhat suppress the ill feeling he felt. He rushed back toward the Unit as if pleased they were all there.

"Hello, my name is Will Stevens. I run this facility. A facility built with you in mind. I hope the projects we have developed here can aid you in your job to protect us all."

With a quick look over his shoulder, Will could see the colonel and Ray now close together, taking in his upbeat speech to the troops.

The colonel motioned for Will to move to the side so he could take over. As Will stepped away, the colonel and Ray walked over to the tables and stood in front of the Unit. The members of the Unit became divided in their attention. Half faced the colonel and Ray; the other half had their heads tilted toward the man named Will. When the colonel began to speak, they all gave him their full attention.

"You've been gathered together again because of an intended strike to the homeland. Two separate UAVs have captured evidence of a new extremist group in Afghanistan that has been moving what we have been told are, and what appear to be, disassembled surface-to-surface missiles they designed all on their own. Four to six is the number we are getting. Insurgents, recruited to look like your average middle-class Americans, are waiting in the mountains surrounding Kabul and will be the ones smuggling the missiles out somehow. Their plan is to position the missiles within range of US seaports and to attack, showing the world just how vulnerable the nation is. How they intend to maneuver and then launch the missiles is all a mystery. But as of now, the first part of their plan is underway."

The colonel regarded the men and women taking on this mission with the look of a man willing to protect his family at any cost—his family being the citizens of America.

"They have just settled at a new location. The weapons are moved every three weeks like clockwork. You will stop the further transport of the missiles by any means—no quarter for those involved. One of the men traveling with the missiles is believed to be the designer. EOD will take the missiles off your hands, and we'll see what this asshole actually created. The rest of the op will be finding the group waiting on the missiles. Alive if possible. We need to find out exactly how they intended to infiltrate the country by sea and how they planned to launch the SSMs."

Another man entered the room, a white lab coat draped over his thin frame. He appeared upon first impression to be skeletal, weak. However, once he took two steps toward the Unit, his face and body came to life with an explosion of anxious, almost giddy emotions he'd been trying to hold back. A few in the Unit almost laughed out loud at how this guy from the lab seemed so genuinely happy to see them. He sure wasn't like the other dick named Will—that much was clear to the Unit.

The man in the white coat started to reach out to shake hands with the members of the Unit but then quickly stopped. He turned and walked over to Colonel Adams, trying to take on a professional appearance while standing beside the colonel. However, to the Unit, he still seemed giddy as a gamer alone inside a testing room with his favorite console, a stack of unknown new games to test, and a cheese pizza on the way.

The colonel introduced the man.

"Unit 10, meet Rydel Scott. He is the top scientist here at Genesis. In the last three years, he has been the one who has significantly improved the gear that keeps all of you safe."

Rydel looked eagerly at Colonel Adams. The colonel smiled and nodded toward the Unit. Rydel tried to restrain the spring in his step while making his way toward the men and women he so obviously wanted to converse with from the moment he stepped into the room. He stood at the head of the table and let it all come out in a sort of controlled blabbering.

"So…so, how are the new sunglasses and the foot warmers in the cold? How about the I-C helmets—do they meet your standards?"

The operators nodded at Rydel and then turned their attention to Ray, standing off to the side, all saying with their eyes: Um…what the heck is up with this super-excited guy, Ray?

Rydel caught their reaction and met the eyes of the colonel, wanting to know if he should continue with his questions.

"Go on, Rydel. Talk to them."

Rydel moved closer, quickly glancing over the men and women. "How is the skin armor I designed working in the field?" Rydel asked. "Is it too hot? I'm working on that."

Ben, dark skin, hazel eyes—and, although he was seated, you could tell he was an extremely tall man—looked at the men and women around the table, their faces softening toward this scientist trying so hard to impress. Ben turned to Rydel and answered for the group.

"They're a little warm. It's all good. Sal over there"—Ben pointed his thumb at Sal behind him (a thick-bodied guy with longish hair reaching his eyebrows)—"yeah, he took a bullet from a distance that got under the side of his vest. A couple of stitches and he was good to go."

Sal pointed at Rydel. "You invented that? You're a brilliant motherfucker. Thanks, Doc."

"You're welcome," Rydel said, his now soft voice just loud enough to be heard. Rydel's eyes drifted down toward the white floor below him. He was quick to compliment others; however, he was not a man able to receive praise himself, something everyone in the room noticed. After a brief moment, Rydel got that excited look on his face once more and continued.

"I have other projects to protect all of you. Colonel Adams tells me you need my best work here at Genesis for your upcoming mission." Rydel folded his arms across his chest to exude confidence. "I will not disappoint."

—

Two days later, Rydel, Ray, and the members of Ray's Unit stood over a white table inside a white room. On the table, wrapped around a clear plastic stand, an almost transparent, paper-thin-looking balaclava stared up at the group. A tint of blue pulsed randomly through the mask's pinholed, mesh-like material (the mask had no eyeholes or back to it; only the neck wrapped entirely around). No one in the Unit, including Ray, could take their eyes off the odd-looking thing. Rydel's eyes sparkled—he had their attention.

"You want to blend in during the day on your next mission—this will do it. Put one of these masks on, and you will be just like them," Rydel stated.

Out of all in the Unit, Carrie, a slim woman with spiked red hair and sleeve tattoos covering both arms, was the only one able to take her attention away from the pulsing blue mask. "How is that? How will we be just like them?" she asked, staring at Rydel.

With an eager-to-explain look on his face, Rydel continued. "Stealth Imaging. Once you put on this blue-tinted mask, we can alter your appearance from here so that you look like any man or woman in Afghanistan—you can change your appearance multiple times, if need be. We can change your eyes, nose, and skin tone at any time. Dress like the locals to cover your body, and we will do the rest."

Ray finally pulled his attention away from the mask on the table.

"Well, that would be amazing. And something I would really like to see a demonstration of beforehand," Ray said to Rydel with a little skepticism in his voice.

"I can demonstrate Stealth Imaging today, if you would like, sir."

Ray turned to face his second in command, Todd. Having just turned thirty, Todd's full face and shaved head were incongruous with his lean, gangly body. He raised his left eyebrow at Ray, impressed with the scientist, very much wanting to see a demonstration. Ray returned his attention to Rydel.

"Call me Ray, Rydel. We've been going over your projects here all day. Everyone in my Unit calls me Ray; you can do the same."

"Okay, Ray."

Janice, a big, broad woman with full features, patted Rydel on the chest. "Pretty fucking cool, man. If it works."

"It works," Rydel said confidently.

Next to Janice, Adriana smiled, her rolled-up sleeves reaching biceps as chiseled as the rest of her body. "Amazing," Adriana said softly to Rydel.

Four Unit members across the table from Adriana shared the same look; they were unimpressed. Martinez, a stocky Mexican dubbed "Talker" because he barely had more than two words to say during a conversation, just shook his head and turned to Jack. Jack, a man who could pass for actor Edward Norton in his late twenties, whispered something to Kevin, a medium-sized operator with a thin face and premature gray tinting his cropped hair. Kevin shook his head and looked at Steve. Steve looked like a banker dressed in black military fatigues. He had a smirk on his face and seemed to be fighting the urge to laugh.

Not having the same feelings as the four doubters in the Unit, Sal walked over and put a hand on Rydel's shoulder.

"I love you, Doctor G."

"Doctor G? No, my last name is Scott, Sal."

"No, you are Doctor G. You own this Genesis lab. Look at what you invented for us. I love you."

Rydel's eyes stopped blinking, and his body stiffened, not sure how to react to Sal's sudden feelings toward him.

"I really don't know how to respond, Sal. We've known each other for a couple of days. And I do like you very much, but—"

Sal put up his right hand for Rydel to stop talking. "You don't have to love me, G. Just know that I love you. I'm good with that."

"Okay, Sal. Thank you."

Rydel looked over the rest of the Unit staring at him.

"I have other projects that could be beneficial to your next mission." Rydel looked at his watch. "But right now, Mr. Stevens would like to see all of you again about one of his projects."

—

In another stark white room at the lab, Ray and the members of his Unit stood before Will Stevens, who was seated behind a white table. He sat at the table without speaking for a good three minutes, working on a laptop (white as well) in front of him. He looked up from the computer.

"So, no problems with your new Smartround weapons on your last mission out, correct?" Will asked.

Ray and the members of his Unit shook their heads.

"No, I didn't think so. Soon…a Smartround rifle will have backup capabilities if you run out of rounds. Solar-powered rounds. However, that is a novelty for another day."

Will stood up from the table, taking slow, deliberate steps toward the group with his hands folded together in front of him. "All of you have been fitted for a translator and received them this morning. Please put them on now like I showed you."

Ray and his team reached inside their cargo pants pockets and pulled out what appeared to be an oxygen mask with a black round speaker affixed to the front of it. The operators put them on, the masks covering their faces from nose to chin. On either side of the translator was a short hose with a round earbud at the end. Each earbud had a slit up the middle. The black hoses with the earbuds reached their ears with a little slack at each side. Ray and the others squeezed the two halves of the earbuds together on their earlobes, attaching them magnetically. As one, they tapped a button on the side of their translators to turn them on.

Will examined Ray and the members of the Unit, taking his time with his prized project. He returned to the white table and sat down. Will leaned forward, facing Ray, and then briefly looked at each Unit member.

"Three thousand years' worth of spoken language has been stored in your translators. Wherever your missions take you in the world, you will understand the language and be able to speak it as well. When you activate your translator, whatever foreign language it detects before you will unscramble and be understood through your receiver buds. Yes, if there are multiple people speaking in different languages, it might become confusing. Get close to the person or persons of interest and the translation will be clear. It will take a moment for the words you speak to translate. And your words will not overlap, if that is what all of you are thinking right now. Once the translator is in place, only your recorded simulated voice can be heard. If you want to communicate in English, simply turn the translator off or remove it from your mouth and clasp the buds around your neck. I will test them now."

Will chose one of the many languages he was fluent in that he knew Ray and the Unit would not understand. Speaking in French: "Are any in this Unit, including its commander, frightened about their next mission in any way? Don't lie."

It took a moment for what Will had said to translate to Ray and the others and for them to understand. And when the translation came through, the members of the Unit glanced at Ray, looking a little pissed off. With the difficult missions they were assigned to complete, look at this pompous prick in front of them now.

With their translators ready to respond to Will's question, Ray nodded at Todd to answer for both himself and the Unit. Ray was the commander. But to think no one else had a say in this elite group of men and women gathered together would be as stupid as this dumbass with his stupid-ass questions.

All have a say.

Todd took three quick strides and stood before Will. Will looked past him at Ray, puzzled, expecting Ray to answer for the Unit. Todd waved a hand in front of Will's face to get his attention. The response coming from Todd in French was delayed. You could tell that he was talking by the movement at each side of his face and throat. When the words came out, his voice sounded like a computer—understandable, but definitely off-key. It worked, but it sounded like shit.

"The answer to your question," Todd said to Will, "is *yes*. There is fear with every mission out; we are human. We would all be lying if we said no. You, however, get to stay here in this lab and monitor the mission. And that's what gives you the balls to ask such a question. Doesn't it, Mr. Stevens?"

Todd's response translated back to Ray and the others after a few seconds, and they removed their translators, a murmuring laugh coming from most Unit members.

Satisfied, Will stood up from the table and walked toward the door to the room. "Functioning well."

All were quiet, listening to Will's footfalls outside the room fading away. Jack then said aloud how they felt about the man.

"'Functioning well.' What a dick."

—

The next day at the Genesis lab, Rydel stood smiling in front of Ray and the Unit seated around another white table the lab furnished proudly inside yet another nondescript white room.

Rydel stuck out a finger on his right hand.

"What is on the tip of my finger can save lives in the field."

Ray looked over the men and women in his command and then turned back to Rydel.

"That would be great. But you do understand you're giving us the finger right now, don't you?"

Rydel looked down at the tiny chip on the tip of his middle finger. "Oh, yes, I am. That's not the way I planned this out. Sorry." Rydel carefully slid the chip over to his forefinger using the middle finger on his other hand. And then the words poured out of him.

"If a bullet from a point-blank shot gets through your skin armor or you are wounded by an explosive, this chip I'm holding, once implanted, will put a soldier's body on ice until medical help can be reached."

Rydel stepped closer to Ray at the head of the table. "This chip will save soldiers' lives."

Ray looked at Rydel's finger with the chip, not sure what to make of it and definitely not sure if he wanted it implanted inside him after all that Rydel had rambled on about so damn quickly. He got most of what Rydel was talking about from his mile-a-minute mouth. But the man needed to articulate a little bit better before Ray would let this chip be put inside him—or inside anyone in his Unit.

"Yeah…Rydel, you are going to have to explain a little more and speak a bit more slowly before I—or any member of my Unit—have this chip implanted in us."

Rydel reached for a small black box in his lab coat pocket and placed the chip inside. He held up his hands and slowly lowered them in a gesture of understanding, knowing that he needed to slow it down.

"I know, I know. I get excited about the projects I've developed here to keep soldiers like you and the members of your Unit safe."

"You are doing great things here, Rydel," Ray acknowledged. "We all know that. Just slow it down a little, and give us a little more background on this chip you are talking about."

"Shutdown," Rydel calmly said. "Once implanted, the chip inside will monitor a soldier's body. In the event of a near-fatal wound, the chip will slow down all vital organs. The chip, in a way, will put a dying soldier's body on ice until he or she can be evacuated to a field hospital."

With the calm and confident way Rydel spoke, Ray and the Unit waited patiently to hear more. They had all seen what Rydel was talking about in the field too many times. However, Rydel was finished explaining.

"You invented this for us?" Ben asked.

"Yes. That's the bulk of my work here. What I am best at. Trying to protect soldiers any way I can."

There were no more questions from Ray or the others.

—

Later, Ray and his Unit sat at a table eating lunch in one of the two cafeterias located inside the lab that was, yes, white from floor to ceiling.

Janice swiveled her head left and right, taking in the spotless cafeteria. "We should have a food fight and see if the table and walls actually do get stained—or will the stains just dissolve and go away from one of the freak-ass projects they have here?"

"Mind if I join you?"

Ray and the members of his Unit turned to see Rydel holding a tray of food near the far end of the cafeteria, standing in the doorway, waiting for permission to enter.

"Sit your ass down, Doc!" Sal yelled.

Rydel waited to make sure Ray and the rest agreed with Sal's gregarious invitation, and Ray waved Rydel over. Sal slid over to make room at the table, and Rydel sat next to Sal silently for a few seconds before looking at Ben seated across from him.

"Ben…Ben Howard, right?"

Ben looked up from his meatloaf lunch, staring at Rydel. "That's me."

"I just found out your dad, Jacob, trained in special ops out of Maryland with my dad. They would fish together sometimes on leave when I was a kid."

"Yeah, well, maybe they're fishing together now in their retirement. I haven't spoken to the old man in a long time."

"No. My father died in combat while I was in college. I enlisted after that. I was sent here because of my science background."

Ben, along with Ray and the others, fixed their eyes on Rydel. Rydel looked down at his food, pushing around the cornbread and the meatloaf on his plate, realizing everyone at the table was now staring at him. He wanted to stare down at his food until they looked away. This was too much attention coming from all of them at once when not talking about one of his projects. However, to crawl back into a shell around these men and women would be so disrespectful to his father. His father deserved more, deserved to be remembered. Rydel wanted them to know what kind of man his father was. A man not as sought out for such missions and regarded like Ray and the members of his Unit, but a great man.

"He was a wonderful father, a great soldier, protecting Americans and others around the world. I was lucky to have him in my life for nineteen years."

Rydel took two small bites of the meal in front of him and pushed the plate away.

"The food is not very good here at the cafeteria, as you can tell. Can I interest all of you in a well-cooked meal for dinner later this evening?

"Dinner it is, G," Sal shouted, accepting Rydel's invite for himself, Ray, and the others.

—

In a breezy green meadow, the tip of the sun began to slip behind towering trees in the distance while Ray and his Unit followed Rydel. Rydel walked them down a dirt path with knee-high grass at either side. The dirt path led toward a forest, the approaching treetops ahead tinged blood-orange by the sunset. Ray and the others continued to follow Rydel into the forest, disappearing into darkness. The fading sunlight barely filtered through the overhead leaf-thick tree branches, the scent of the forest growing stronger as the group walked on. They made their way out of the other side of the forest five minutes later. In front of them was a row of outdoor benches and tables surrounded by a landscaped meadow. Above the benches and tables, a canopy supported by white metal beams stretched one hundred feet across. The large canopy puffed up and down in the wind as if taking in and letting out a calming breath.

Trees circled the entire meadow, giving the area a feeling of an island paradise just being discovered after stepping out from the forest. The benches and tables were sparkling white. Centered about twenty feet away from the canopy was a red brick-faced fire pit reaching ten feet across. Two large white refrigerators were sunk into the brick pit at either side. The refrigerators and the unlit lights inside the canopy were powered by a white shed covered in solar panels in the distance. Having led Ray and his Unit to this hidden sanctuary, Rydel turned around to face them all before he reached the benches.

"This is one of the getaways for the workers to unwind when we have the time. Nice, isn't it?" Rydel asked Ray and the others.

Ray and the rest all shared the same opinion: it was awesome—a beautiful, tranquil place. Sal got a look at the fire pit and pointed at it. "Holy shit, look—something not sparkling white that the people here are so anal about. Look everybody—it's the color red!"

Rydel glanced toward the fire pit behind him and turned back to Sal. "Yes, we are a little anal about our cleanliness here. Aren't we, Sal?"

"Just a little."

"The refrigerators are full of beers, burgers, chicken breasts, steaks, and other refreshments. I grill a mean steak if anyone is interested," Rydel was proud to say.

"Well, Doctor G, I drink a mean beer," Sal was proud to divulge as well. "So let's get things started. Light up that big red fucker."

—

Night had fallen. Plates with nothing but bones from T-bone steaks lined the long bench behind Rydel, Ray, and the members of the Unit. All had a beer in hand as they stared at the flames blazing in the pit. Everyone took in the fire for a few minutes without speaking, and then Kevin was the first to start a conversation.

“Rydel, when do you get to leave this place?"

Rydel slightly shrugged at Kevin seated near the end of the bench. "Leaving is not really an option for me anymore with the projects going on here. I have a room that they set up for me. I'm the only permanent resident. Some of the other scientists stay here during the week and fly out to their families on the weekends."

Seated next to Kevin, Janice craned her head around him to get a look at Rydel. "So you never get to leave this place?" Janice asked with a little beer buzz in her voice.

Rydel smiled down at Janice. "On occasion I get time."

Sitting beside Rydel, Carrie leaned in closer. "So I'm guessing you're not married?"

Rydel shook his head.

Janice belched, letting out the aroma of the two T-bone steaks she took down, and then shouted to Rydel from the other end of the bench. "Got a girlfriend here, Rydel?"

Rydel shook his head again. Ray and a few of the others in the Unit could see Rydel was beginning to become embarrassed by the questions. Ray was about to change the subject but wasn't quick enough, as Carrie let out the first thing that came to her mind.

"So, what…do they bring in a girl for you or something? You gotta be, like, seriously horned up."

The comment from Carrie lowered Rydel's head and seemed to put him in a silky-spun cocoon, not responding in any way to Carrie's inquiry.

Steve stood up from the table to get another beer and tried to take some of the attention away from Rydel, seeing that the man was humiliated.

"Wow, real class act there, Carrie. We all go out on long missions. We all cope. Well, except for you, I guess. Like when Sal and I caught you humping your hand in your tent after only three days out last year in Afghanistan."

Carrie gave Steve the finger and looked back at Rydel. "Sorry, didn't mean to offend you there, Rydel. But, shit, he's right. I did get all worked up after only three days out that time because I hadn't seen my boyfriend in, like, two weeks. I *can't imagine* what you're going through, man."

An embarrassing situation started to become worse for Rydel. He tried to reply to Carrie but couldn't. His words got caught in his throat; he was too embarrassed to speak. So Ray stood up from the bench.

"Carrie." Ray's voice was flat and direct as he spoke her name.

Carrie shot up out of her seat at the sound of her name—and because of the way Ray had spoken to her, like it was an order.

"Yes, Ray?"

"Go get another beer."

Carrie walked toward the refrigerators to get a beer without saying another word. With Carrie and her to-the-point conversation out of the way, Adriana stood up from the table and took a seat next to Rydel.

"They do let you out of here, though, don't they?"

"I go out sometimes. It's not like they're keeping me behind bars."

"Got family?" Adriana asked Rydel.

Rydel gave Adriana a thankful smile for her questions, which seemed to be going in a different direction, even if the last question she had just asked opened another topic he was uncomfortable talking about. One not embarrassing, but painful.

"My mother passed away two years ago," Rydel said bluntly and stopped talking. After a few seconds, he straightened up into a proud posture. "I have a sister. She took the path of religion. She is a nun. A beautiful soul."

Carrie made her way back with a beer in her hand, but then she stopped and turned around, walking toward the surrounding forest. "Oh shit, a nun? Guess I'm going to hell for the horned-up remark I made to you, Doc. I'm gonna take a piss in the woods."

"There are lavatories to your left, just up ahead," Rydel yelled out to Carrie.

Carrie held up a hand as she continued to walk away. "No, that's okay, Doc. I just need to pee, not shit." Carrie slipped through the trees in front of her and was gone. Rydel was shocked and amused by Carrie's frankness. He wanted very much to know all about these men and women. However, his social skills were lacking when it came to a person like Carrie saying exactly what she was feeling. People were like that on the outside, but not at the lab. Nobody associated with the lab really spoke about how they felt. All waited before answering a question, choosing their words carefully.

Ray noticed Rydel lost in his thoughts, staring blankly at where Carrie had been before she disappeared into the woods.

"Yeah, Carrie just says it like it is, Rydel. She may cross the line a couple of times, but you'll always know where you stand with her."

Rydel slowly turned his head toward Ray.

"Sorry. I must seem kind of out there to you guys," Rydel said, his eyes on Ray before glancing at the others. "I think the way she says what's on her mind is fantastic. It's just not like that here. Sorry."

"No reason to be sorry, Rydel," Ray said.

"I don't get out that much…as I'm sure you can all tell."

Ray stood and grabbed a split oak log, placed it on top of the fire, and sat back down. It was quiet, only the sounds of crackling wood burning in the fire pit and birds singing their last songs to the night could be heard over a soft breeze rippling along the canopy. Adriana then asked Rydel another question.

"What age did your sister take the vow?"

The question by Adriana seemed to strip away some of the shyness Rydel had when talking about himself.

"Seventeen," Rydel said. "Right after she graduated high school. She just knew."

"That's awesome, Rydel."

"I think so. Every Christmas Eve I visit her in New York City."

All were quiet again, taking in the fire Ray had built up. Martinez stretched his arms toward the sky and looked over at Rydel.

"Anything else to do around here for fun, Rydel?" Martinez asked.

"Yes. With the seclusion and the time away from the outside world, we do have other amenities to help us unwind. There's a basketball court, gym, and three hot tubs located on two levels inside the lab that all of you haven't seen yet."

"Let's go, then," Martinez said, standing up.

Rydel flashed one of his eager-to-please smiles at Martinez. "There's also a fully stocked bar and a pool table."

All in the Unit cheered, ready to seek out the two-level super rec room that Rydel was talking about with a fully stocked bar. All were ready to let go for a little while, as high-fives and fist bumps were shared with one another.

Todd noticed Ray seated stoically, staring at them all. A ripple effect went through the rest of the Unit so fast that the sound of them celebrating cutting loose for a night turned into a moment of silence. Unaware of what was going on around him, Rydel continued to celebrate by himself, with his awkward little fist-pumps pumping in the air.

The abrupt quietness by the rest soon confused Rydel. He looked over the faces of the men and women around him and finally turned his attention toward Ray sitting alone. Ray leaned back, stared at the stars above, and spoke to the members of his Unit.

"We'll enjoy tonight. But tomorrow we start to prep. We are leaving Thursday."

—

Two days later, Rydel entered one of the rooms at the lab that was not white from wall-to-wall to show off its cleanliness—something Will was oh-so adamant about when it came to the lab's appearance. The room had tan walls, a brown floor, and three black tables.

Ray and the members of the Unit stood at the tables, packing their new gear provided by Genesis into black military bags. They all noticed Rydel enter the room and gave him only slight nods.

They were different now. Rydel was almost afraid…it was as if he meant nothing to them after the time they had shared at the lab. He was hurt. He came to wish them all the best. Maybe reminisce with a story or two about their time together, like the fire-pit steaks or playing pool later that night. Rydel flashed back in his mind to Sal singing into his ear the theme song from The Jeffersons for some strange reason, trying to make him miss on the eight ball.

Sal's singing had only made him concentrate that much more, sending the winning ball across the pool table on its way to victory…right-side pocket. Rydel found it funny as hell later recalling Sal singing in a whisper into his ear: Now we're up in the big leagues.

Sal was generations removed from the show, just as Rydel was; however, both had connected with the show through reruns.

Rydel felt he had a bit of a connection with them all (more so with Sal and Ray). But maybe I'm wrong, Rydel thought as he stood in front of Ray and the others. They seemed distant, almost bothered by him being there.

"Sorry to just walk in like this. I—I…I just wanted to say good-bye and good luck. The time we've had here…I feel very close to all of you."

Unresponsive, Ray and the Unit continued to ready themselves for their next mission without even a glance at Rydel. And then it hit Rydel: no matter what kind of friendship he thought he had forged with these people, he should not overstep the line. He was intruding.

Rydel shook his head and turned away, his eyes focused on the floor, knowing he had made a mistake by coming here to wish them all a safe mission. At the door, Adriana and Todd stood guard, making it so Rydel couldn't leave the room. How the heck did they get there so fast without making a sound, Rydel's confused mind asked as his heart pounded inside his chest.

Rydel felt a hand on his shoulder and spun to face Ray standing with the rest of the Unit, all glaring at him.

"Payback."

"Huh?" Rydel squeaked out.

"That's for beating our asses in pool. We're a proud group, Rydel. That ass-kicking was a bitter pill for us to take, you hustler."

The relief on Rydel's face was priceless to the Unit, all laughing and cheering, getting one over on the Doc.

"Okay, you got me. I thought that maybe I crossed the line coming in here to wish you good luck. Thinking we were…"

Rydel was unable to finish what he wanted to say, as the members of Ray's Unit had stopped laughing and cheering. "Thinking we were what, Rydel?" Janice asked.

"Friends."

"We are friends, Rydel," Adriana said, speaking for Ray and the others.

Sal walked over to Rydel and, with both hands, drew Rydel's head closer, kissing him on the forehead. "Fucking love this guy. We'll see you again, Doctor G. Count on it."

—

Colonel John Adams sat behind his desk in his office at the Genesis lab. Two sharp knocks on the office door turned his attention away from the laptop in front of him.

"Come in."

Ray entered the office, closed the door, and stood where he was, looking over the room of burgundy with two framed paintings. On one wall, a painting of a lone soldier walking out of an apocalyptic battlefield set against the dying rays of the sun. Glancing over at the other wall, Ray observed a painting of a blazing fire in the middle of an empty desert.

Behind the desk where the colonel sat, a floor-to-ceiling window splashed sunlight over the room. Outside, armed soldiers patrolled the area.

"I'm guessing that guy Will running the lab doesn't have the best room in the house anymore since you got here, does he, Colonel Adams?" Ray asked as he continued to stare at the desert painting.

"Fuck no."

The colonel stood up from behind his desk and met Ray where he stood, wrapping him in a bear hug. Easing away from the embrace, John smiled at Ray.

"My brother."

"Guess it did pay off to marry the sister of a colonel. Thanks for all the new toys."

"That wasn't me. That would be the general. Dowling knows how important you and the members of your Unit are."

"Really?"

"I might have had Rydel add a couple of things here and there that are still in development but are ready to go for you and your Unit."

"Where the hell have you been for the past few days, man?" Ray asked.

"Yeah, had to get back to Ridge so I could oversee how your mission is playing out. Good to go…good to go."

John stepped closer and put his hands on Ray's shoulders. Ray knew John was worried by the way he said "good to go" and waited for him to say what he really wanted to say.

"Careful, hear me? You come home safe."

# Afghanistan

The thin-clouded half-moon in the sky lit only the tip of the mountaintop, leaving the rest of the mountain in near blackness. A whispering breeze rustled a few loose pebbles on the mountain's precipice. Other than that, nothing moved.

Out of the blackness surrounding the mountain, a hand reached out and settled on moonlit shale. The hand lay unmoving, and then an arm emerged from the dark, fingers digging into pebbles and dirt. Reaching hands started to slip out from the darkness, and from the shadows, Ray's Unit (in their head-to-toe new Genesis gear) slowly crawled into the light of the moon and ascended the narrow tip of the mountain. With Ray leading the way, he quickly motioned for all behind him to stop and stay down. Ray eased himself forward to get a look over at the other side of the mountain.

Below, rudimentary barbed-wire fencing surrounded three lamplit tents in a mobile-looking compound with three dirt-crusted, beaten-up trucks. No one guarded the compound's perimeter. As he stared down, Ray heard the words clearly in his head.

Wrong, too easy. Are we being baited by this crude compound—a way to draw us in and be taken out by explosives? Smartround guns can detect IEDs, but not ones dug deep enough into the ground.

Too easy.

This devastating threat to the nation, deep here in the desert with its half-assed compound, looked and felt wrong. Ray decided he would have to go down alone.

"Todd."

Crawling, Todd joined Ray at his side.

"I have to go down alone."

"You have to what?" Todd quickly replied.

"It can't be this easy. We're being baited."

"Send Sal."

"No. Have Adriana and Steve track me."

Without further discussion, Ray started his descent down the mountain, quickly and quietly.

He made it to the bottom without being blown up, which was a good thing, Ray thought. Ray scanned the ground ahead of him using a slide-out screen on his Smartround gun. He then circled the entire compound on his elbows and knees, taking it all in at ground level with his rifle. The Smartround rifle: black and boxy with a short stock, compartments on each side of the action, a long barrel, and a large muzzle.

Ray finished his recon around the compound's perimeter and confirmed that what was in front of him was exactly what he'd initially thought—a half-assed compound. Crawling, he returned to where he'd started and then stood up, raising his right hand toward the night sky with his middle and ring finger pressed against the palm of his hand.

The Unit crawled down the mountain on their stomachs, taking less than two minutes to join Ray. They stood behind him and waited for orders.

Ray nodded at Carrie.

"The gate."

Carrie ran without a sound toward the compound and stopped alongside the gate leading inside. A sturdy iron lock held two thick wood-framed, chicken-wire doors together. Carrie removed a handheld blowtorch from her cargo pants pocket and melted the lock's shackle, and it fell to the sandy ground. She then held up her left arm with her fist clenched tight, signaling the others.

Ray and the rest of the Unit joined Carrie at the gate. Ray pointed ahead, and the Unit slipped through the gate one by one into the compound. Ray took a few steps to his left into a pocket of darkness and slowly moved his Smartround gun over the compound—the rifle's small screen, sliding out from the side of the weapon, outlined the members of his Unit in blue. Aiming his rifle at one of the tents, a boxed-in image of his Unit shot up toward the top right-hand corner of the screen. Ray scanned the tent with his gun, and a larger image of three men outlined in red flashed on the slide-out screen. Ray spoke into his headset:

"Tent on the left. Three targets. All appear to be sleeping. Weapons leaning by their sides."

Each Unit member received Ray's message.

The Unit approached the three ragged tents set up in the middle of this nowhere desert they found themselves in and lowered their night-vision goggles into place, moving forward with their backs to Ray. The silhouetted Unit closed in on the far tent as Todd pointed at Ben and Steve to enter. Ben reached inside his cargo pants pocket, pulled out his KA-BAR knife, and silently slit a long L-shaped entryway.

The quick cutoff of three men taking their last breath could barely be heard. Ben and Steve slipped out the same way they had entered and met up with Todd, both giving Todd a slight nod.

Todd and the rest hustled back to Ray, who was standing by the edge of the compound.

"Targets down," Todd confirmed.

Ray waved at Kevin and Janice to join up with him. "You two come with me." He then tapped Todd on his shoulder. "Stay here with the rest. Cover us."

Kevin and Janice followed Ray as he led the two back to the tents. The three lifted their Smartround guns and aimed them at the tents, the screens on the side of their guns sliding out. All three tents now appeared to be devoid of any living humans.

Ray stopped, looked over his shoulder at Kevin and Janice, and pointed at one of the tents, the largest of the three. Kevin and Janice jogged toward the tent without making a sound and stood in front of the zip-up entrance, waiting. Ray joined them and eased his way into the tent first.

Inside, the three adjusted the night-vision apparatus strapped to their helmets and quickly searched the spacious, dark tent. After a minute, Ray flipped up his night-vision goggles.

"Janice, light it, right corner," Ray ordered from out of the dark.

Janice, then Kevin, flipped up their goggles as Janice lit up the right side of the tent with her flashlight. Ray took a couple of steps and then stopped. In front of him was a line of disassembled missiles supported by a wooden rack. Next to the wooden rack were tools, along with casings to fit each missile part. Were they still a work in progress laid out like this? Ray thought as he heard Kevin and Janice move closer.

"Fuck," Janice whispered.

Ray wasn't sure why Janice sounded so shocked. Yeah, they looked real. They might work. But how the hell would they know? Surface-to-surface missile authentication was not in any way their forte.

"Move out. Next tent," Ray ordered.

Outside, the three reached the middle tent, entered, and found nothing. Stepping back outside, they reached the last tent. Inside the tent, a lone lantern close to extinguishing trickled a weak flame. Three deceased men, twenty-five, twenty-eight at the most, lay on thin mattresses with their throats recently cut. Janice, Kevin, and Ray performed a sweep of the tent. After a two-minute search, the three began to file out of the tent. Kevin exited first, then Ray. Janice started to make her way out when a sound stopped her. She looked at Ray, who was already looking back inside the tent. He pointed for her to light the tent with her flashlight—then quickly gestured for Janice to kill the light. The two lowered their night-vision goggles.

In the weak light coming from the flickering lantern, the two could see crystal-clear through their goggles that the sand floor was beginning to rise. The sound of pouring sand grew louder in the tent. Ray tapped Janice on her shoulder, and the two slipped outside.

A trapdoor in the floor inside the tent opened and an arm reached out. A man clothed in black started to emerge from an underground wood-framed safe room. Able to make out some images from a simple surveillance camera below, he now could see that the men he traveled with were dead. Their throats undeniably cut. The handsome man with a ducktail beard reached inside his black jacket and slowly left the tent.

Outside, there was nobody to be seen. The man held a grenade in his hand, knowing the soldiers were still here in the compound somewhere. He had only one way to fight them, and that was with the grenade. The compound was just what it appeared to be—primitive. A place going unnoticed until the missiles of his creation could be relocated, which was scheduled to occur only days from now. The missiles had to keep moving at all times. They had been successful in hiding them for over six months and were so close to deployment.

Above all, though, he must survive. The grenade will help do just that. The ones who attacked had to be waiting at the gate, Morteza surmised.

A sudden memory flashed in Morteza's mind. A time when he was a child, running with his younger sisters up one of the looming mountains behind his home, a race to the top they could never finish. And then it came to him, as he felt solace from the memory, his mind and body at peace. He would survive, and this race he had started with so many believers by his side would continue onward and upward.

A war unlike any other was coming. They were an unknown group, unlike the Taliban or ISIS. In no way would credit be taken for their acts until all worldwide targets were hit. Once the vicious attacks were completed, Morteza and his army would grace nations of interest with options—insider agreements the people of the world would never know about.

America, the first target, would not pay. America was to be but a demonstration of power. Once other smaller, wealthy nations were hit—like sheep sent to be slaughtered—they would not know what to do. Powerless, held to ransom. Failure to pay would result in repeated hits until submission, the method of attack never the same. The cause was for one thing, and one thing only—power and riches. Being recognized, feared, and a dominant player on the world stage—albeit behind the scenes—was fine with Morteza and his entrepreneur army.

He found it puzzling at times why others in the world could not also design the weapons he was able to create with such minimal expense, materials, and ease. After a while, he concluded there just really were no more geniuses left in the world.

As if walking on the moon, Morteza took each step in almost slow motion toward the gate leading out of the compound. He stopped walking when a shadow, and then another, crossed over him. He held the grenade up over his head and fixed his eyes on two soldiers in the dark. He was not trained for this. He was the brains, not the brawn. The grenade will save me, Morteza repeated in his head. Escape and design more missiles for the cause. Just get them to back off, and I can run into the desert to the next safe room buried in the ground. There is no way possible they could know the location.

Yes, he had made a mistake, one of the very few in his life. He should not have left the safe room. They may not have found him.

The two soldiers stepped out of the shadows and into the light of the now cloudless moon. Their mouths were covered with what reminded Morteza of a scuba diving regulator—a quick image flashed in his head of scuba diving while vacationing with his parents in Jamaica as a child. He then noticed the eyes of the two soldiers were covered by a type of night-vision goggles he had never seen before.

"Let me go. Right now!" Morteza shouted in Dari to the soldiers in front of him. From what he could make out of the two soldiers and the way they were armed, he assumed they were Americans, so he tried to speak what limited English he knew while sweeping his free arm in the air like a windshield wiper for them to back away.

"Me go. Go me!"

"We understood you the first time. Stop trying to speak English, asshole," Janice replied in Dari, her voice sounding a bit like an old computer. Janice, like some others out on the mission, had decided to test her translator. Language skills were not her strong suit; her Pashto and Dari sucked.

Morteza reached for the grenade pin. Just as he did, his body spun around, and his arm felt like it had caught fire, the grenade falling to the ground somewhere. He fell on his hands and knees with his back to the soldiers. Morteza could see where the grenade had landed in the sand right in front of him. He was able to pull the pin after grabbing the grenade with the hand of his good arm. Looking over his shoulder, he threw it toward the soldiers. He took a bullet to his head, and everything went black.

With the distinct sound of the spoon popping off, the grenade Morteza threw hit the ground in front of Janice. With Kevin by her side, Janice saw the grenade in the sand, and she sprinted away.

Janice ran toward Ray, who suddenly flew past her. She tried to reach out and grab Ray, but he was gone. Turning, she looked back to see Kevin down on the ground where the grenade had landed.

What the fuck?

While trying to figure out what happened to Kevin, Janice felt hands on her shoulders. Todd and Carrie grabbed her from behind and dragged her away. The two, like the rest, had seen Kevin trip and fall to the ground, the laces on Kevin's right boot snagging on a piece of chicken wire in the sand that had broken away from the compound fence.

Ray reached Kevin and put his arms around his shoulders. Disoriented after hitting his head on a rock when he fell, Kevin attempted to get up but couldn't. Ray started to drag him away and then saw the live grenade near Kevin's boot. Kevin looked at Ray and then looked down at the grenade. They were out of time; both of them knew it.

But nothing happened.

Ray got Kevin up to his feet fast, and the two ran, reaching the others. Kevin ripped off his translator and let out a beyond-relieved sigh. Janice ran at the two with her translator dangling around her neck and wrapped Kevin in a hug for unintentionally leaving him the way she did.

"Fuck, I'm sorry, Kevin. I didn't know."

Kevin gently broke away from the embrace with Janice. With his body slightly shaking and his eyes still wide from having a grenade about to rip him apart, he approached Ray, taking each step cautiously, his mind and body still recovering.

Ray gave him a tap on the shoulder.

"A dud. Someone above was looking out for us tonight, Kevin."

Walking away, Ray called out to Todd.

"Todd, call EOD to come pick up their missiles and check on that grenade."

# Camp Constellation

Miles away from the location where the new power-hungry radicals of the world thought they were being so clever to hide their weapons, a military base had recently been established right under their noses, away from any sort of city or homes. Two gray AH-1Z Viper helicopters flew off into the sky—the heavily armed, slim-bodied copters benefiting from a recent upgrade from the Genesis lab: their choppy whisper mode replaced by what sounded like nothing more than a gust of wind outside your bedroom window.

Kevin sat on the ground, leaning against the back of one of the tents, watching the helicopters fade away in the sky without a sound. Recalling what had happened just four hours ago, Kevin rubbed the stubble on his head and face repeatedly.

The sound of shifting sand jerked Kevin's head to his left, and he saw no one. Turning to his right, he saw Ray standing next to one of the tents just ahead.

"You okay there, Kevin?"

Kevin nodded, took a breath, and answered Ray honestly. "I'm a little fucked up with what happened."

Ray walked over and sat down next to Kevin, and the two took in the morning sun rising ahead. Ray reached into his left cargo pants pocket, pulled out two Budweisers and handed one to Kevin.

"We don't go out for another day or two, still tracking the transporters hiding in the mountains. So, I thought you could use one."

Ray could see Kevin's body was trembling.

"You're okay, Kevin, you're all right," Ray said in a calming voice.

The words and tone of Ray's voice seemed to calm Kevin, as he controlled his shaking body somewhat. Kevin clasped down on the back of his neck with both hands and then looked over at Ray holding out the beer.

"I could actually use a whole case after what happened, Ray."

"I've got more."

After taking the beer and putting it up to his lips, Kevin laughed and spit out the small sip he had taken, the beer running over his chin as what Ray had just said registered inside his brain. Kevin stared down at his boots, beer slowly dripping from his face.

"No way…there's no way you could've known that the grenade wouldn't go off. I…"

Kevin tried to speak once more, but nothing came out, only an exhaled breath. He lifted his head to face Ray, staring at him with grateful eyes.

Ray tilted his beer and tapped it against the Budweiser in Kevin's hand. "To another day alive."

"To another day alive, Ray."

# Mountains of Kabul

Two days had passed, and Ray and the members of his Unit were sent back out to finish their mission. They walked in the light of dawn on a rough gravel path precariously close to the edge of the mountain. The mountainside of rock, smooth and flat in places, protruding and jagged in others, the mix of tan- and off-black-colored stones touched by the sunrise.

Ray held out a hand for all in his Unit to come to a stop.

"It's time," Ray said.

Ray and the Unit, clothed in turbans and local garb for authenticity, reached under the loose garments they now wore and removed Stealth Imaging masks—one of Rydel's many projects at the lab. Everyone stared at Ray with unenthusiastic expressions while holding the masks.

Ray was the first to place the mask on. The pulsing blue mask sucked down on every contour of his face, ears, and entire neck. With his blue face, Ray looked over the worried men and women staring back at him and gave them all a thumbs-up. "I'm still breathing. Put them on."

The Unit, having seen a demonstration at Genesis and still unnerved by it, stared at their commanding officer's blue sucked-in face. However, he was still breathing and speaking, so one by one they all started to put the masks on. Adriana, one of the last to place a mask on her face, reached down to her chest for her crucifix beneath her tunic, raised it to her lips, and kissed it. Ray notified Genesis that the masks were in place and their blue faces morphed to resemble the people of the region.

They traveled on.

Ray and his Unit continued up the mountain's winding path for just over two hours. Up ahead, they spotted a man traveling in the same direction on the same narrow passage, the first person Ray and his Unit had encountered. Moving closer to get a better look at him, they could make out the bent-over figure of an old man dressed in baggy black clothing with a narrow, light-brown pack on his back—the top of the pack reaching all the way to his head, and the bottom ending at the back of his knees. Laboriously, at a crawl, the man stomped forward with his left leg and then slowly with his right, fighting the weight on his back and the uphill climb.

Ray pointed for Sal to move in on the old man's left and then pointed for Kevin to pull up along the right side of the old man. The two did so without making a sound, flanking the old man, walking side by side with him. The old man dropped the giant backpack from his shoulders and looked up. His mouth slowly formed into a circle O of surprise as his ocean-blue eyes went back and forth between the two men now alongside him.

"Who are you?" the old man asked Kevin and Sal in Dari.

"Do you need help?" Sal replied in Dari, his language skills excellent.

The old man shook his head and started to reach for his backpack on the ground, getting a hand on it. Kevin shot the old man in the leg with a sedation round from his Smartround rifle—the weapon making a barely audible high-pitched whooshing sound.

Ray and the rest of the Unit, with their altered faces, joined Kevin and Sal by the unconscious old man.

"Scan it for IEDs," Ray ordered Kevin and Sal. The two scanned the long backpack with their Smartround guns. Finished, Sal turned to Ray.

"Clear."

Ray pointed at the backpack with the muzzle of his Smartround gun.

"What's inside?"

Sal opened the pack on the ground and searched its contents.

"Just food. Shitload of naan, some—"

The road began to rip open in a Y-shaped line of explosions making their way toward Ray and the rest of the Unit. They all took cover against the side of the mountain, and the explosions came to a sudden stop. Ray pointed for all to follow as he ran up the blasted, churned-up dirt road, making his way toward a bend in the road only a few yards ahead. Ray stopped just shy of rounding the curve, taking cover against the mountain's rock wall. Todd joined Ray, leaning against the mountain.

Another blast hit the dirt road ahead of Ray and Todd, knocking them back, with Todd falling to the ground. Behind the two, the rest of the Unit had their backs pinned against the mountain's rocky slope and were safe.

Ray reached down and helped Todd to his feet. As his head cleared from the blast, Todd tapped Ray's left shoulder, thanking him with the gesture.

"Ray, you have something sticking out of your shoulder."

Ray suddenly felt the pain that had, until now, been masked by the adrenaline rush of being in combat. A glance at his right shoulder confirmed that a branch had embedded itself in his flesh. He ripped the branch out of his shoulder, and a stream of blood trickled down his chest. Todd reached under Ray's clothing and placed a blue patch on his shoulder, wrapping it in tape.

"I'm good, Todd."

Looking above and ahead, Ray studied the mountain quickly, glanced back to his Unit, and then faced Todd. "Either it was the old man, or it doesn't matter how we appear—we are too close to where they are. We could be overrun now that they know we're here. Call in an air strike. Have them blast the mountain. We'll salvage whatever intel we can get after."

As Todd called in the air strike, three men dressed head-to-toe in black came into sight up ahead and fired on Ray and Todd but missed. One of the men quickly threw a grenade way the hell off its mark, the explosive flying over Ray and Todd. The grenade exploded just as it fell on the dirt road, the mountain absorbing most of the blast. Ray and Todd returned gunfire, taking the three men down with lethal Smartround headshots. The men crumbled to the ground like puppets cut from their strings.

Todd reached under his clothing and took out a pair of binoculars provided by the Genesis lab, strapping them around his head. He ordered a search through the binoculars' headmic, glancing left and right.

Todd spun to face Ray. "We're clear for nine hundred and fifty-six yards. Human movement picks up after that, a gathering with weapons coming our way. Air support, ETA five minutes away, has their location."

Past Todd, Ray could see Janice, in her altered appearance, running toward the two.

"Ray! Martinez and Ben have been hit!"

Ray and Todd ran back to where the rest of the Unit had taken cover. Ben and Martinez lay on the ground under a rocky overhang carved into the mountain—both men had decided to opt out of wearing Rydel's skin armor because of the heat. On her knees, Adriana applied pressure to Ben's shoulder. She quickly glanced up at Ray and Todd as they came into view.

"I think Ben's on ice."

Ray and Todd rushed over to Martinez, who was on the ground and surrounded by the rest of the Unit. Ray could see it right away: a headshot right above Martinez's right temple. Martinez also had a wound on the side of his body, and from what Ray could see, it was most likely from the overthrown grenade that had flown past him and Todd.

Ray dropped to his knees next to Martinez.

Seeing the wounds, Todd bowed his head like the rest of the Unit surrounding Martinez. They all waited silently on Ray, knowing they were safe for the moment.

Ray lowered his head and made the sign of the cross. He reached out to touch Martinez's shoulder, and Martinez's body shuddered in an epileptic-like seizure.

Martinez disappeared.

Ray, Todd, and the rest of the team surrounding the now-empty spot where Martinez had been stared with wide-open eyes. Then they all felt the ground shake—the mountain above erupting into a wall of fire.

The approaching enemy—from Todd's last reading on his strap-on binoculars—was swept up in a fire cloud, half of them turning instantly into ash.

It was over. The mountain above Ray and his Unit glowed in a deep-orange sunburst.

The air strike had burned the entire top of the mountain. Three Viper helicopters circled above, hawk-like, as if searching for prey, making sure the area was clear…and then faded away into the blue sky.

## Rydel Working off the Clock

Rydel worked on one of his laptops inside his off-hours quarters at the Genesis lab, the computer's screen providing the only light inside the room at the late hour. It was almost midnight. He went over his notes, along with statements taken from two high-ranking military officers afflicted with PTSD. After counseling and other medications had come up short, the two men had volunteered to test a new injectable drug developed at Genesis, and they remained symptom-free for what was now nine months. The one-time injection did not eradicate the memories of what had happened during their tours of duty, but the images and thoughts of war no longer continually raged inside each man's mind anymore and were manageable if they did surface. No more dependency on pills like Zoloft and Prazosin when the images of warfare flared up because you forgot to take your meds. The two men now fully functional in society and with loved ones.

Pounding inside his room—loud.

Rydel let out a startled gasp. He rushed to the door to his room, unlocked it, and began to open it slowly. John Adams stood in the doorway. He had a look on his face Rydel had never seen before—the man was worried.

"What's wrong?"

"A malfunction of some kind with Shutdown. We need to get to Afghanistan right now."

"What went wrong—"

"Now, Rydel, let's go. We are on a plane in five minutes."

Rydel looked around his room. "Okay, okay. Do I need to pack supplies for—"

John Adams took three steps closer to Rydel, grabbed him, and pushed Rydel out the door.

"We're leaving, Rydel!"

# Deathbed

After a flight lasting half a day, John and Rydel entered a desert-tan military tent to find Ray waiting, seated at the end of a cot. The tent housed four Marines in the comfortable space. Three cots with mattresses before Ray were empty and neatly made, sheets of gray tucked in tightly at the sides. The only cot disturbed was the one Ray sat on, with the visible shape of someone under the sheets.

John and Rydel reached the cot and waited for Ray to say something. Ray spoke to the two without looking up. "He disappeared right in front of us, and this is where we found him. Had the docs here confirm DOA. After that, I made sure he was not touched. I didn't want him moved. Wanted both of you to see just how we found him."

After letting Ray's words sink in, John and Rydel turned their attention toward the shape in the bed. Ray pulled the sheet back on the cot. John and Rydel stared down at a deceased Martinez.

Ray finally looked up at Rydel.

"What the hell did that chip do?"

"I'm sorry, Ray. I have no idea how this happened. I…"

Members of a medical team made their way inside the tent behind the three and looked at Ray. Ray held up a hand for them to stop.

"Can they take him, Rydel? Is there anything you need to do here?"

Rydel nodded that it would be all right to move Martinez. "An autopsy, a thorough one, will have to be done, lasting days, weeks maybe, depending on what they find…but you can move him now. His family will be upset. They will not be able to bury him for some time—"

"Martinez has no family to speak of," Ray abruptly said, cutting off Rydel. "Only a girlfriend he broke up with. She can wait for now. His real family were the members of the Unit. He spent most of his off time with them back home."

Ray looked back down at the body of Martinez. "Let's just get him home then, Rydel."

"Okay, Ray."

Both John and Rydel could see the pain of loss on Ray's face. With his shoulders hunched over, Ray looked like he had just lost a family member and seemed to be guarding Martinez's body. John met Rydel's eyes and nodded toward the tent's entrance for Rydel to leave. Rydel exited the tent, followed by the medical team, leaving John and Ray alone with Martinez's body.

"You okay, Ray?"

"No, not really."

"I know. I'm sorry. The first one you've lost in your Unit after three years. I understand, Ray."

"No. You do not understand."

Ray stood and walked away. He stopped, shook his head, and then walked back to John. "I'm sorry I said that, John. You've lost people under your command close to you—"

"But not as close as you were to Martinez…and how close you are with the members of your Unit. I know how you feel about them. You're right. I don't understand what you're going through right now."

"There were no survivors of the air strike, as I'm sure you know by now. We salvaged three working laptops from a mountain hideout. One laptop details how they intended to infiltrate and detonate the missiles. Their plan was good…disturbingly ingenious. You'll see when you take a look."

"Okay."

With nothing else to say, the two turned to leave, with Ray out in front. John made sure he was the last to exit the tent and gave a look back at Martinez's body, then slipped outside.

—

Hours later inside the same tent, three men from the base's medical team prepared Martinez's body to be sent back home. Once finished, the three-man team looked behind them, and there was Ray again, standing alongside the next bunk.

"Just give me a minute here alone, and then you can take him," Ray said, glancing at each man after he spoke.

The three left the tent.

Ray took a knee by the side of Martinez's bunk and placed a hand on the fallen operator's forehead. "I'm sorry I failed you, Paul."

Ray stood and turned to walk away. At the tent's entrance, Rydel waited silently for him.

"I'm the one that failed him, Ray."

Ray joined Rydel where he stood and could tell that the man was remorseful, shaken. He grasped Rydel's shoulder and drew him closer. "Hey…Shutdown worked on Ben. He would've died from his wounds if he wasn't put on ice."

Both men glanced back to Martinez's body.

"What happened? What did this to him, Rydel?"

"I don’t know. But I promise you, Ray, I *will* find out."

# The Discovery

Two weeks. That's how long it had been since Rydel had last left his private room at the lab. Rydel himself wasn't quite sure how long it had been. As he woke up, eyes fixed on his computer's screen saver, Rydel realized he was hungry.

Rydel stood and stumble-walked over to a mini refrigerator, grabbed a Dannon yogurt without checking the expiration date, and wandered back to his computer. It was 3:33 p.m. on Sunday. He had been at his desk since almost everyone at the lab left for the weekend—the weekend before Thanksgiving, Rydel remembered. A few of the scientists he worked with had stopped by, wishing him Happy Thanksgiving before leaving the lab. John Adams was the last to say good-bye on Saturday, a concerned look on his face. Even you are permitted to take time, if you want, John had told him. But there was no way Rydel was leaving Genesis. He had to find out what happened to Martinez.

Thoughts of what he had been working on began to crawl back inside Rydel's mind. Fumbling with the yogurt lid, he walked back to get a damn spoon for the thing and stopped, looking like he'd run into an invisible wall.

I wrote a note to myself. The note!

He had been unable to keep his eyes open for more than twenty seconds as he worked, head bobbing up and down. Although dead tired, he was aware enough to be worried about slipping and hitting a wrong key on the keypad and losing everything he'd been working on. He'd known that he needed to stop and rest. And that was when the thought had come to him. As he'd lowered his head and reclined in his chair to close his weary eyes and mind, a flash of insight came to him on what he was overlooking. Rydel wrote down his last thought on what had happened to Martinez on a piece of paper to look at when he woke up. He now remembered writing down a revealing theory but had no clue what that theory was; his mind was still rebooting from waking up.

A piece of paper was tucked under his desk lamp, along with a pen, supporting the lamp haphazardly. Rydel shook his head as to why he would do such a thing. This all-important epiphany note appeared to be hidden from anyone who might see it. He knew he had the lab all to himself. Why be so covertly cautious? Rydel realized his better judgment was taking a beating from lack of sleep as he stared at the note under the lamp. He was now probably doing more damage than good in his attempts to find out what happened to Martinez.

However, he could not shake the feeling of importance regarding the note. Rydel slipped the paper out from its lame hideaway under the lamp and read the seven words he had left for himself. He read them once more and fell to his knees. "My God..."

# Back to Genesis

John had the itch to get back to the lab during drinks before Thanksgiving dinner. He hated feeling eager to get back, especially during a holiday when he was able to be with Kate and Ray. The days they had each year with one another were everything to him. This night was different, though. Rydel was at Genesis, working alone since John had left him Saturday, still trying to figure out what happened to Martinez. He couldn't leave Rydel by himself any longer.

So John kissed his sister good-bye and whispered to Ray where he was going. Outside in his SUV, with a slice of pie and a turkey sandwich Ray had whipped up for Rydel (a turkey sandwich with stuffing, mayonnaise, and cranberry sauce), John started to pull away from the curb outside his sister's home. He tapped on the break, bringing the SUV to a slow stop. Through the home's bay window, John watched as Ray waved his sister away from the table so that he could clean up. Kate kissed Ray on the forehead and took a seat by the fire in the living room.

Having a brother-in-law you get along with so well is pure luck. Knowing that the man married to your sister could disarm, subdue, or kill any intruder (or multiple intruders) entering her household, and at the same time clean up after Thanksgiving dinner, was a pretty awesome and comforting feeling.

He fucking loved the guy.

John grinned at the bay-window scene before him for a few more seconds, eased off the brake, and drove away.

He drove his SUV down a side street off his sister's block, then headed toward the parkway, which he could see through a line of trees outside the passenger's window, the sound of only a few cars whooshing by. The roads were clear; John estimated he would be back at the lab in less than three hours.

And, making great time, he was right. He pulled into the lab's near-empty parking lot in less than two-and-a-half hours. John parked and caught sight of snow starting to fall in the glow of the yellow-lit lamppost above.

"Just in time," John said aloud, grateful to not be driving in an early-season snowstorm that the radio was building up to be a blizzard within the next hour. Out of his SUV, he jogged to the Genesis lab, a seven-story white structure with black windows circling the building like streams of satin ribbon. There were no partitions or spaces in the black glass.

The residents of Masonville all had their ghost stories about the place located in the hills of their small town—a lot of activity with unmarked trucks coming and going during the late hours of the night. It would be the security of the place, however, that was outright scary to most people in town. Arrests had been made for trespassing as far as a mile away from the establishment. That's why, for the most part, people stayed away—far away.

Setup of the research lab in the sleepy little town in upstate New York had been well planned by the military. In the first year after construction, local politicians, inquiring minds, and a few drunks tried to wander onto the property. But not anymore. It was understood by everyone, even the animals, to stay away; it just wasn't worth it.

John approached the lab's tinted black glass entrance door. No key, no voice command, the thick door just parted in the middle, and he walked inside. It closed immediately behind him. There was no chance of anyone or anything being able to slip inside without an entrance chip like the one John had under his skin, authorizing admittance. A mosquito couldn't get in without an implanted chip.

John made his way down a long white hallway with artless walls. He reached a Coke machine at the end of the hallway and tapped the Dasani bar. With his water in hand, he stepped inside an elevator that opened without him having to push a button. He was linked into everything inside the lab. One of Rydel's access-body chips gave John free rein to every room and anything inside the lab.

Out of the elevator, Colonel Adams walked down another long hallway toward Rydel's private room and knocked. Concerned, getting no response, he turned the doorknob and slowly entered.

"Rydel!"

In front of his computer, Rydel lay facedown on the floor, something deep-red trailing from his head and staining the floor.

Blood—he's bleeding.

John ran over to Rydel, fell to his knees, and quickly—but gently—turned Rydel over. Rydel was bleeding, but not much. He had a little cut under his right ear with a piece of metal sticking out of it. His nose was also bleeding. The color of blood on the floor mostly mixed in with the contents of a now-empty energy-drink container beside Rydel. John removed the aluminum tab behind Rydel's ear, which had been causing most of the bleeding, and carefully eased him up against his desk.

"Rydel...hey, hey. Come on, wake up."

John held up his hand and was about to give Rydel a gentle smack to wake him up but then thought better.

How hard did he hit his head on the floor?

After lifting himself to his haunches, John checked Rydel's pulse and listened to his breathing for a good thirty seconds. He stood and looked around for the Dasani water bottle he had been holding just seconds before, spotting it by the door. After retrieving the bottle, John took off his jacket, ripped the sleeve off his white dress shirt, and doused it with water. He knelt back down next to Rydel and gently patted the wet sleeve on Rydel's forehead.

Rydel's eyes popped open with a look of amazement and shock. He reached out for John, grabbing onto his shoulders.

"John—John, you're here!"

"Yeah, easy, Rydel, easy! Shit, you had me fucking worried. What the hell happened?"

"We need to talk, John."

"We *are* talking, Rydel."

"No. We need to talk about what happened to Martinez."

"All right. Just calm down, and let me help you up."

John carefully led Rydel to his office and, once inside, sat Rydel down on a couch across from his desk. Rydel pinched the bridge of his nose to stop the bleeding as John searched for tissues inside his desk. Finding them, he grabbed a handful and rushed back to Rydel. Twisting a few, he inserted the tissues gently inside Rydel's nose.

"It looks like it's slowing. I'm gonna get some ice, and that should do it." As John started to walk away, Rydel's hand clamped down hard on the colonel's arm, bringing him to a stop. Surprised by Rydel's strength, a stunned smile spread across Adams's face. He was about to speak—but Rydel brazenly put up a hand for Colonel Adams to be quiet.

"Stop, I'm fine. Forget the ice. You need to listen to me now. I found something, John. Something that could change everything we do here."

Rydel coughed, and some of the air pushed through his nose, causing the tissues to fall to the ground and the bleeding to start up again. John used what tissues he had left in his hand to clean Rydel up.

"Easy, Rydel. Just take it easy. Whatever you need to tell me can wait. We're not going anywhere tonight. A damn blizzard is moving in, and we're the only two people here in the lab besides security. So relax, man. I'm going to get you some—"

"John—I believe I found a way to go back from what was recovered on Martinez's Shutdown chip."

"A way to go back? Back where, Rydel?"

"I'm not sure yet."

—

Half an hour later, Rydel's nose finally stopped bleeding, and John had replaced his ripped shirt. The two sat side by side on the couch in the colonel's office while Rydel began explaining to John what had happened to Martinez.

Taking a moment to let the colonel process everything he had told him so far, Rydel stood up and threw the bloody tissues into a trash can by the side of the desk. Rydel sat back down and continued his conversation with the colonel about what he had found on the Martinez chip.

"The Shutdown chip that sent Martinez away had a small fragment inside it from the grenade, too small to be seen with the naked eye, causing the chip to malfunction the way it did," Rydel said. "The chip began to search for another way to save Martinez because it was unable to put his body on ice."

Shaking his head, John asked, "Save him how?"

"The Shutdown chip, for some reason I don't understand yet, started to probe into all areas of Martinez's brain and tapped into this ability—an incredible ability we might all have as humans. One that we obviously cannot access at will. A way to…I'm not sure how to say this…the chip found a way to somehow teleport Martinez's body organically—an act of self-defense, I believe. Well, in the case of Martinez it was. The chip used this ability to try to save Martinez."

"The Shutdown chip did what?" John said, barely voicing the words.

Rydel took a moment, his eyes alive with fascination as he stared at John. Leaning in closer, Rydel continued to explain to the colonel what he'd discovered.

"The areas of the brain the chip had time to gain access to were too severely damaged. Therefore, it was only able to recall one image from Martinez. And that was of the camp. The chip sent his deceased body there in present time, unable to do anymore."

"You are so losing me here, Rydel."

Rydel stood up from the couch and got himself a bottled water from a small refrigerator behind the colonel's desk. He became fixated on the bottle of water in his hand, lost in his thoughts, eyes focused on a few tiny air bubbles rising to the top. Rydel returned his attention to where he was now, inside the colonel's office, and smiled at John.

"I believe what the Shutdown chip tried to do was recall any sort of stored long-term memory it could from Martinez and use it to send him back to a time in his past so that Martinez would not be on that mountain where he died. And that way…he would be saved. It was the only solution the altered Shutdown chip could come up with to save an unsavable life. Tapping into Martinez's somewhat still-functioning brain with all its power and complexity, an organ of the body we are still mystified by. The altered chip kept referring to it as Rebegin. I had no idea what to make of it until Sunday. I don't think it would have saved Martinez; his lifeless body would have just traveled back to a time from his past. But maybe…someday…we might be able to save him. Because what we have now is something incredibly different from what I first designed. All because of that grenade fragment causing the malfunction…or maybe a better way of putting it is that it caused the Shutdown chip's incredible progression. Now it could be a way to go back."

John was beginning to understand what Rydel was talking about—and the good it could do for the people he protected. The colonel stood up and stepped closer to Rydel, placing both hands on the scientist's slight shoulders.

"Are you saying what I think you're saying, Rydel? Are you sure?"

"I'm saying I should drop everything else I'm working on here at the lab and work only on the Martinez chip. I think we might have a way to go back to a time of our choosing and potentially correct mistakes we've made in the past."

"Time travel?"

"The beginning of it, I believe. Yes."

"You're right. You now have only one job here at Genesis—working on that chip."

"Oh, shit yes I only have one job here now! It's absolutely amazing, John! Amazing!"

John joined in on Rydel's excitement and smiled a crazy smile—like he had hit the lottery and then won Olympic gold. "Okay, let's take a break before my head implodes. Ray and my sister packed you up a turkey sandwich and some dessert. Eat something, Rydel."

"You brought me Thanksgiving leftovers?"

"I did."

Tears started to stream down each side of Rydel's face. He smiled at John while still crying. And it became apparent to John that the scientist in front of him had *no idea* he was crying.

"Okay, Rydel, easy now. It's just a turkey sandwich and a slice of pie. Why don't you just eat something and rest for a bit."

"Sleep and a turkey sandwich would be nice, John."

"Okay then, let's help you out with that."

"I haven't had a Thanksgiving meal in a long time. A turkey sandwich and…and did you say pie too?"

"I did, Rydel. Pie as well, so come on, now, and let's get you set up."

Yes, Rydel was starting to lose it, John could see it; he had seen it before. Get Rydel rested and treated by the doctors here at the lab, John thought. Because if there was any truth to what Rydel was rambling on about with the Martinez chip, the country and the people he swore to protect could truly sleep in peace.

The two made their way down the hallway outside the colonel's office. Rydel stopped suddenly and placed a hand on John's chest.

"Do you have any idea what we have here, John?"

"I'm starting to have an idea, if everything you told me is true, Rydel."

"It is, John. It's true. It's really true!"

# Fourth of July

Bursting fireworks began to light the deep orange-red sky. This wasn't just your local neighborhood gathering with firecrackers and bottle rockets celebrating the evening—the sky over Ray Catlin's backyard glowed in amazing colors of red, white, and blue. Being in the military had benefits—like the ass-kicking fireworks the Catlins got their hands on to shoot off every Fourth of July. No one within a three-block radius ever missed the display in the sky above the Catlins' home.

After shooting off the fireworks, Ray turned to the large gathering of friends and neighbors in his white-fenced, perfectly landscaped backyard and held up his arms as the cheers around him grew.

"Okay, that's just the first wave. More to come after we have some of the ribs Mike has been cooking in my yard all afternoon. Let's eat!"

The guests of the Catlins' Fourth of July party started to file toward the barbecue pit set deep in the corner of the yard. At the other end of the yard, John Adams, wearing khaki shorts and a black T-shirt that was unable to hide the man's huge shoulders and arms, quickly walked up behind Ray and tugged on his shirt.

"Hey, need to talk to you alone for a second."

"Cool, I need to talk to you alone for a second."

The two started to walk away from the rest. Ray placed an arm of affection over John's shoulders, gazing at him with his beer-induced happy eyes.

"Hey, what do you think of Ashley, John?"

"Huh?"

"My next-door neighbor. I think you met her when you got here, she was just standing over there with Kate."

"She's nice, I guess."

"Nice enough to take out on a date? She hasn't stop looking at you, and she won't stop talking to Kate about you. She's recently divorced. No children, husband went to jail for insider trading. Guy was ass-wrong from the first time I met him, just weird. And he always smelled like cat food every time I talked to him. Ashley, right now, is just waiting for the right guy to come along."

"Are you trying to set me up?"

"Yep."

"Come with me, Ray—please."

John walked Ray out to the front yard and gestured toward a large willow tree on the front lawn. The tree leaned to one side, its branches reaching the ground. At the other side was an opening like something out of a J. R. R. Tolkien book—the limbs parted at the center, revealing the tree's gnarled trunk. John pointed toward the opening between the branches, and the two made their way under the tree to talk privately.

"Rydel discovered something from Martinez's Shutdown chip, Ray. Something we have been developing at Genesis. When the time is right, I'll be able to tell you more—"

Confused, Ray held up his hands for John to stop. "Whoa, whoa. Developing? From the chip? What do you mean?"

"My brother hitting on you again, Ray?"

John and Ray spun around to see Kate standing outside the branches; both men were surprised they hadn't heard her approach.

"Get over it, John. He's mine."

Kate walked through the opening and wrapped her arms around Ray's waist from behind, kissing him on the cheek and then dragging him away.

"Both of you, back to the party, right now. You two are off the clock. Whatever is so important can wait, unless we are going to war."

Ray glanced back at John with a look—Not much I can do here—letting Kate drag him back to the party. John raised a finger and pressed it to his lips. Ray nodded, understanding completely.

## One Year and One Week Later

Colonel John Adams, Rydel, and Will sat at a white oval table inside another ubiquitous white room at the Genesis lab. Rydel had asked the two men to meet him in the room. Time had taken a toll on Rydel, his body now dangerously thin. There was also something with his eyes; they looked eager and at the same time hollow. Rydel held his hands up to his lips as if he were praying and then lowered his hands on the white table before him.

"Placement is ready," Rydel said in a matter-of-fact tone. "We've had two successful times out. Now is the time for Placement to do what it was meant to do."

The colonel clasped his hands behind his head, leaning back in his chair. "Rydel, we didn't change anything in the past. We only traveled back."

"By traveling back, didn't we in some way change the past by us just being there, John? There's really no more testing we can do. It's safe."

Colonel Adams turned in his chair to face Will, seated next to him. "Will, your thoughts here?"

"I agree with Rydel."

Rydel leaned closer to the colonel. "It is time, John."

The colonel stood up.

"I'll talk to the general. If it's a go, we will test it in Japan. I have to be at Blackburn next week. And I'll be one of the ones going out to oversee what we change in the past."

The colonel left the room and was on a private jet twenty minutes later, ready for takeoff.

—

The jet had him in Arizona in less than five hours. When John called the general, the man set aside everything he was working on and told John to meet him ASAP to go over Placement's next stage. The general, like John, knew the day would be approaching soon for Placement to be fully tested. But both had their reservations.

After the jet touched down in Arizona, a tan JLTV truck drove John to the general's location twenty-five minutes away at a military base nestled between twin mountain peaks. Their towering presence gave the appearance they were guarding the base named Mountain Peaks 1776, nicknamed Ridge. With the advanced technology and number of men overlooking Ridge from the twin peaks, that was exactly what the mountains were doing.

General Dowling, a man of medium build with thick gray hair and blue eyes and dressed in uniform, greeted John as he stepped out of the truck.

"John."

"Hey, Lyle."

"Let's take a walk."

After walking just over a mile, the two had made it halfway up one of the guardian mountains before the first word was spoken.

"It's up ahead," the general said.

"What is, Lyle?"

"The only place around here I feel comfortable talking about Placement."

The two walked on for another twenty minutes and reached a mountain cave. Just as they entered the cave, the general held up a hand for John to stop.

"Here is good."

Enough sunlight from outside lit up the cave so the two could still see each other and a little of what was behind them. Standing by the cave's round opening, they were able to see the base below lit by the afternoon sun.

"So Rydel and Will want to change something in the past," the general bluntly said.

John sighed a little. "They do."

"You sound as excited about the idea as I am. Do you think it's time? Has every possible test been done to make sure it's safe, John?"

"Will and Rydel believe they are at the point with Placement where the next step has to be taken. They have nothing left to test. However, I will be going back with two other men. And I'll decide what we will change in the past, making sure it's an obscure moment in time."

General Dowling took a couple of steps away from John and stared down at the base, casually kicking away a few small rocks by his feet. With his back to John, he nodded. "Do it," he said, and began to make his way back to the base below. John followed.

—

By nightfall, six hours later, John was on a jet headed back to Genesis. Looking at the moon outside the private jet's window, John felt he had somehow let the general down with the way he was handling Placement. Lyle was a friend away from the job; they were close. Both felt more testing should be done, but John did not have a valid reason to wait any longer. He had overseen the project for almost two years now. It was time to use it. As for the general having the same feelings about holding off until further testing could be done…it was disconcerting. Everybody else involved with Placement seemed gung-ho for the next step to be taken with the project.

It was a gut feeling both men had. But Rydel was right; it had to be used to its full potential eventually. And the scientists, along with Rydel and Will, were exasperated. There were no more tests to be done. It was time.

# Japan

At the American military base in Japan named Blackburn, a lab was located two levels underground. Inside, techs sat at a black table, each one in front of a computer monitor. Off to the side, behind the lab personnel, Rydel and Will stood staring down at a blank laptop computer screen on a black table of their own. The two waited.

The laptop came to life with individual pulsing red lights appearing on the screen. "They're back. Inside sleeping quarters 19," Will said to Rydel.

A booming sound sent Will and Rydel falling to their knees. The half-dozen lab techs in front of them hit the floor hard, and then they were all in the dark. Above, emergency lighting sputtered on. Another sound, like water inside a washing machine, filled the room, followed by silence.

Rydel and Will were the first to rise from the floor. Rydel looked around at the others to see if anyone was injured.

"Rydel, let's go!" Will screamed.

"Wait, we need to check on the others."

"Now, Rydel!"

Will turned and ran toward the room's twin doors, opened them, and waited for Rydel to join him.

"Move, Rydel."

Rydel reluctantly started to walk toward Will and then stopped.

"No, Will."

Rydel ran back to the other lab techs on the floor and began to check each one, taking in the seriousness of their injuries.

"Rydel, let's go—let's go!" Will shouted, his voice angry and desperate.

Without looking back at Will, Rydel shouted just as intensely. "I can't!"

Three of the lab techs started to rise to their feet, staring blankly at Rydel. Rydel scampered over to the other techs unconscious on the floor. The last tech that he placed his hands on wasn't breathing. Rydel began CPR on the man just as another boom sent the lab into darkness for a few seconds, then the lights returned. Will had seen and had enough. He slipped out of the lab's twin doors and started to make his way to the panic room. Fluorescent lights, flickering off and on, lit his way down the hallway. He turned at the corner, slammed open the door to his right, and ran into John Adams's chest.

Two men stood behind John, eyeing Will. John grabbed Will's arms.

"What the hell's happening outside, Will?"

"I—uh...I don't know."

"You don't know—what the hell do you mean you don't know?"

"The lab got hit by something outside. Some are hurt—"

John sunk his fingers into Will's arms, and the man lowered to the ground from the pain inflicted. "Where's Rydel?"

"Still inside the lab."

John looked over his shoulder at the two men standing behind him. "You two look after him. Take him below—*do not* take your eyes off him."

"Why are you making me out to be the one that did something wrong?" Will meekly asked John.

John motioned for the two men to take Will away—right now. Both men, military-trained with beefy bodies and thick necks, took Will by each arm and led him away. John ran down the hallway and, in under a minute, reached and entered the lab to find Rydel leaning over a lab tech who'd just recently been stationed here. Jay Harold—a fellow New York Giants fan John would talk football with, primarily about how their team was going in the wrong damn direction.

Rydel lifted his head and spotted John out of the corner of his eye. "Heart attack, I believe. He's breathing now, John. But we need to get him proper medical."

# Upstate New York

Rydel and Will sat at a table in one of the Genesis lab's white rooms as John paced back and forth behind them. Printouts took up all the space on the table in front of Rydel and Will. Both men had their eyes fixed on the papers.

John glared down at the two studying the printouts. "That would be the death toll as of yesterday. Before I made it to this room, I was told five more bodies had been recovered. That makes it three thousand and sixty-six lives lost."

The colonel began to snatch up each printout in front of Rydel and Will. The two could see and feel the anger coming off John; they neither moved nor looked up at him as he ripped the printouts away.

"Look what we did by going back and giving a man just one more minute to live."

Finally, Rydel had the courage to speak up for himself, and for Will, on their decision to test Placement the way the two had agreed it needed to be tested.

"I pray for the souls of the tsunami victims each day, John. But Placement had nothing to do with what happened. Placement is meant to save lives. I know it."

"That's what we thought when you first discovered it, Rydel. But not now."

"The tsunami was nothing more than a coincidence."

"Coincidence? It hit at the exact second we returned from the past. Without any sort of warning. I think that's a little bit more than a fucking coincidence!" John walked over to where Will was seated and stood over him.

"Anything to add, Will? Anything at all?"

"Maybe another mission out. We can—"

"No! No more! The general has shut down that part of the program. No further missions out until we are certain that changing the past had nothing to do with this disaster killing thousands. And just let me repeat that to the both of you—thousands. Thousands of lives were lost."

Will leaned on the conference table with a hand on each side of his face, rubbing his temples and lowering his head, his body language agreeing with John. Rydel stood up from the table and left the room. With Rydel now gone, John sat down next to Will.

"How is he, Will?"

"I don't know yet."

"You better fucking know! You run everything here. Rydel looks and seems off. Am I wrong?"

"No, you are not wrong."

—

John and Will gave Rydel some time alone. After two days of leaving Rydel to himself, John decided Will could use some time off—a full week. When Will argued that he thought time away from the lab would be a bad idea now, John tacked on another seven days and ordered Will to take a two-week vacation. Will was, without a doubt, one to watch. John knew his reason for being on this earth was to protect humanity. But there was always the flip side of the coin—and John usually could sense the people who hated their own kind. John wasn't sure if Will fit the criteria of that kind of person yet, but he had his concerns. Unlike Rydel, Will seemed only to be invested in his projects to prove what he could do with his gifted mind.

Rydel's mind was different. John knew it, and Will sure as shit knew it. And there was something inherently good about Rydel. Hell, the colonel had been on a first-name basis with Rydel after only knowing the man for a month—it did not matter who was in the room. Not only was Rydel exceptionally talented at what he did, his heart was huge when it came to humanity. Not so with Will. These two men with their incredible minds—their country needed them both. But Rydel came first. He had to be protected at all costs; he was too damn gifted.

John kept away from Rydel for almost a week into Will's forced vacation until a custodian named Dan knocked on his office door and told him Rydel had not left his workplace for three days. Rydel would always ask Dan about his daughter Jamie and how she was doing at Cambridge.

"He's just in there like he's in some kind of coma or something," Dan had said to John with concern.

So John rushed to Rydel's workplace with the custodian behind him. He had no time to tell the man to back off and could not come up with a reason why he should. The two entered the room and found Rydel facedown on the keyboard of his computer. John hurried over and eased Rydel back, checking his pulse. Feeling the beat of Rydel's heart, John spoke loudly, trying to wake him.

"Rydel! Hey—Rydel, wake up!"

Rydel snapped his head up and stared at John as if he didn't recognize him. The colonel could see Rydel was completely burned out, his glassy eyes staring back at him.

"Enough. You need to rest. You're no good to yourself—or to the lab—working like this." The colonel eased Rydel up to his feet.

"Come on, Rydel."

—

In his private room at Genesis, Rydel was on his tenth hour of undisturbed sleep when his cell phone woke him. The buzzing of the phone vibrating on the nightstand next to his bed finally broke Rydel away from his vampire-like slumber. The room was dark with the exception of two laptops and their streaming aquatic deep-blue screensavers. He turned his head toward the nightstand and, on the eighth vibration, opened his eyes.

Three missed calls.

Rydel tapped his phone and focused on the number repeatedly calling him. As he tried to shake off the deep sleep he'd been awakened from, Rydel could see the three missed calls had a 212 area code. Rydel bolted upright.

Karen.

Karen was the only person he knew in New York, but the number was different.

The phone vibrated again. Rydel turned on the lamp next to his bed and snatched his cell phone off the table.

"Hello?"

"Rydel Scott?"

"Yes—who is this?"

"Karen's mother superior. We've met. A few years ago when you came to see your sister on Christmas Eve."

"Yes, I remember you. Is everything all right?"

"When was the last time you spoke to Karen?"

Still groggy, Rydel could not help being a bit angry that the woman didn't answer his question.

"My sister, is she okay?"

"No. She is not okay."

—

John Adams sat behind his desk, taking a little break, doing some online Christmas shopping for his sister. Rydel walked into John's office without knocking—looking like he hadn't slept again for weeks, his eyes puffy and his clothes crumpled.

"Shit, Rydel! I ordered you to get some sleep. You can't work like this—"

"My sister is sick. I have to go. I have to go now!"

"Hold on. Tell me what's going on."

"Cancer. She's dying. I haven't seen her in almost a year. I just got a call from her mother superior. She thought I knew Karen was sick and just didn't visit for some reason. Christ, I don't know what the hell's going on there!"

"All right, I'll drive you in."

Rydel shook his head. "No, I'm okay. Just drop me off at the train station. Please, John. I need time to be alone."

"Okay, Rydel. Okay."

# Karen

Rydel stepped out of the taxi and looked up at the white brick church wedged between two red brick buildings. It wasn't Saint Patrick's, but it was a well-kept church many Catholics in the city chose because of its simplistic beauty. It was for those who truly just wanted to pray, confess, and feel closer to God.

Rydel walked up the church steps and entered. Inside, candles adorned each wall around the church. Stations of the Cross, the paintings counting down Jesus's Fate, lined the walls on either side. Rydel stood before the pews in front of him and waited. When she'd called, Karen's mother superior told Rydel over the phone where to meet her. She would not give the name of the hospital Karen was in or any other information before hanging up. Karen had not been admitted to the few hospitals he was able to call on the train ride in. Taking a vow for religion is one thing, but keeping information about a family member is another, Rydel furiously thought as he waited.

He heard light footsteps from behind and turned to face a woman in her mid-fifties dressed in a black shirt and black pants. As she approached, the woman's eyes, ice blue, looked just as hard and angry as Rydel felt. And it gave him a moment of pause. Just seconds before, he wanted to scream at this woman for not telling him over the phone where he could find his sister—who was very sick, as the woman put it. But now, the woman—unlike the last time they had met—looked at him like he was shit on her heels.

"Hello, Rydel. I wanted to meet you here because—you might laugh—by some miracle from God, I was able to find the number to reach you so that we could talk."

"For security reasons, my cell phone is the only number I can be reached at."

"I understand that. And as your sister's condition worsened, she refused to give me that number. I found her cell phone hidden under her mattress while she was asleep and got your number. When we first met, I got the impression you two were close?"

"We are close."

"Did you have a falling-out?"

"No!"

"I find it hard to believe Karen would not want the only family member she has left in this world to be by her bedside now."

"You find it hard to believe because it's not true. And if you do not take me to my sister right now, the people I work for will make sure you do. I can have them here in minutes. Where is my sister?" Rydel shouted, his voice echoing throughout the church.

"Why would you threaten me like that? I reached out to you to see if there was a way you could forgive whatever quarrel the two of you may have had…to see if there was a way for you to get away from this all-important job of yours to be with Karen in her worsening condition."

"Of course I can. She's all I have. She…"

Rydel stopped talking. It was starting to make sense. He took a seat in a pew to his right and stared up at the cross hanging above the altar.

"Is that what she told you? She was worried about what might happen if I left my job…what kind of trouble I would be in, what kind of danger."

Karen's mother superior shook her head.

"No. She told me you knew about the illness."

"What?"

"She said you knew."

"I didn't know a thing about it—what the hell *is* going on here?"

—

Rydel sat restlessly in the back seat of a cab on his way to Lenox Hill Hospital. Karen's mother superior was glad to give Rydel the address of Karen's hospital once it became clear to her it had all been a misunderstanding, a very convoluted misunderstanding. Maybe in her condition, Karen was not in her right mind. With the church and its secrecy, this all could have gone another way, Rydel knew. Therefore, he set aside his feelings of anger toward Karen's mother superior, who had finally introduced herself as Grace Rose.

As the lights of the city passed over his face, Rydel could not get her words or the look on Grace Rose's face out of his head. She really thought he was a brother wanting nothing to do with his own flesh and blood. The woman was obviously protecting one of her own. But why? Why would Karen make this woman think they had such a bad falling-out?

The cab pulled up a few feet away from the entrance to the hospital. Rydel paid the driver with a fifty-dollar bill and stepped out of the cab without bothering with the change for a $19.60 fare.

Through the parting hospital doors, Rydel approached the receptionist's desk. A woman in her thirties with jet-black hair, heavy makeup, and a gummy smile spoke to Rydel in a smoky voice.

"How can I help you, sir?"

"I'm here to see Karen Scott. I'm her brother."

After finishing all the formalities, proving he was who he said he was, Rydel was told the floor and room where his sister was located.

On the eleventh floor, Rydel looked for room 18. As he walked down the hallway, most of the doors he passed were open; his sister's door was closed. Hand on the doorknob, Rydel opened the door, not knowing what to expect.

"Jesus."

His sister lay asleep on the hospital bed. Her body, half-covered in bedsheets, showed the frail shape of a woman Rydel was having a hard time recognizing—a dying woman withered and weak. The air she took in appeared to be a hardship with each single breath.

Karen opened her eyes and tilted her head toward Rydel. Her eyes were in contrast to her body; her eyes were alive, alert, and excited to see him. She smiled.

"Hey." The rasping voice that came out of his sister sounded alien to Rydel.

He rushed over to the bed and almost grabbed hold of his sister to hug her tightly, but he stopped himself. Fiercely embracing Karen probably would have ended her life—her body was so utterly frail, ghost-like.

Rydel dropped to one knee by the side of the bed and shook his head, not understanding. Karen reached out, and Rydel gently cupped her hand in his.

"Karen, why didn't you let me know you were sick? Why have you been hiding it from me?"

"Later, Rydel. I will tell you later."

Her breathing labored, her body fighting to stay alive, Karen closed her eyes and slept.

—

Five hours passed, and Rydel never left the room once. A nurse named Peggy tried to convince Rydel to go home (having no idea how far away his home was) and get some rest. It took Rydel only a few minutes to convince the nurse he would not be going anywhere—that he would be here as long as he needed to be—and asked her to bring some things to make himself somewhat comfortable.

Near the window inside the room, the nurse and her superior set up a chair with a footstool, blankets, and pillows and brought in a bedside table with wheels. They also placed a nightlight in an outlet below the window for Rydel to see where he could plug in the laptop he'd brought with him in a shoulder bag. He finally left the room briefly while Peggy changed his sister's bedding.

Now alone with Karen, the first sound of thunder finally came. Rydel stood by the window for over half an hour, watching the gray clouds form above the city, listening to his sister fighting to breathe behind him. Another rumbling sound as light-tapping rain hit the pane of glass in front of him. He almost began to cry along with the rain—but held it back. Another feeling started to take over, a feeling of contempt toward this God his sister devoutly served with everything she had in her beautiful soul. And this is what she received for her complete devotion—to suffer in a wasted shell of a body at the age of twenty-seven.

How incredibly cruel, he thought. Suddenly, Rydel's awareness of his surroundings alarmed him that something was wrong. He could not hear Karen breathing anymore.

Turning, he came face-to-face with Karen standing in front of him and took a startled step backward. Not just because of the sight of his sister out of bed—but her appearance. She looked healthy, vibrant. Karen reached out with both hands and touched Rydel's face.

"He came to me. He has been guiding you these past few years. At last, finding the right soul to give the knowledge to, the one who will help save His Son. He told me about your Placement."

"How? How do you know about Placement?"

"By the broken fence leading to the field where we would play as kids…there is something He needs to show you, Rydel."

"Who?"

Karen closed her eyes and slowly fell forward into Rydel's open arms. Rydel carried Karen back to the bed, placing her down softly, staring down at his sister as her body continued to heal right in front of him. Rydel moved away from the bed and stumbled out of the room, running toward the nurses on duty just down the hallway, the two talking quietly to each other.

Rydel had met the nurses before, but now, frantic, he could not recall their names.

"Nurse!"

"Mr. Scott—what is it?" the taller of the two nurses, Jackie, asked.

"Something has happened to my sister!" Rydel shouted.

Rydel spun away from the two women and ran back inside Karen's room. The two nurses ran after him, both sharing the same thought—the vital signs monitor had gone down (happening only one time on record at the hospital five years ago) and Karen had passed without anyone noticing but her brother, watching over her in the room.

The two women entered the room to see Rydel kneeling at his sister's bedside with his head lowered. They looked over the patient, then the machines in the room, and everything seemed to be working.

Rydel quickly turned toward the two.

"No, no, no! She wasn't like this before!"

"Calm down, Mr. Scott. She wasn't like what? What did you see—what happened?" Jackie asked.

"She wasn't dying! She was cured!"

—

Early the next day, Rydel sat alone and impatiently in an office, waiting for Karen's doctor, the sunlight streaming through the windows behind an oak desk in front of him. A man in his forties with sandy hair entered the office. He walked behind the desk and eased down into a high-back gray swivel chair.

Lee Stepneake was a man with an excellent reputation not only for saving lives but also for his amazing bedside manner. It was a blessing the way Dr. Stepneake cared for a dying patient as well as for their family.

Knowing Rydel was a man of science—having talked with him briefly—Lee saw no need to comfort Rydel and therefore skipped the approach he was well regarded for by so many. He was at the end of a twenty-hour shift; he was tired and hungry and wanted to go home.

"Your sister has only weeks to live. I am sorry."

Another doctor entered the room—a woman with frazzled hair and eyes that seemed almost halfway shut. Rydel knew the look all too well with the hours he put in at the lab. The woman walked over and stood next to Dr. Stepneake without saying a word.

Rydel nodded a hello toward the woman, acknowledging her, and returned his attention to Dr. Stepneake.

"She got out of her bed. Coherent. Healthy, it seemed. Somehow, something is happening inside her that's trying to fight off the illness. I saw it happen."

The half-awake woman glanced down at Dr. Stepneake and then stepped closer to Rydel. "Mr. Scott, she hasn't been able to get out of her bed for over two months now. You are tired. Believe me, I understand. The mind can play cruel tricks when a loved one is dying."

Rydel quickly stood up and paced in front of the two doctors, shaking his head, knowing very well what the two were trying to do with him now. He came to an abrupt stop and pointed a finger in the face of the woman doctor with the slept-in hair and droopy eyes.

"Don't talk to me like that, damn it! I know what I saw. I didn't imagine what happened. I'm not crazy!"

"No, you are not. However, the way you are screaming right now, you do sound a little crazy."

Frustrated, Rydel turned away and bolted toward the office door. On his way out, he suddenly stopped.

"I know what I saw."

—

Rydel spent the morning and afternoon with his sleeping sister. By early evening, he was out of the Hertz car-rental office on 76th Street and in his rented Chevrolet Impala, navigating the streets of Manhattan.

He was heading back to his childhood home in New Jersey.

The hour-long drive seemed like the first time in years he felt calm and at ease. A soothing, whispering voice was calling him to the place his sister had told him to go. He had complete fluidity in his thoughts and a feeling of peacefulness flowing throughout his body.

Everything he was working on at the lab pushed its way out of his mind, and a calming presence began to wash over him. Now his work wasn't all-consuming. Those thoughts were put aside—not gone, but on the back burner.

Where he was going became all that mattered. Where he was going would give Karen what she needed. Rydel had no idea what that was, but he knew he had to reach the place his sister had talked about, hoping that the fence and the field would still be there.

The field and remnants of the old broken fence were still there. Nothing much had changed. The house looked different on the property, refurbished. However, the large backyard property line of his childhood home had not changed at all. The homeowners of the present, feeling it was also too much of a hassle to landscape the entire acreage of the property, ignored the fact that the overgrown, weed-strewn wasteland with tall trees dotted here and there was theirs to upkeep.

Standing in the knee-high grass with a half-dead tree behind him, Rydel took it all in. Memories of being a young boy playing hide-and-seek with friends, running after his sister, times when they would—

"Remember playing out here when we were kids, Rydel?"

Rydel turned around so fast he lost his footing and went down on his knees. He lifted his head to see his sister in her hospital nightgown, smiling down at him. Small patches of moonlight lit her face, and thin tree-limb shadows covered her body.

On his feet, Rydel clumsily stepped closer toward Karen, his legs unsure and his head trying to process what he was seeing. She's not here. She can't be—your mind is not working properly. Too much work. Too much to take, knowing Karen is going to die. Too much!

Rydel closed his eyes, feeling the wind move over him, seeing and thinking nothing, taking time to calm his mind. He breathed in the air passing over him, and the smell of the greenery around him began to make him feel better.

A hand touched the side of Rydel's right cheek, and his eyes snapped open. He was now standing face-to-face with his sister.

"This can't be possible."

"God has given me an extension of life in this world. My life should have ended by now, Rydel. This night is why I kept my illness from you—to show you God's miracle. To make sure you do what needs to be done. There is a reason you discovered Placement. You need to follow me now."

Karen let her hand fall slowly away from the side of Rydel's face. She walked past him into the field, and Rydel followed. She walked toward a circular clearing with a sky-reaching dawn redwood placed in the middle of the overgrown landscape.

Rydel stopped and rubbed his eyes. And when he was finished, Karen was suddenly sitting under the towering redwood with her back against the tree, sixty feet away.

"Come sit with me, Rydel," she called out.

Fear hit Rydel hard. He feared not just for himself but also for what he could do to help others with his mind's abilities, saving lives with his work.

God, I'm losing my mind.

"You *are not* losing your mind, Rydel. Come and sit with me. We have a lot to talk about," Karen said, just loud enough to be heard.

The inflection changed in her voice. She spoke in her normal speaking voice from before she became ill; however, there was now this underlying warmth coming from her. With the soothing tone of voice drawing him in, Rydel was starting to peacefully accept what was happening.

Rydel smiled back at his sister, who still sat sixty feet away, and walked over to her. After lowering himself and leaning against the tree, Rydel touched Karen's face, the face of a healthy twenty-seven-year-old woman.

"You're cured. How?"

"By God."

"I don't understand."

As he faced his sister, Rydel's mind began to question what he was seeing. This is not your sister. You are just seeing what you want to see. You are imagining this image of her.

"You're not imagining what you are seeing, Rydel. I am healed right here in front of you now."

"That's not possible. My mind has just created you. I wish to God you were cured, Karen. But I'm starting to understand what is happening. The doctors were right. I am worn out. I'm surprised I made it here without getting in some sort of accident. You are back at the hospital, you are dying, and I will always miss you."

Rydel got back up on his feet and turned away from his sister. After taking three steps, the redwood tree he had been leaning against landed on each side of him, perfectly halved. One tree branch struck his lower cheek, and his cheek began to bleed slightly. The tree never made a sound; it just split perfectly in half from the ground up and fell forward.

Body and face trembling, Rydel looked over his shoulder. Standing between each half of the tree, Karen nodded for Rydel to join her, and he did, moving closer with robotic legs he no longer controlled until he stood in front of his sister.

"A war is coming, Rydel. One you have to help stop."

"A war?" Rydel replied.

Karen slowly nodded three times. "Yes. The one war that will turn the earth into a literal hell. The Other will wipe out humanity. Christ's Second Coming has to be done in His time to save us from that. We let Him die on the cross as a people. We have to save Him."

"Save Him?"

"The earth will burn, Rydel. Did you really believe it was just you creating Placement? God's hand was guiding you to save our Savior."

"Placement is dangerous—"

"It is not dangerous," Karen quickly said. "And you know it. It will save humanity…once He is saved. The message Christ was sent to deliver to the world has to be known in our time. He was crucified before He was able to finish what He was sent here to do."

"You want me to go back in time and save Jesus Christ?"

"You will," Karen said confidently. "God chose you to go back and save His Son."

Karen took two steps closer to her brother.

"I'm going to show you something important now, Rydel. Something to put your worried mind at ease." Karen stepped backward between the split redwood tree. From the ground up, the tree mended itself back together in front of Rydel.

She was gone. Disappearing behind the tree—or inside of it—Rydel could not be sure which of the two.

Emotionally drained, Rydel gazed almost drunkenly at the tree as a leaf drifted down and landed at his feet. He let out a sort of half-mad laugh at the leaf now resting on his dirt-caked shoe. The sound of a child giggling whipped Rydel's head back up at the redwood in front of him.

A young girl walked out from behind the redwood and skipped over to Rydel, then stopped and stood in front of him.

"Let's run together and explore like we did when we were kids, Rydel. One last time."

Rydel dropped to his knees and touched the young girl's face. "My God, what am I seeing here?"

"It's me, Rydel—it's Karen. Come on!"

Karen, who now appeared to be about ten years old, ran off into the field. Rydel stood and took a couple of steps forward like a fawn on the day of its birth, got his legs under him, then followed after her.

—

Two days later at the Genesis lab, Rydel sat hunched over his desk, scribbling on a notepad, when a knock at the door spun his head around. He slipped the notepad into the desk drawer and combed back his hair with both hands.

"Come in."

Will entered. His eyes darted around the way they always did when he was inside Rydel's private room at the lab. He then gave Rydel a look of compassion that almost made Rydel laugh out loud.

"Adams told me about the condition of your sister. My sympathies."

"I'm putting in some hours—but she needs me now. After I leave today, I can't say when I'll be back working like I was before," Rydel bluntly said.

"I understand. I have people I care about as well."

Will took one more discreet glance around the room and gave Rydel what he thought resembled a smile, his lips barely moving. He then exited the room. The look he had given Rydel was unsettling—his face almost inelastic. They'd been colleagues for years, yet Rydel still wondered how Will could work at a place benefiting, for the most part, the quality of human life when the man clearly had no concern for humanity at all.

As years passed, Rydel realized what was driving Will—and that was control. Will had the final say when projects got the green light. He loved having the power over whether the soldiers in the field or innocent civilians in war-torn countries deserved the benefit of the projects he supervised. Once Colonel Adams arrived at Genesis, he had stepped in a few times and disagreed with Will, but for the most part, Will had the final word.

Sensing that Will had gone and wasn't waiting by the door to pop back inside, Rydel slipped the notepad back out from his desk drawer. Fearing hackers, he did not want to use his computer for what he was doing.

Rydel went over his notes one more time before finishing up for the night.

"Two more days," Rydel whispered to himself.

He slipped the notepad inside his lab coat and shut down his computer. Everything was falling into place for his mission that no one at the lab would ever know about.

# The Return

Ten minutes after he returned from the past, Rydel's jumbled mind finally came back to him. For the next two hours, he sat in the back seat of another car he had rented, piecing together what he had witnessed and what he was able to find out, working on a laptop purchased weeks ago with cash. He had taken from the lab only what he absolutely needed for his mission and paid cash for the rest.

While typing his notes, Rydel glanced at the date on the bottom-right-hand corner of the laptop. He'd only been gone just shy of five days. Good. The lab did not hear from him in that time, which would be understandable because of his sister's condition but still unusual for him. He needed to get back to Genesis soon, not wanting to raise suspicion—and to do what needed to be done. But first he needed to see his sister. She had to know what went wrong.

In his rented Pathfinder, it took Rydel only an hour from where he had used Placement—the field where his sister showed him the miracle—to reach the hospital.

Rydel walked down the hallway and reached his sister's room. The dying young woman lay on the bed, waiting, the miracle of being cured now gone. The only semblance of life came from her eyes, pleading to know how the journey back in time went. Rydel reached the bed and knelt by Karen's side. He held her hand and swept away a strand of hair curling down her face.

"Rydel."

His name sounded as if she'd been given a small glass of sand to drink. Regardless of the pain she was in, she smiled at him. How much strength did it take to smile, Rydel asked himself. He bent forward and touched his forehead to his sister's, wishing he had better news for her. Joined together by the touch, he remained that way for a few seconds with his eyes closed and then raised his head. He had to tell her what had happened in the past and what had to be done next.

"I'm sorry. The date I told you, from what I'd learned, was wrong, Karen. He'd been crucified already. But now I know the correct time—I am leaving again."

"Go, Rydel. Save Him."

—

With the moon still visible in the sky, the dawn started to outline the surrounding trees behind the Genesis lab in purple and deep orange.

Parked in his rented Pathfinder, Rydel stared down at the lab with heavy-lidded eyes through a pair of Genesis binoculars. Three men Rydel knew by name stood waiting at the lab's entrance: Bob Clancy, Neil Mitchell, and Paul Rogers. The doors opened, and a shift change took place. Three men who had just finished their shifts walked to the parking lot, got into their black SUVs (provided by Genesis), merged onto the road leading out, and drove away.

Rydel's Pathfinder made its way toward the lab. As luck—or maybe destiny—would have it, today happened to be Will's one day off. Unlike Rydel, Will did not live at the lab; he had a place in town. But if Rydel had returned to the lab before Clancy, Mitchell, and Rogers were on duty, a call most likely would have been placed to Will, since Rydel was technically on leave. The three men now on duty would only ask how his sister was doing and carry on with their day-to-day routine. A couple of the projects at the lab had helped family members of Clancy and Rogers. Mitchell himself had also benefited from Rydel's work. They would say nothing to Rydel or to anyone else about him being inside the lab when he was not scheduled to be.

Rydel had planned for only the one time out with Placement—a chip he was able to make on his own. There was no way he could make another chip without resources from the lab. He could no longer hide his intentions—he had to take what he needed from Genesis.

Inside the lab, Rydel was met with consoling looks and words of support regarding his dying sister from scientists he worked with. Rydel entered the hallway leading to the guts of the working lab and stopped, staring at the three from security who, he was sure just shortly before, would have let him breeze on by. The men, however, now stood in a line as if waiting for him, blocking the entrance to the hallway. Rydel tried to suppress a sudden feeling of trepidation and walked toward the men.

"Hey, guys."

The widest of the three, Bob Clancy, glanced at the other two men with him and then looked back at Rydel.

"Rydel, why are you here?" Bob asked.

Rydel wasn't sure how to interpret the unemotional way Bob spoke to him, so he just kind of shook his head and replied just as flatly.

"I have to work."

With his intimidating form, Bob moved closer and placed a hand on Rydel's shoulder.

"No, Rydel, you should not be here now."

He now had a decision to make in just seconds. Before arriving, he had tucked a handgun into the back of his waistband in case something like this happened. Realistically, Rydel knew he probably could not even shoot one of these three men before being taken down. He was not a trained soldier—the three in front of him were. And in the pause Rydel had taken to consider his options, Bob spoke again.

"You should be with your sister now, Rydel. Your work here can wait. I lost my mother while in Iraq. I should've been with her. The time you are spending here is time you will never get back with your sister."

"Thank you, Bob. You're right. But the work I need to complete here saves lives. I cannot keep myself away from it. My sister understands. She's the one who sent me away to continue with my work—for just a little while. But like you said, I don't intend on being here long. I will be back with my sister tonight. I will not let her be alone at a time when she needs family the most."

The three in front of Rydel glanced at one another. Bob then spoke once more.

"You're a good man, Rydel."

"So are you, Bob."

—

Rydel entered his room at the lab an hour later. After wiping out all his work on Placement on every Genesis computer, he finished placing the destination into the chip he would confiscate for his mission. He could gain access to the chips from his computer after hours at the lab if a flash of inspiration came, but he could not get to them physically; only John and Will could. However, he was able to get to the secret project Will was hiding. He couldn't destroy it. That would have attracted unwanted attention. Does the man really think I am that gullible?

Rydel removed a clear plastic bag from his desk drawer. The bag contained what looked like a human hand. He had lifted Will's fingerprints off a coffee mug in the cafeteria weeks ago and transferred the prints onto a synthetic hand he was working on for amputees.

Once inside the lab, security and the scanners became a bit more lax so that the doctors could move from room to room. The scanners in the lab would never know a synthetic hand was being used—the scanners could not detect liveness. He couldn't use a chip like the one John Adams had implanted to gain access to every room—that required minor surgery.

In the hallway leading away from his room at Genesis, Rydel made his way toward the rooms inside the lab he was not authorized to enter. He already had S-7 (a drug used to control a person completely, body and mind) and a translator. No one had noticed that both had been missing for weeks now.

They would, however, know in minutes what was taken tonight—minutes if he was lucky, Rydel knew. But it didn't matter anymore—this time out would make all the difference. Whether he made it back to this place in time or not was secondary.

The first room he needed to get to would be the black room. Just fifty feet away, the black room was where the Placement chips were stored after he was finished working on them for the day—only Will and Colonel Adams had access to the room. Rydel had no idea why the hell they called it the black room.

He placed the thumb of the synthetic hand on the red scanner, and the door opened. The black room was black: black walls, black desks, and black computers. A wall to the right of Rydel stretched across the room with what looked like black safety deposit boxes facing him.

"I guess this is why they call it the black room," Rydel said to himself.

He hurried over and touched the side of one of the black safety-deposit-looking boxes with all five fingertips on the artificial hand. A tray slid out from the wall with black pills in glass cylinders. Rydel took one of the glass cylinders and removed the pill from inside, looked it over, and placed it in a plastic baggie. He gathered up the rest of the glass cylinders, stuffed them in his pockets, and tapped the timer on his wristwatch. He knew wherever Will was tonight, the man would now know the black room had been breached because of the men monitoring everything in the Overlook. Rydel figured he had about two more minutes to reach the weapons room before being taken down. On his first attempt to save Christ, he had gone unarmed. He would not make the same mistake again. If he went back and was somehow off on the time once more—with maybe Jesus on his way to be crucified—he would need to take down anyone near Christ.

Down one empty hallway and into another, Rydel raced toward the weapons-room door and scanned himself in using the ring finger on the synthetic hand. The weapons room, with a large white table in the middle, stored state-of-the-art weaponry inside black-tinted glass cabinets mounted on each of the four walls. Rydel was able to open most of the cabinet doors, searching for what he needed; he knew the doors were unlocked on select weapons still in development. At one of the cabinets, Rydel grabbed a new prototype Smartround rifle Will was just about finished working on, a recent handgun version of the rifle, and magazines for the guns. He placed everything on the white table, then went back and closed the glass door. After running back to the table, Rydel reached under his coat for a duffel bag and started to place the guns and ammo inside as the alarms went off. The inside of the weapons room went dark. In the darkness, Rydel slung the duffel bag over his shoulder, reached into his coat pocket, and pulled out the plastic baggie. Then he swallowed the Placement pill he had programmed just minutes ago.

The weapons room door burst open. His three friends from security rushed toward him, now dressed in black protective gear, guns drawn. The light inside the room returned as the three moved in on Rydel.

"On the ground, Rydel! On your knees—down, down—down!"

It sounds like Bob behind the black face mask I designed, the quick thought flashing in and out of Rydel's brain.

Rydel did as he was told and knelt on the floor. The three moved closer, cautiously, and it was Bob behind the mask who spoke again.

"Arms above your head, Rydel. Do it."

Rydel started to lift his arms but then stopped his hands near his chest, his palms open and facing out.

"Over your head, Rydel—arms up!"

Rydel dropped his left hand to his side and made the sign of the cross with his right hand.

"Rydel, don't—"

Rydel vanished in front of the three, taking the floor tiles he knelt on with him. The sound of the tiles being pulled up from the floor and of siphoned air filled the room for a split second. All that remained of him was a small white swirling hole, which eventually disappeared. The three armed men stepped closer to where Rydel had been and suddenly stopped. With all the rumors of what went on here at Genesis, who knew what the hell just happened to Rydel. They sure as shit didn't want to be exposed to whatever just made him disappear.

# Rydel's Whereabouts in Time

The three security men on duty at Genesis stood off to the side in the white-ceilinged, white-floored, white-walled security room at the lab, as the Overlook at Genesis was off-limits to them. Will sat behind a desk in front of thirty monitors, shaking his head as the images of Rydel popped up. The sound of footfalls and the repeated usage of the word "sir" turned the attention of the four toward the room's closed door. The door flew open so hard the knob stuck into the wall as John Adams entered. He yanked the knob out of the drywall and slammed the door shut. The colonel looked over the three security men while walking toward the monitoring desk. He stood over Will and slowly enunciated every word to him:

"What…the…hell…happened here, Will?"

"Rydel stole and used Placement. He's gone."

The colonel slammed his fist on the desk, and Will jumped a little in his seat. "Where did he go?" the colonel asked quietly and intensely.

"I don't know yet, sir."

—

In Colonel Adams's office twenty minutes later, Will sat expressionless in front of the colonel's desk. Colonel Adams paced behind Will, waiting for an explanation. Will blankly stared out the window behind the colonel's desk. He wanted to relieve John Adams of his revolver concealed under his black peacoat and shoot him between the eyes for actually insinuating this was somehow his fault. But he knew he would die attempting such a thing.

Bide your time, Will reminded himself.

"Only the thirteen chips that we copied from Rydel's work as backups are left. Rydel took the rest from the lab and crashed all his work here at Genesis."

John Adams stopped pacing and stared out the same window Will had fixed his own attention on.

"Of all people. Fuck!" The colonel closed his eyes and pinched the bridge of his nose. He remained that way for thirty seconds. He opened his eyes and stared down at Will. "Okay, send me back to when Rydel entered the lab tonight."

"Yes, sir."

—

The colonel looked out the window behind his desk with his arms folded across his chest, waiting. It had been over half an hour since Will had left the room. He turned to reach for the phone on his desk, and just as he did, Will entered the room. The look on the man's face told the story.

"What is it, Will?"

"Rydel got to the backup chips."

"Destroyed?"

"No."

"Damaged? How bad?"

"I can't send you back the way you want. He altered every chip to make sure that could not happen. A virus of some kind. But Rydel wasn't able to totally ruin my backups because of a backdoor I installed into the program. I don't trust anyone, sir. Let us be grateful for that. But we need to know where he went. And as of now, I can only send you back fifteen, maybe twenty years because of the virus, if that is of any help. I can't do any better. It would take months or even longer to undo what Rydel has done. He got to the weapons room as well, sir. I haven't had a chance to check what is missing yet."

"Let's go."

The two made their way to the weapons room without saying a word. Will opened the door and led the way inside. Following behind, John slipped his hand around the grip of his gun under the long coat he had on.

He had no idea what was going on tonight or whom to trust. But he knew for sure not to trust the asshole in front of him. Not one bit.

Will started to open the black glass cabinet doors around the room. He stopped after opening the eighth door, revealing empty black foam cavities where ammunition and weapons were once stored. John joined Will at his side and looked over what was missing. Unsure, he turned to Will for an explanation.

"He's got the prototype Smartround LM rifle, a large number of rounds, and the Smartround handgun I was working on."

John took in the situation, breaking it down in his head. "I need to use some of your S-7 you say is now ready, Will. You're coming with me to find out exactly where Rydel went back to in time."

—

The rain, which almost seemed to be coming sideways, slammed into John and Will as they ran toward the entrance to Lenox Hill Hospital. Undetected upon entering because of a planned disturbance between four screaming women, John and Will walked over to the elevators. They knew what room the woman they wanted to see would be in and would not be denied because of the late hour or for not being blood relatives.

The elevator doors opened, and as luck would have it, an empty hallway faced the two. John and Will approached a room to their left. The two quietly slipped inside.

The woman in the room slept on a slightly raised bed facing a window, her body fighting to take in each breath. John let out a sigh of disappointment for having to do what he was about to do. He then nodded at Will without further reflection of his feelings.

"Okay, Will. Do it."

Will fell to one knee by the side of the bed and from his coat pocket removed a small clear cylinder with what looked like a four-inch black pushpin inside. Will slid S-7 out from the cylinder. He took the woman's limp left arm and stuck the black pushpin into it. He stood up and waited.

Karen turned her head away from the window and opened her eyes, staring up at the two. John stepped closer to the bed. Karen's head tilted slightly, and John's gaze connected with hers.

"Hello, Karen," John said in a calm, reassuring voice.

"Hello…" Karen replied weakly.

John glanced at Will. Will administered the rest of the S-7 drug into Karen's arm, and her eyes changed. The only part of Karen that hadn't succumbed to sickness were her vibrant blue eyes. That vibrancy was now gone as the drug took complete hold. Her blue eyes became the eyes of a doll with the ability to blink, which they did at John in slow intervals.

Will removed the S-7 needle from Karen's arm. "She's completely under. Since you were the one to speak to her first, you now control her. Ask her anything."

Staring down at Karen in her zombie-like appearance, John felt something break away from the pride he took in defending the people of America he cared so much about: a woman with maybe weeks to live put into this hypnotic state. Regrettably, this scenario, like others, would always be part of the job. What Rydel took could possibly cause the death of hundreds of thousands of men, women, and children he'd sworn to protect. Sometimes, difficult choices had to be made, like doing this to a dying young woman looking at him with her vacant eyes.

"Karen, tell us the exact date Rydel traveled back to in time. And the reason why Rydel stole Placement. Tell me now, Karen."

Karen's doll eyes closed for five seconds and then snapped wide open.

"Okay. I will tell you."

—

John and Will were over Manhattan inside a private jet two hours later, headed back to Genesis. With the aircraft to themselves, the two sat across from each other, staring out of their respective passenger windows. What Karen had told the two was starting to sink in, as both men sat in a daze. John finally turned to Will.

"I talked with General Dowling before takeoff. He wants Ray and his Unit on this so we can find Rydel fast. You are a part of this, Will. I'll need your help to get Rydel back."

Will turned away from the window beside him to face John. "Of course."

"I don't want anyone in Ray's Unit knowing where or when we are traveling back to. Including Ray—understand?"

"I understand. I'll need at least three days to make sure the chips—"

"You have two days. No more."

Back at Genesis an hour later, Will and a team of techs went to work on the remaining chips, working through the night.

Later, as the dawn lit the east side of the lab, John walked outside onto the lab's helipad and stood in the light of a new day. After a few peaceful minutes alone, staring at a grouping of emerald-green treetops swaying in the wind below, the sound of an incoming helicopter broke the morning silence. John stepped back a few feet and waited to greet Ray and the members of his Unit.

—

By late afternoon, the members of Ray's Unit were situated inside an airplane hangar located near the back of the lab, all seated on folding chairs. The Unit stared at John and Will standing in front of them, with Ray standing off to the side.

"We've had a breach in weapons. It was Rydel," John said to Ray's Unit point-blank.

John waited before speaking again. He wanted to take in the reaction of the members of Ray's Unit, knowing how most of them felt about Rydel. And what he saw were their subtle, shifty looks at one another, the Unit confident the colonel had not picked up on it—but he had. John was not surprised. He knew he had some convincing to do.

"I know how all of you feel about Rydel. I feel the same way. He's a good man, but a man who has lost his way."

John looked at the operators in front of him, slowly making eye contact with each one. "Although it is confidential and understood never to be spoken of again, you all remember what happened to Martinez with Shutdown. Correct?"

John waited for a response, and all in the Unit replied back with a "Yes, sir" at the same time.

"From that, we discovered something here at Genesis that has not been fully tested yet. Placement…sending someone back in time to try to correct a situation that's already occurred."

Ray's Unit stared blankly at John. Out of the nine now making up the Unit, Ben was the first to comprehend what Colonel Adams just said.

"I'm sorry…time travel, Colonel?" Ben asked.

"Placement. A way to go back to a certain time in the past and make corrections when the worst has happened to our nation," John answered. "You are all here because we need to find Rydel fast. Changing events in the past with Placement at this time is extremely dangerous to the American people here in the present."

John turned to Will with a slight nod for him to explain the dangers of Placement to the men and women of the Unit. Will tried to smile at the Unit as a hello, only to come off looking creepy as fuck. He spoke in the monotone voice they all remembered and found disturbing about the man from their first days at the lab.

"It appears to be fortuitous for all of you that one of my projects here at Genesis is ahead of schedule. S-7 will change everything about getting the information you need out of an individual. I will show all of you how to use S-7 today; it will help in your mission like nothing before. As for Placement, during a previous test run, we changed something in the past that affected just one person. By doing so, we believe it caused an incident of severe damage to the present. Lives were lost. We have no idea what Rydel wants to change in the past. You people have to find him, and find him fast."

Mistake, John quickly realized.

"Thank you, Will." John motioned for Will to fall back, and he did. John didn't like the way "you people" sounded when Will said it, and neither did anyone in Ray's Unit. He said it as though they were something created here at the lab. Will always reminded John of the android no one knew about on the ship in the first Alien movie. Shit, maybe Will was an android.

With Will now standing behind him, John took over and continued to explain the situation to the members of the Unit.

"We tested Placement three times. The first two times, we changed nothing. The third time out, using Shutdown, we gave a man in the past one more minute to live. And the tsunami that hit our base in Japan happened the second we returned after altering what we thought would be something minor in time. We were fine when we returned because the base in Japan is underground. For those above, you know what happened. If Rydel changes something significant in the past and is able to return, just imagine the damage it will cause to the world. Questions?"

Jack cleared his throat, paused, and then spoke. "So…um, I can't believe I am saying this…when in time are you sending us back to…to hunt Rydel down?"

John took a moment before answering. "Rydel erased the time on the chip he stole from the lab. However, the chip he took went through one of Will's projects here—a computer keeping all the chips in line as to where they are going. We will program that information into backup chips we have that will take us exactly where Rydel traveled back to in time. From what Will has been able to find out so far"—the colonel held up his hands, a calm gesture for all not to freak out—"he thinks it is in the range of over a thousand years back in time, maybe a little more. We will dress you as best as we can to blend in with the people of the time. Unlike the backup chips all of you will use, which can't be tracked, you can track Rydel by the Placement chip inside him. He had no time to alter the chip he took in any way before he used it. Any other questions?"

Silence. They all looked a little overwhelmed. John glanced at Ray standing off to the side and gave him a slight smile. The colonel returned his attention back to the Unit.

"The scientists here need maybe another day to make sure Rydel did not tamper with the remaining backup chips we will use. So now all I need from each one of you is your favorite meal and adult beverage so we can set it up in this hangar tonight."

In front of John, Sal leaned back in his seat and clasped his hands together behind his head. "Sending us out in style, sir?"

"Abso-fucking-lutely."

# Rydel in the Past

As Rydel sat on the slanted ground with his head lowered, the sun began its descent behind the distant mountains to his right. The clothing and footwear he had chosen to wear to blend in for this trip were flawless because he stole the whole getup once he arrived. No one gave him any sort of odd look as if he did not belong in this time or was in some way out of place.

Rydel lifted his head, watching the sunset beside him. He gave the sunset a few more seconds of his time and then rose to his feet. He took six steps up the mountain, reached down for a shrub, and pulled it out from the ground with ease, then placed it off to the side, leaving a large hole in the ground. He reached in the hole and pulled out the Smartround rifle he had stolen from the lab, leaving behind the magazines—each holding one thousand smartrounds—for the weapon. He stood up with the gun in his hands and pressed a black button on the side of the weapon. A small screen with a mini keypad slid out from the side of the gun. Rydel stared down at the flashing red lettering:

Record targets?

He lifted the weapon up to his eyes and scanned over the ancient city of Jerusalem below. Behind the walls of the city, torchlights began to ignite sporadically in orange-shaped spheres here and there as night approached.

Rydel took in the city of Jerusalem with the gun's slide-out screen, closing in on the scattered people walking the streets.

Satisfied with his test run of the weapon, he lowered the gun and typed in a response of No on the keypad's small black keys. He placed the gun back in the hole in the ground. Rydel knelt down and reached deeper inside, then removed the smaller handgun version of the weapon and placed it under his cloak.

Back on his feet, Rydel turned to walk away and spotted a shadowed man standing near the top of the mountain, looking down at him. He blinked, and the man was gone. He was alone.

Rydel closed his eyes. He was tired, weary. His mind—his best asset—was begging for sleep. His thoughts needed to be clear and sharp to do what had to be done.

Rydel opened his eyes and made his way to his camp with the lean-to he had set up and got the rest he needed.

# Brothers

Colonel John Adams sat behind his desk, typing on his computer, when a knock at the door took him away from his work. He let out a frustrated grunt, saved what he was working on, and acknowledged the person on the other side of his office door.

"Come in."

Ray opened the door and shut it behind him.

"Oh, it's you. The hell did you knock for?"

Ray glanced up at the office ceiling, then at the walls and the door behind him before looking back at John, shrugging his shoulders, a gesture saying, You never know who is listening.

John waved a dismissive hand at Ray's worries. "Not in my office, brother. Speak as fucking freely as you want."

"Okay, I will. Go over again with me how this Placement works."

"I'll show you."

—

The overhead lights inside the Viewing Room at the lab came to life one section at a time.

To the right of the now bright room that resembled a theater with auditorium seating, John and Ray entered through a side door. A giant black screen waited. The two took seats in the front row with a console between them. John hit a button on the console, and the room went dark as the screen glowed light blue. A scruffily bearded man in his late twenties appeared on the screen with mountain topography behind him. To the left of the man, a pitched tent flapped in the breeze alongside a smoldering fire.

John hit a button on the console as he turned to Ray, and the image of the man froze on the screen.

"First one to use Placement. A volunteer here at the lab. Had the campsite set up months before, and I told him not to move from it," John said.

John hit another button, and the man on the screen slowly lifted a black pill in the palm of his right hand. The man raised his eyebrows and grinned at the camera taping him. Smiling a cocky smile, the man on the screen swallowed the black pill and closed his eyes. He then disappeared. A patch of the dirt ground he stood on sent up a swirling cone of soil five feet high. The dust settled, and there was nothing left of the man.

Ray stared down at his clenched fists for a moment, remembering what had happened to Martinez. He then turned to John seated next to him.

"The pill dissolves quickly once you swallow it," John said. "Rydel encased the chip in a pill because it needs to reach and attach to the stomach wall. And when it does, rock and roll. And it won't just plop you into a pool party surrounded with people or place you in the middle of a tree. Remember, its origin was Shutdown; it will keep you safe and alone when you arrive. The time travelers themselves may be a little scattered, but they're generally in the same area. After the chip returns you to where you came from, it detaches and, well, you know what happens. It's useless, but just make sure to double flush."

A slow smile started to spread across John's face.

"Now take a look at the video from a micro camera Will had inserted into a specific area of the man's brain that actually caught a glimpse of him being sent back in time."

John pressed another button on the console, holding it down for a few seconds.

"Take a look at this."

Ray fixed his attention on the screen fading to black. After staring at the black screen with nothing happening, Ray was about to turn back to John and ask him what exactly he was supposed to be looking at, and then it started to come into view in front of him: dotted lights on the screen. A constellation of stars in deep space is what Ray thought he was looking at, with a turning, tornado-like black circle in the middle of it all.

Ray turned to John and at the same time tried to keep an eye on the screen, stunned at what he was seeing.

"That's time travel?" Ray mumbled.

"A form of it. Not where we want it to be yet, but he sure as hell went back in time."

Ray's eyes drifted back to the screen. "The paradox of time travel? The grandfather thing?" Ray asked.

John nodded. "That's the whole point; we don't know yet. We can travel back, but as for changing anything in the past, hell no! Not after what happened the third time out testing Placement."

Ray adjusted himself in his seat so he could face John. "How do we get back?"

"It lasts anywhere from four to fourteen days. Taking you back to roughly the same place that you left from. It does not return you to an exact time and date. Rydel can't figure it out yet."

John stood up, staring down at Ray.

"But once we find Rydel and get him back working again at Genesis, just imagine what Placement can do."

"A weapon."

"The best defense in the world, brother. Think about it—no more 9/11s, bombings, the threat of an EMP—which is bound to happen."

Ray glanced back at the huge screen once more and then looked back at John, speechless.

"But it is beyond dangerous to change the past now, Ray. And we cannot go on any further without Rydel. We need to get him back."

John could see Ray struggling with everything he had just seen and everything he had just been told. "I know. A lot to take in. Let's get a beer and check in on your team."

## Sending Them Out in Style

Inside the lab's hangar they had all sat in hours before, Ray's Unit now gathered around a long table set up for a large sit-down meal with their beverages of choice in hand. The hangar doors opened, and military personnel walked in, making their way over to the table. The six men carried pizza boxes, Chinese cartons, McDonald's bags, Taco Bell bags—and one man held a tray with a roasted duck.

Jack looked over the members of the Unit at the table.

"Who ordered the duck?"

Sal raised his hand. "I did. They said anything we wanted; never had duck before. And with what they plan to do with us, I may never get a chance again."

Across from Sal, Janice shook her head. "Had to know it was Sal—who the hell else would order a fucking duck."

The military personnel placed the meals in front of each Unit member at the table, getting each dinner order right without having to ask. Then as a group, the military food-delivery service made their way out of the hangar. As the hangar doors closed, Todd stood and held up his Budweiser bottle, and the rest of the Unit did the same. No words—they just raised their drinks in a toast.

"Let's eat," Todd simply said and sat back down.

Sitting with their backs against the hangar, which was partially underground, John and Ray peeked through a window at the Unit seated around the table, a bucket of ice with a six-pack of beer placed between the two men. The two reached for a beer, taking in what was going on inside the hangar. John and Ray leaned away from the window and twisted the bottle caps off their beers, grinning.

"To be their age again…right, Ray?"

"Nope. Only wanna take this journey once and then take the next."

"I wish I had your faith, brother. I really do."

"There is something waiting for us after we die, John. There has to be."

After slugging down his beer in three sips, John reached for another in the ice bucket, twisted the cap off, and flipped it away with his thumb, the cap landing on a rock path leading away from the hangar. John lifted the beer to take a sip and stopped, the bottle inches from his lips. His eyes fixed on the bottle cap reflecting the light of the sun lowering over the hills around Genesis—just the slightest trace of sunlight on the bottle cap recalling a long-buried memory.

The light under the door…the only light.

Ray reached over for another beer and noticed the look on his brother-in-law's face.

"John, you okay? You—"

"I just don't believe like you and Kate do. I never will, Ray. Would a caring God leave two children in a basement to starve to death? Put there by their own father."

Ray's head dropped. He knew not to try to come up with a comforting response. He just sat and waited for John to speak about what he had been subjected to, something John never spoke of but something Ray knew a lot about, being married to his sister. There were many late nights holding Kate in his arms, her screaming as if he wasn't there…unable to shake the nightmares.

"He laughed at us," John said in a voice cracked with emotion.

Squinting from the lowering sun, Ray looked over at John. "What was that, John?"

"As he closed the basement door on us after smashing all the light bulbs, my dad was laughing as he walked away. A malicious sort of laugh I'd never heard come out of the man."

As John stared out at the woods surrounding the lab, Ray noticed that John's eyes seemed to be searching for something. Reaching back to the past, reliving the horror he went through with Kate.

John's face suddenly changed. Coming back from where his mind had traveled to, he looked at Ray. "I'm glad Kate was able to find religion after what we went through. But I'll never take comfort in any kind of God. Never."

"You two got out."

"Clawing away at the bottom of the door like two wild animals, which I guess we were by then, starving down there. No God helped us, Ray. Only a survival instinct saved us, with our fingernails ripped off, fingers sliced down the middle. A will to survive."

"Doesn't that will you're talking about have to come from somewhere?" Ray asked.

"Not from your God. It's just something every living thing has."

John took a long swallow from his beer.

"But if you are right and I'm wrong, and there is a God like you and Kate believe in—I want nothing to do with it. Nothing at all, brother."

## Rydel in the City of Jerusalem

Rydel walked among the people of Jerusalem and blended in perfectly with his pilfered clothing. He kept his head low and slowly walked through the crowd inside the stone city, eyeing a possible candidate ahead to help him. At a corner fish market, a man was looking at the selection on the table. Rydel approached the man and tapped him on the shoulder. The man turned around, facing Rydel with an angry, weathered face cracked deeply by the sun.

Rydel lowered his head and made a peaceful gesture with his arms raised, and the man calmed down. With his head down and his translator covered by both the hood of his garment and his keffiyeh, Rydel spoke to the man in Aramaic.

"The Nazareth man Jesus, the preaching man. Can you tell me where I can find him?" Rydel asked.

The man shook his head and nudged Rydel out of the way so he could choose and purchase the fish for his family's supper.

Rydel blended back into the crowd, hustling his way through the streets of the city. He continued his search for just one person with information on Jesus—one he could control to help him on his mission to rescue Christ.

Through the congested city, walking almost elbow to elbow with the people of the time, Rydel reached out for a lean-looking man walking toward him and tapped him on the shoulder. Before Rydel could get the words out through his translator, the man brushed him aside and looked back with a warning glare.

Rydel stepped aside from the busy horde of people and leaned against a tan wicker basket outside a tent selling meats. The proprietor stood at the other end of a long table under the tent, busy with a line of waiting customers. Rydel took it all in. The place was a metropolis much like Manhattan; the way they were all hustling and bustling—truly amazing. Not much has changed, Rydel thought to himself, and then he saw the man in the black cloak. A large black hood concealed the man's face; however, Rydel could feel the man staring at him through the black fabric.

The man folded his arms over his chest and continued to focus on Rydel without revealing his face from under the hood of his jet-black cloak. He stood out from the rest because of his garment's inky color, unlike anything worn by the people in the city. The man also had an allotted space to himself—not crammed in with the others fighting for room in the marketplace. He stood alone, his back against a stone wall. Rydel watched as people walked toward the space the man had to himself but then would inexplicably turn away and bump into one another—almost fleeing.

Rydel realized the people did not see the man—the people just knew instinctively to stay away.

Fear stiffened Rydel's body. He was able to take a few lumbering steps, his whole body shaking as he did. With the temperature in the city reaching at least ninety degrees, Rydel felt cold. His body felt as though he had been sprayed down with water and thrown out into a winter storm. Something inside of him also felt off—a wave of nausea. He felt the urge to throw up, but couldn't. It felt as if whatever started to come up out of his stomach was being thrust back down again to make him feel even worse.

Rydel's mind and body pleaded with him to do one thing—run. He quickly turned so he could escape from the black-cloaked man and ran into a tall man standing right behind him. The man looked down at Rydel, his face shadowed by the lowering sun.

"I overheard you speaking with the rude man and followed you." The man's soft-spoken Aramaic was translated back to Rydel. "I know the man Jesus. I'm a follower."

From under his cloak, Rydel slipped out S-7 and stuck it into the man's arm.

# Countdown

Ray's Unit sat at a table inside another white room at the lab. Above them, skylight windows dripped beads of rain from a heavy storm outside. Colonel Adams stood at the head of the table, flanked by Ray and Will. The colonel looked over the men and women of the Unit, all appearing to be unfazed about traveling back in time.

"You need to put aside the way you feel about Rydel. He's become completely unhinged. He is not the man you met before. I want you all to remember that," the colonel reminded them.

Will moved closer to the table.

"Understand, only two Placement chips will be left after we send all of you out to find Rydel. I hope you realize the importance of getting Rydel back," Will stated.

Sal raised his hand like a fourth-grader, his enthusiastic arm waving left and right to get Will's attention.

"Yes, you have a question?" Will asked Sal.

"Do we go nude?" Sal bluntly asked. "I'm thinking like in The Terminator movie, you know, where the Terminator ends up in some back alley on one knee with his ass crack taking in a stiff breeze. I mean, hey, I'm comfortable with it. I'm just asking for the others who are maybe too shy to ask."

Sal pointed his thumb behind him at Janice and whispered, "Rumor has it that Janice behind me doesn't shave her legs or anything else while she's out on a mission. It could be embarrassing for her. She's Greek."

"Fuck you and the small sack of old-man balls you got cursed with, Sal," Janice said, her face flushed.

Sal looked over his shoulder. "What? Easy, Janice. We're all family here. I was giving you a heads-up, that's all. My balls are small, but they're not old. Don't be mean."

Sal returned his attention back to Will.

"So…how about it, do we go nude?

"Anything touching you will go," Will curtly said. "Even the part of the floor you stand on will be sent back in time with you. Strap down tight everything you take. If something separates from you while traveling, it will follow you to the time you travel to—but you will have to search for it when you get there."

A slim lab tech in her thirties entered the room and walked over to John Adams.

"The chips are ready, Colonel.

—

Ray and the members of his Unit filed into an octagonal white room at the lab. They were all dressed up in cloaks of light and dark brown with large hoods draped over their shoulders and tan shemaghs around their necks to hide their translators. The weapons they carried were hidden under the cloaks they wore—all except for Sal, who had his gun and a tan bag slung over his back. Each member of Ray's Unit carried a sizable tan duffel bag with the exception of Steve and Ben. The two men each held a duffel bag in one hand and had two larger ones strapped to their backs. John and Will sat at the one table inside the room, John wearing a cloak like the others, waiting for Ray and his Unit. In front of John and Will was a line of small black boxes.

Ray and his team lined up at the table. The colonel grabbed a tan duffel bag by his feet, stood up, and joined them at the other side. They all waited silently for the colonel to speak.

"We find Rydel and avoid the people in the past at all costs. Let's hope we're not too late."

John took a black pill out of one of the boxes on the table. He walked away from the table to the opposite side of the room, turned around, and met the eyes of the others. He swallowed the pill, remained where he was for a moment, and then disappeared—along with some of the floor tiles he had been standing on. A small white hole floated and lingered in midair until it evaporated like curling smoke, twisting itself into nothingness.

Ray took his black pill out of one of the boxes. "Anyone wants out, I'll understand. And so will the colonel. He told me he would—"

"Adams said nothing about this to me, Catlin. All must go," Will said in a raised voice.

All in the room turned toward Will.

"What you need to do now is leave the room. *I am* in charge at the moment," Ray said, glaring at Will, the look in his eyes telling Will he really should leave—now.

"But—"

One word was all Will was able to get out. He noticed the members of Ray's Unit, as one, walking his way to remove him from the room. Before they could, Will shot up out of his seat and was gone. With Will out of the room, the members of the Unit turned back to face Ray. Janice was the first to speak.

"You're lying about the colonel, Ray. Why?"

"When I reach him, I'll explain I gave all of you a second chance to think about it, and that it was my call. I need to make sure all of you want to do this. In no way will your military careers suffer if any of you say no. I'll make Colonel Adams understand because…well, shit, as only you guys and General Dowling know, he's my brother-in-law. It's all good. So for anyone having second thoughts, stay behind. I'm ordering you."

"You're trying to protect us, Ray," Steve said.

"It's what he always does," Adriana said, agreeing with Steve.

"I have to go. I believe John and I can find Rydel alone. It is an overabundance of resources sending all of you out."

"Shit, he's lying to us all right!" Sal said, looking over the others in the Unit. He then looked back at Ray. "You never lie, Ray. And, man, let me tell you something, you suck at it."

Yeah, he was lying, and they all knew it—he was bad at it. Ray glared at Sal for a split second, then looked over the faces of the others in the Unit.

"Okay, maybe I'm not being completely forthcoming about my—"

"Uh-oh. Forthcoming. Ray said forthcoming on top of the phrase overabundance of resources," Sal blurted out and then continued: "Yep, I feel another lie coming."

Arm straight out, Ray pointed at Sal. "Sal, shut up."

Glancing at the members of his Unit one more time, Ray took a few steps away from the table and swallowed the pill he held in his hand.

"Stay. You all don't have to do this—"

Ray disappeared just like John before him, the tiles where he stood going with him.

The members of Ray's Unit stood where they were for a few seconds. They reached out and took their assigned pills out of the black boxes.

They all swallowed the pills at the same time.

# The Messiah

The faithful entered the arched gateway into the Holy City of Jerusalem all crammed together, barely having room to lift their arms from their sides. Behind the flow of humanity entering the city, a man on a donkey approached and waited to enter, His followers flanking Him. Men and women of all ages seemed to notice the man on the small animal at the same time without anyone saying a word to one another. The people inside the bustling stone city made a path as best as they could so that the man could enter. Then, as one, the crowd screamed in heightened joy at the sight of the man—the Holy Man unlike any other before—slowly entering the city of Jerusalem.

Toward the back of the crowd, Rydel watched the man make His way through the city. No matter how hard he tried to get closer, he could not take more than three to four steps at a time. He was the last man in the back of the crowd—too far away. He watched the man he had come back in time to save slipping out of sight through the crowd.

Rydel tried once more to pass the people in front of him and accidentally pushed over a small child standing next to her mother. He gasped at what he'd done and lifted the girl off the ground, brushing the dirt off the back and front of her knee-length tunic. The stunned child moved closer to her mother, looking up at her. The child's mother, caught up in watching the miracle man enter the city, did not realize that her little girl had fallen to the ground. But she did suddenly notice Rydel standing close and smiled at him.

"They say he's cured a man from death. Do you believe?" the woman asked Rydel in Aramaic.

Rydel took in the language through the translator hidden under his keffiyeh and nodded at the woman. The child pulled on Rydel's cloak. He tilted his head down at the girl, who was now by his side.

"I believe," the little girl said, her words translating to Rydel in English.

Rydel smiled down at the young girl, the sweet child not caring that he had just accidentally pushed her down moments before. Rydel looked back up and took in the last glimpse of the celebrated man moving deeper inside the city against the late afternoon sun.

Rydel felt a pull on his cloak again and looked down at the little girl beside him. The sweet girl now tugged on his cloak with a serpent's tongue—the girl's face reddened in rage—the pupils of her eyes slits of black. The snake-like tongue recoiled and slid back into the little girl's mouth. The face of the child, beautiful and innocent seconds ago in front of Rydel, started to crack by her eyes and cheeks, blood running freely. The little girl grinned at Rydel with her reptilian face.

"He dies," she said to Rydel in a soulless voice, speaking the words in English.

The little girl's tongue slowly rolled out of her mouth, red and elongated, flickering at the tip. She started to lick Rydel's groin area in a sick, seductive way. Pulling away, Rydel fell to the ground, his arms flailing to protect himself as he landed. The demonic child squatted in front of Rydel and slapped him across the face. She then disappeared in a swirling mist of dust.

Rydel stood up and quickly spun around, searching for the thing that was a little girl just minutes before. Coming to a stop, he faced the child's mother staring at him with concern. The woman placed a hand on his shoulder.

"Are you all right?" the woman asked. Rydel waited for the words to translate and noticed the little girl standing by her mother's side—normal, as she was before.

The child's mother took a step closer. Rydel stumbled backward, distancing himself from the woman. He fell to his knees and shot right back up to his feet, turning away from the woman and the child, running toward a side street. Rydel ran down the empty street, faster than he ever thought possible, fear pushing him forward. He ran for as long as he could and finally stopped to catch his breath, bending at the waist. After taking in all the air it took to breathe normally, Rydel raised his body upright.

At the end of the deserted stone-walled side street, the cloaked man, again with his face hidden under his charcoal-black hood, waited for Rydel.

Fear took over Rydel's body again—his body shaking in intermittent spasms, quickly coming and going. All that was in front of him was a man in black. Just a man! Nothing to fear, Rydel reasoned with himself, trying to shake the foreboding grip over his body.

Another man in a brownish tunic trotted quickly toward the man in black, shuffling on his hands and feet—his back awkwardly arched. He sat by the feet of the black-cloaked man like a beaten dog.

"My God—is that a man?" Rydel said in a whimpering voice to no one, the words just coming out of him.

The man in the black cloak pointed a spearhead-like black finger at Rydel and lowered his hooded head, looking down at the thing, the man-dog, waiting by his feet. He then spoke to it in Aramaic.

"Eat him."

The man's legs ripped through the tattered tunic he wore. The thing galloped like a rabid animal toward Rydel. The man-dog ran at a freakish angle, its arms and legs almost running sideways—but still coming straight toward Rydel. Fast.

Rydel fumbled with his Smartround handgun under his cloak as the crazed beast leaped in the air and landed on him. As they scampered for position on the ground, the man-dog bit into Rydel's left arm and pulled away its mouth—a chunk of cloth and a piece of flesh tearing from Rydel's arm.

Rydel let out a scream and swung his right arm at the crazed thing, hitting it on the head with the butt of his Smartround handgun. He quickly fired two rounds into its chest. The man-dog fell to its side and began clawing at its chest in an attempt to extract the rounds. After ripping through its clothing and reaching the smartrounds, the thing stopped moving.

With his throat feeling as if he had swallowed sand, Rydel weakly rose to one knee and heard laughter coming from the other end of the narrow street—the man in the black cloak, laughing an eerie, screeching laugh. Frozen by fear on one knee, staring at the black-cloaked man, Rydel could make out the man's eyes from under the black hood. The ice-blue eyes he saw sent another wave of fearful spasms shuddering through his body, urging him to vomit, which he was finally able to do in two rapid, bursting thrusts. What came out of his mouth and spilled on the ground was a black fluid that began to crawl back toward him, reaching out for Rydel.

Rydel's body broke free from its paralysis at the sight of what was reaching out for him. He bolted toward the other end of the street, away from the regurgitated living black liquid crawling after him.

## The Arrival

Through arched gateways, a line of people made its way into a lengthy stone courtyard surrounded by white pillars. Tables for exchanging coins, and open-sided tents with merchants selling animals in small wooden crates, lined the pillared courtyard.

A man's angry shout turned the people around. There was not one person—with all the commotion going on in the courtyard—who did not hear the man's voice.

A man in an off-white hooded cloak covering His face down to His lips walked straight toward the money-changing tables. No one in the dense crowd got in His way or touched Him as He moved forward.

The man reached the tables and started flipping them over. Just as He did, a stream of white light flashed in the sky above.

—

Inside a small stone passageway half-lit by the sun, the sound of whooshing air could be heard as members of Ray's Unit started to appear in flashing spheres of bright white light. Four members of Ray's Unit materialized with their knees on the ground and heads lowered, the hoods of their cloaks hiding their faces. The white light sending the four back in time receded into the blue sky above the passageway and vanished.

Todd was the first to raise his head and take in his surroundings. After releasing his tight grip on the duffel-bag strap he held onto with one hand, he looked over at the other three Unit operators with him, hidden under their hooded cloaks. Beneath each hood, all three had their chins pressed against their chests and eyes closed tightly, unsure if the journey back in time was over.

"Guys, we're here," Todd quietly said.

Adriana, Janice, and Sal lifted their heads, following the direction of Todd's voice. The three stared wide-eyed at Todd. Steve and Jack lumbered out of the dark in a daze, followed by Ben, the men making their way over to Todd. Adriana got it together and started to search the stone passageway with quick looks over her shoulder, then turned back to Todd. "Ray and Adams aren't here."

"Carrie and Kevin are also missing—" Janice started to say.

Todd held up a hand at the two. "We wait. Nobody move. Quiet."

"Todd—"

Todd turned to face Sal, now standing by his side.

"I said quiet, Sal."

"Todd…my gun and the extra ammo aren't here either."

Todd glanced over the alley, mumbling to himself.

"Shit."

—

They were alone in the dark.

Ray waited in the shadows for a few minutes with Carrie and Kevin after arriving, the eyes of the three adjusting to the darkness with only slight fragments of light ahead. Ray then ventured out of the dark into a stone passageway, placing his foot across a barely inch-thick shaft of light streaming from above. Ahead, Ray could see the way out of the narrow stone passageway—an opening outlined in sunlight was just forty feet away. He turned to where Carrie and Kevin waited in the dark.

"Stay there."

Ray ran and reached the end of the passageway, then leaned his back against the left side of the curved structure of stone leading out, closing his eyes for a few seconds. He then tilted his head around the corner.

Outside the passageway, men and women were making a path to allow a hooded man to leave a very crowded courtyard. The hood of the man's cloak concealed His face as the people continued to step out of the man's way. A man of power, maybe a politician in this time, Ray thought at first.

However, there was something else about Him. A feeling of purity Ray felt—an indescribably comforting feeling of warmth radiating from the man.

Red-flag warnings began to go off in Ray's mind as his military senses kicked back in, telling him to ignore these emotions he should not be having while out on a mission.

"What is this? What's happening to me?" Ray said aloud.

A flash of movement caught Ray's attention. An obese man, whose weight was not hidden by the brown tunic covering his bloated body, dragged a woman into a stone passageway directly across from where Ray stood. The way he moved the woman against her will, without anyone else seeming to notice—it was clear to Ray the woman was about to be violated in some way or killed. John's orders to avoid contact with the people of this time repeated in Ray's head: Just get Rydel back. Ray was about to take a step out into the courtyard, disobeying orders he knew he should follow, then stopped. Suddenly it hit him what ramifications his actions might have on the people back home, just as John had warned about. So Ray turned his back on the woman and fucking hated doing it.

As he turned away, Ray caught a glimpse of another man. The shrouded man entered the passageway where the obese man had dragged the woman. A sudden gust of wind lifted the hood of the newcomer's cloak—exposing a flash of his face to Ray.

"Rydel…?"

The man Ray caught a glimpse of slipped into the alley like a ghost. Not sure what he had seen, Ray sprinted back down the narrow stone passageway to check on Carrie and Kevin. The two stepped out of the dark, hearing Ray approach, and stood in front of him.

"Stay hidden. I need to check something out in an alley across from this one. I won't be long." Ray put on his translator and wrapped his shemagh around his neck to hide the device.

He ran off, leaving Carrie and Kevin once more. The two slowly eased back into the darkness around them. A hand reached out from the blackness behind the two and rested on Carrie's shoulder. Carrie spun around and threw a wild roundhouse punch at the person, which was batted away.

Kevin stepped around Carrie with his elbow held high, ready to strike.

"Lower your arm, Kevin."

Kevin lowered his arm, recognizing the voice, and was now able to make out the colonel in the limited light.

Carrie and Kevin stood in front of John Adams, both relieved, waiting for orders.

"Did you two see the rest yet?"

"Just Ray," Carrie said. "He saw something. Went to check it out—an alley like this across from where we are. Told us to stay put."

"Rydel?" John asked, hoping.

Carrie shrugged, glanced at Kevin for a second, then looked back at the colonel, answering him. "Don't know."

John ran down the stone passageway, yelling back to the two. "Stay here—do not move."

Ordered yet again to stay where they were after traveling back in time, Carrie and Kevin were more than happy to take a knee and wait.

With his translator hidden and in place, John slowly stepped out of the passageway, spotted the alley Carrie had described, and began to make his way over to the other side of the courtyard, walking at a brisk pace. The colonel slowed down a bit as people started to notice him—not paying much attention, but enough. He walked the rest of the way across and entered the dark passageway. Inside, shafts of sunlight made their way in from above, and he was able to find Ray at once. He was just standing there in the light, unmoving. The colonel ran over and grabbed Ray, spinning him around. He then shut off his translator so he could speak to Ray in English.

"Ray!"

With his translator hanging around his neck, Ray looked at John, dejected. "Thought I saw Rydel heading in here, but it wasn't him, and I came across this—"

"Came across what?"

Ray nodded past the streaming sunlight. John followed Ray's eyes and saw it—a pair of bloodied legs on the ground, lit by the sun. The rest of the body cut off by the darkness inside the stone passageway. John had no idea if there was anything left in the dark connecting the legs to a body.

Out of the shadows, the obese man walked into the light, knelt down, and reached for the other half of the dead woman in the dark, bringing her into his arms, holding her tight. John could now see that the woman's throat was slit open.

The sight was gruesome. The slash to the woman's throat almost completely encircled her head. There was also another wound in the center of her stomach—a crimson gash dripping blood.

At the same time, John turned on his translator, and Ray placed his translator back over his mouth.

The obese man lowered his head and wept over the woman, letting the knife that he killed her with fall to the ground. He began to speak to the dead woman in Aramaic.

"I loved you..."

"And she loved you," a different, deep voice said in Aramaic from somewhere inside the darkness around them.

The words came from behind John and Ray, and the two stared at each other, confused. They turned in the direction of the voice as the man who had tipped over the tables in the courtyard earlier stepped out of the dark. With the hood of His cloak covering His face, the man walked toward John and Ray. As He did, the man placed a hand on Ray's shoulder in a polite gesture to give Him some room so He could make His way between the two.

The hooded man slipped between John and Ray, reaching the obese man with the dead woman. The man knelt by the dead woman's side, His black-rope gartel reaching the ground. He looked up at the corpulent murderer.

"Why?"

"She...she was talking with another man, talking in a way I did not like. It...it...it hurt to see," the man uttered.

"You ended her life for talking with another man?" the hooded man asked incredulously. He glanced back down at the slaughtered mess the obese man had made out of the woman.

The hooded man raised His head up again, and the murderer let the woman slip out of his arms. The large man ran away. The hooded man returned His attention back to the dead woman on the ground.

The obese man ran by John and Ray, not noticing the two in any way, wanting to escape from what he had done—the remorse now caving in on him.

John and Ray turned, watching the murderer run toward the other end of the alley. Ray turned his attention back to the hooded individual with the dead woman.

John made sure that the obese man was gone before spinning around. He reached for Ray's translator, shut it off, did the same with his, and grabbed Ray by the arm.

"He didn't see us. He's gone—let's get out of here, Ray." The colonel tried pulling Ray away, but he couldn't move him.

"Ray—now!"

"John…the man and the woman—"

"She's dead, Ray! C'mon!"

"Look."

John looked back at the dead woman on the ground. The hooded man had both hands splayed out over her wounds, blood oozing between His fingers, dripping down the backs of His hands. A light brightened the passageway and seemed to shift toward the man's hands—too fast and too white to be descending sunlight, and the dead woman's wounds seemed to burn in the white light.

The woman sat up, jolted by life.

The blinding light faded. John and Ray lowered their arms that were covering their faces—both had instinctively shielded their eyes from the piercing brightness. The two stared at the man in natural sunlight, now standing with the woman, a woman who had been dead just moments before. John and Ray turned their translators back on.

The man spoke to the woman, and His words translated back to John and Ray after a few seconds.

"Go home. Your child is hungry and alone. Your husband is now leaving the city. You will never see him again. People will say he abandoned you and the child. You and your child will be cared for."

The woman stood in front of the man for a moment and then clumsily walked away.

Witnessing the miracle, Ray's eyes were wide open in shock. John stood, confused, not sure what had just happened.

The woman, healed of her throat and stomach wounds, walked past John and Ray. She, like the man who had killed her just minutes before, did not notice the two. John and Ray watched from over their shoulders as the woman reentered the courtyard.

The two turned toward the healing man, who was now staring back at them. The man then made His way down to the opposite end of the stone passageway, fading into darkness. John and Ray followed in a fog, both drawn to Him.

With their translators off and hidden under their shemaghs, John and Ray walked deeper into the darkening passage. Light began to appear up ahead, leading toward another way out. The man stepped out of the alleyway into the light and could be seen no more. Ray quickly ran ahead. Surprised by Ray taking off so fast, John stumbled a couple of steps forward and sprinted after Ray.

For almost half an hour, John fought with Ray to turn back, but he wouldn't. Ray would push John away when he grabbed hold of him and wouldn't listen when being ordered to stop.

So John had no choice but to follow Ray for over an hour, surrounded by the people of the past. Reaching a dirt road outside the stone city they had traveled through, Ray followed it toward a hillside and finally came to a stop. John grabbed him by the arm.

"Goddammit, Ray, stop already!"

"He's up there, on the dirt path circling the hill. See Him?"

"Ray, listen! Listen!"

"He touched me," Ray whispered to himself.

John shook his head, not hearing Ray.

"What—what did you say?"

Ray broke away from John and started to go up the hillside, the man almost out of sight. John reached out and grabbed Ray once more.

"Ray, stop—stop. What the fuck is wrong with you!"

Ray stared at John with unresponsive, void-like eyes, then looked away, searching for the man on the hillside who was now out of sight. Tears fell down Ray's face as he dropped down on one knee. John crouched beside Ray, still holding his arm tightly, and tried a different approach to snap Ray out of whatever was going on in his head.

"Ray…come back to me here, brother. I need you—and your team needs you. Some are missing."

John's words got Ray's attention.

"Missing? Who?"

"Ray—for the safety of your Unit—you need to come with me. Right now!"

—

John and Ray reached the passageway where they had left Carrie and Kevin to wait. The fragmented sunlight coming in from above had just about slipped away.

"What happened?"

The sound of Kevin's voice, spoken softly from out of the engulfing darkness, spun John and Ray around in a defensive manner, both pointing their sidearms at Kevin's head outlined in remnants of sunlight with Carrie by his side. John and Ray lowered their weapons and pulled back their hoods, the two men unable to hide being unnerved.

"What is it, Ray?" Carrie asked, her voice high, worried. She'd never seen Ray in the condition he was in now while out on a mission. In the last shafts of light receding from inside the stone passageway, Carrie could see that Ray's body was shaking.

Kevin stepped toward Ray.

"You okay there, Ray?"

Ray fought to calm his trembling body—and did so for the most part—as Kevin took another step closer. Ray nodded to Kevin that he was fine, stepped around him, and stood in front of Carrie, inches away from her face.

"Communication yet, Carrie?"

"Yeah, I got hold of Todd. He's with the others, waiting for your orders."

Ray reached into the pocket of his cargo pants and took out his Genesis-enhanced headset, adjusting it to his head with hands beginning to tremble again.

"Todd..."

Todd's voice came back immediately and urgently. "Hey, what's going on—did you find Rydel already?"

John joined Ray by his side, listening in. "Thought I saw him, but no. Stay where you are. We'll track you through your gun."

"Sal's gun and our backup ammo are missing, Ray."

"Just stay where you are."

Ray removed his headset, and John walked him away from Carrie and Kevin to talk privately. The colonel turned and pointed back at Carrie and Kevin.

"You two stay there."

Carrie and Kevin stood where they were, watching John walk Ray out of earshot. Thirty feet away, John stopped and pulled Ray closer to him. Although dark, there was enough light to make out that John was furious.

"Ray, you need to get your shit together, and I mean now. Carrie and Kevin can tell you're starting to lose it." John glanced back at Carrie and Kevin, took a few seconds, calmed down, and placed a hand on Ray's shoulder.

Ray stared at John, lost and confused.

"But what about what we saw? The woman? She—"

"We saw nothing. Nothing, Ray. Now let's get the rest of your team together, find Rydel, and wait to be taken back."

John turned away from Ray and walked back to Carrie and Kevin. Two of America's most elite operators now looked shaken, which was to be expected traveling back in time. But what worried John was they also looked leaderless—both staring at John for answers while Ray stood behind the three in the darkness. Carrie and Kevin glanced over John's shoulder to see where Ray was, the two looking like abandoned children.

The colonel stepped closer.

"Ray's coming, give him a second. You two follow me, keep your heads down, and avoid the people like we talked about. Got it?"

Carrie and Kevin nodded.

"Gonna need more than a nod when an order has been given by a colonel—so let's hear it, you two."

Both stood erect and gave the colonel a "Yes, sir" at the same time.

"I understand the situation we are in is unique, but remember the elite operators that you are—better than any in the world."

The mini pump-up speech by John got Carrie and Kevin back and ready. Out of the darkness around them, Ray joined John without saying a word. It seemed to Carrie and Kevin that Ray barely acknowledged they were there. As the two waited for John to give the next order, Carrie and Kevin took in Ray's condition with his distant, faraway gaze.

"You two follow me. Hoods over your heads, sling the duffel bags over your shoulders. Do not walk past me, and listen to everything I say," the colonel said to Carrie and Kevin with assuredness in his voice and eyes.

Carrie and Kevin snapped out another "Yes, sir." Ray just stood by John's side, nodding distractedly.

"Let's move," John said.

The four moved toward the light of a fading day, the sunlight coming from the passageway's arched opening.

Out of the passageway, avoiding scattered men and women inside the stone-pillared open area, the four kept their heads down and pushed slowly forward. No one seemed to give any notice to the tan duffel bags from the future that Carrie and Kevin carried on their backs—the bags blended in with Carrie and Kevin's wardrobe nicely. From under her hooded cloak, Carrie stared down at the slide-out screen on her concealed Smartround gun, tracking the rest in the Unit and getting a fix on them before the others.

She lifted her head slightly and joined the colonel, who was leading the way out in front.

"I have them, sir."

"Stay by my side and lead the way," the colonel ordered.

They all kept their heads down, passing only scattered groups of people here and there as they traveled. At a barely noticeable narrow entrance leading into a stone passageway to their right, Carrie entered the tight space sideways, followed by John and Ray. Kevin trailed behind, making sure nobody followed. Satisfied they were now clear, Kevin quickly stepped inside the passageway.

Led by Carrie, the four walked cautiously—*two steps, stop, two steps, stop*—slowly making their way ahead. Carrie turned on her flashlight, and the four gathered around one another, pulling back their hoods. Carrie pointed a finger in front of her.

"They're up ahead," she said.

Before John could give the next order, Ray spoke.

"Unit."

John turned to Ray, giving him a slight smile.

"You're back?"

"I am, John."

Up ahead, the rest of Ray's Unit began to appear from out of the dark.

## Camp

Logistically, it took over a day and a half to begin the search for Rydel. With a view through his binoculars, Ray looked down from a high ledge jutting out from the deserted mountainside that he and John commandeered. He scanned the city of Jerusalem, only a short walk away, then focused on the members of his Unit below. Sal, Ben, and Steve had set up three tents while Jack finished digging out a second fire pit. Janice and Kevin were away from the rest, searching for firewood. All were doing what they should be doing—all except for him, Ray thought. He had told John he wanted to look over the members of his Unit from above to make sure the pressure of being in another time did not get to some of them. And John bought it.

However, he was standing high above for only one reason—to search for the healing man from the stone alley. He was now connected to the man and could not disregard what had passed through his body, mind, and soul by the simple touch of the man's hand—a hand that had healed a dead woman right before his eyes. He knew he was searching for a needle in a haystack, but it did not matter. All Ray wanted to do now was find Him.

After three years together, the members of his Unit were a family he had adopted, a family that needed his protection. Right now, however, the healing man needed his protection more, for a reason he did not yet understand.

Ray watched the members of his Unit dotting the i's and crossing the t's around the camp, getting ready to hunt Rydel down. Being who-knows-how-many years away from the time they belonged in, each member of the Unit still did not miss a beat. Perfect. Ray programmed his binoculars to search the hill where he had last seen the healing man and again found no human activity.

Ray noticed Adriana a distance away from the rest. She was setting up a tripod-10 tracker—a small tracking system provided by Genesis—so they could better track Rydel and search for Sal's gun and the lost ammo at the same time. Ray scanned the hill once more for the man who had healed the dead woman. He lowered the binoculars and put them in the pocket of his cargo pants. He stared ahead for close to a minute, then turned and walked away with the sun on his back.

—

On a nightscape mountainside miles away from Ray and the rest of the operators hunting him, Rydel ran down a dirt path haphazardly, slipping here and there. He reached the bush where he hid what he had borrowed from the lab for his mission. Rydel felt a wave of relief, knowing he was lucky not to break an ankle on his way down the mountain. Thankful he did not cripple himself. Thankful that he was now only inches away from a weapon. Something was following him, watching him.

He fell to his knees and pushed away a bush in front of him—the bush he had uprooted when he first arrived. He had dug a two-foot hole under it to hide all that he had taken from the present to aid him on his mission here in the past (the hole too far away from his camp, Rydel lambasted himself).

Left in the hole to taunt him was the Smartround rifle he had taken from the lab, placed on two V-shaped branches stuck into the ground—the ammunition and the handgun gone.

Behind him, someone laughed. Rydel spun around to see a shadowed man above him, outlined by the light of the moon. The man in the black cloak, who had been with Rydel from almost the time he had arrived, glared down at him from the mountain's precipice. The man in black lowered to his haunches, fixed on Rydel.

Rydel's bladder failed him, pouring urine down his right leg. He got up and ran as fast as he could down the mountain to escape from the man above, never daring to look back.

—

The moon and stars lit up the mountainside where John and Ray stood. The two men scanned the stone city below with their Smartround guns, searching for Rydel.

"Colonel Adams, Ray…"

John and Ray turned to see Jack coming their way.

"What is it, Jack?" Ray asked.

"Got a slight hit from Rydel's chip. He's on the mountain across from us. And Adriana has tracked down Sal's gun and the lost ammo just outside that city we arrived at."

John and Ray followed Jack back down to the camp. Ray ordered the rest of his Unit to gather by a fire now burning high and snapping, sending swirling sparks into the air.

"Everyone take a knee," Ray quickly said.

The members of Ray's Unit took a knee around the fire. Ray glanced over his shoulder at John standing behind him. John nodded and walked away. Ray turned his attention back to the men and women in front of him.

"Two groups going out. Sal, Todd, you two are coming with me to the city, where Adriana has tracked down the lost ammo and Smartround gun."

Ray waved his index finger in a back-and-forth arc over the others.

"The rest of you will join Colonel Adams and track down Rydel. We leave in ten."

The members of the Unit rose to their feet and hurried back to the tents.

Not seeing John anywhere, Ray began to run. In just under a minute, he stood on a mountain ridge, watching the city below again, a city lit by various methods of fire. The conflicting feelings he was having between leading the members of his Unit and running off in search of the man in the alley were hindering his abilities to focus. Something inside had been altered when the man touched him. Ray could feel the goodness of the man flowing through him—and suddenly he became unequivocally aware of who the man was—it was Jesus Christ. He now knew it was not just some chance encounter with the Messiah; it was meant to happen. He had been chosen.

Earlier, he had tried dismissing what he saw in the alley. But the feeling of what passed between the two had now grown stronger. He was being drawn to Christ.

"Ray?"

Ray turned to see John, not ten feet away, walking toward him. So deep in thought, Ray lost track of time and didn't hear John approach until he was just about on top of him. Normally, Ray could hear and sense a person from over fifty feet away. Now, almost face-to-face with John, Ray knew he could not hide what he was doing up here. It didn't matter. It was time to be honest about the man they encountered in the alley and what He did.

"Ray, what—what the hell is it now? I thought you got your shit back together. You look half-fucking mad. You have any idea how long you've been up here? Your Unit is waiting for you!"

"You know who the man in the alley was, John. You saw what He did," Ray calmly said.

John started to speak but then stopped. He walked toward a ridge overlooking the camp and glanced down, making sure all in Ray's Unit were where he had left them. He walked back to Ray and stood inches away from his face.

"I'm not sure what I saw, Ray. Okay, yeah—saw something messed up, but it doesn't matter. We need to find Rydel before he's able to save this man."

"Rydel wants to save Him?"

John rolled his eyes in frustration and nodded.

"Why?"

"Because Rydel is losing his frigging mind, that's why!"

Ray turned away from John and looked down at the city aglow in candles, fires, and torch-flame.

"So you knew when we were going back in time, and you didn't tell me?"

"Yes."

"Why keep it from me?"

"Because look how you're acting now. I know you have your beliefs, but we cannot let Rydel do this! The devastation could be catastrophic if he succeeds. We have to stop him. Lives back home are at stake here. Please, please do not fucking forget that, Ray."

The tug of war inside Ray eased—the conflict of what he should do fading away. Lives back home may very well be in harm's way if we change anything in this time, Ray reminded himself. He knew John would do anything to protect American lives. The man truly loved the people he protected.

"Okay, John. Let's find Rydel and take him home."

## Clopas

On the mountain he chose for his camp, the rocky terrain now half-lit in moonlight, Rydel sat tucked away in the darkness. The city of Jerusalem below him glowing, the Lower City homes dotted in candlelight and the Upper City palaces blazingly aflame with the use of ornate oil lamps.

Rydel stared at a small fire in front of him, the hood of a second cloak he had had to confiscate covering his face, down to his nose. The superficial bite wounds from the man-dog were no longer painful. The wind cried out, moving over the fire, chilling Rydel, goose bumps spreading over his skin.

A man's deep voice spoke from behind Rydel: "I'm here for you."

Rydel recognized the voice and did not move. He waited for his translator to translate the words. He turned his hooded head around, eyes searching the darkness behind him, seeing no one.

"Let me see you," Rydel said in Aramaic. Peripherally, from under his hood, Rydel caught movement to his left. The darkness around him shifted, and the tall shape of a man walked out of the dark. Rydel kept his head lowered and spoke again through his translator.

"Come…sit with me by the fire."

The black shape emerged from the darkness and walked closer. The firelight reached the man as he moved near, lighting his tall body and face. The forty-year-old man with his sunken, skull-like, deep-tanned face looked down at Rydel with eager eyes that wanted to please.

"Come, Clopas."

Clopas cautiously walked forward and sat on the ground opposite Rydel. The man nodded at Rydel and lowered his head, waiting to be spoken to again.

"Word of where Jesus is now?" Rydel asked Clopas.

"No," Clopas answered.

"His followers?"

Clopas shook his head. "No. When Simon comes to see me again, I will know more."

Rydel leaned closer toward the fire and pulled back the hood of his cloak. There was no need to hide his translator from the man; he was under the influence of S-7, and Rydel had told him to never see it. "Clopas, you told me you knew all there is to know about Jesus!"

Rydel stood up and started pacing back and forth, glaring down at Clopas each time he passed the man seated by the fire.

"Shit," Rydel said to himself. Frustrated, he began to think that he might have wasted S-7 on the wrong person to help him find Jesus. Clopas had helped locate Jesus once, but maybe that was all the information the man had.

Clopas stood, sensing and seeing the anger coming from Rydel. He took a couple of steps toward Rydel, holding his arms out straight with his palms up.

"No one in the city can tell me where they stay during the night. Most only want to talk about the healed one."

As the words translated back, Rydel came to an abrupt stop in front of the fire.

"The healed one?" Rydel asked.

Guarded, but very much wanting to please Rydel, Clopas ventured a couple of steps closer and lowered his head submissively.

"Clopas, lift your head."

Clopas lifted his head. He had a look on his face that was both nervous and eager.

"What you need to do right now is tell me all you know about the healed one people are talking about."

"Lazarus. I know him. A friend. And a very close friend of Jesus. He had passed, and Jesus brought him back, filling his body with life again. I was there. I saw. Lazarus is in hiding now. Many seek him out, wanting to see the miracle of being reborn into the world after death. Others seek him out for different reasons."

Rydel took a couple of slow, deliberate steps and put a hand on Clopas's shoulder, smiling at him. And Clopas returned the smile, eager to please Rydel under S-7's control.

"You know where this man is, Clopas?"

"Yes, he's a friend."
"Take me to him. Now."

# The Overlook

At the lab, seven men were seated at a table in a white room called the Overlook. These scientific laboratory technicians, handpicked by Will, sat in front of security monitoring screens overlooking the entire lab and everything around it. From cameras inside the lab to outside cameras tracking the roads leading up to Genesis—and anything closing in from the sky with its miles of restricted airspace—it was all monitored here. The Overlook also tracked weather conditions.

Will entered the room and walked down the line of techs facing their screens. Not one of the men turned to face him; all kept their attention focused on their appointed posts. Will walked past the seated men, making three passes as he studied each screen, and then stopped, staring over one man's shoulder.

"Remember, even the slightest change in the climate, any storm moving in—I need to know."

"Yes, sir."

Will continued looking over the man's shoulder, leaning closer—so close the tech could feel him breathing on his neck. Will stared at the tech's screen for another minute, pulled himself up straight, and walked out of the room.

Outside the Overlook, Will waited with his ear pressed against the door, listening. Handpicked or not, he trusted no one. Will stayed that way for two minutes, satisfied that the seven men in the room did not speak a word of disrespect toward him. He walked down a white hallway leading away from the Overlook and entered his office a few doors down, locking the door behind him. Will's office at the lab was stark white, spacious, and impressive. What made it seem so grand was the ceiling—at least forty feet from the floor. A black sofa and one large desk reaching thirty feet across faced a window with a view of pine trees on a sloping hill. On Will's desk, three white computers lay idle. Will placed his hand on the computer screen in the middle, and it came alive in a deep red glow.

The red screen on the computer then faded to white. The names of each one sent back in time—with the exception of Rydel—appeared on the screen to show their vital signs. Their vitals came back in a jumbled mess of unusable data. Just like the three times out before, nothing came back. But maybe as the time travelers returned, the safeguard he had added to the backup chips might work.

Will came to realize that not only was he in charge of the lab—but in a delusional grasp for more power—he now thought he was in charge of the mission.

And sometimes, tough decisions must be made.

Like if any dangerous earth activity should make its way toward the lab as the time travelers returned, he would be forced to kill each one with a new project he had just recently designed and added to the replicated chips before the time travelers left. They would not feel a thing. Just like being on ice, their bodies would shut down, but for good—at 1.1 seconds before arriving back in the present. As simple as that, once he decided to upload the program. Saving him and humanity.

## Dawn over Jerusalem

The light of dawn spread out over the mountains and then the stone walls surrounding the city of Jerusalem below. Ray stood and watched the morning light from a mountain crevice he had found. A hideaway from John and the rest of the Unit. He knelt on one knee and made the sign of the cross over his heart.

Up on his feet, Ray emerged from the crevice. As he rounded its rocky exterior, Todd was waiting for him.

"Hey. What're you doing up here, Ray?"

Caught off guard by Todd, Ray kept his surprise from appearing on his face, projecting a calm, passive demeanor.

"Just making sure they all got down the mountain safe."

"They're down, Ray. Well on their way. Sal and I have been waiting for you for over half an hour now. You all right?"

"I'm fine. Let's go."

Ray walked past Todd, and Todd followed him without saying another word.

Ray, Sal, and Todd reached the city of Jerusalem half an hour later. The three, wearing their nondescript cloaks, entered one of the city's arched gates with their heads lowered, looking up just enough to see where they were going. The city in front of them was bustling. The three tried to keep as much distance as they could from the people around them. Cautiously, they continued on until reaching an area of the city that was less crowded. With Sal and Todd close behind him, Ray nodded toward a narrow alley just ahead, and they quickly made their way inside. After making sure nobody had followed them, the three pulled back the hoods of their cloaks and looked around for anyone in the alleyway. It was empty; only at the other end of the alley, where it opened up to the city, could people be seen busily walking by.

Ray pulled out his gun from under his cloak and looked down at the slide-out screen on the weapon.

"We're five hundred yards away from your gun, Sal."

"The ammo?" Sal asked.

"A little farther away from your gun. Let's keep going the way we are—stay away from the people—and we should be back at camp before dark."

The three placed their hoods back over their heads and stepped out of the alley. The street had almost emptied out from just the few minutes spent in the alleyway. They walked on, reaching the city limits. Coming to a stop, the three looked around and saw no one.

They made their way outside the city. Ray held out his gun and jogged at a quick pace, following the reading on his slide-out screen, followed by Sal and Todd. The three reached the top of a small hill. On a mound of dirt formed by the wind, Ray knelt down and uncovered Sal's gun, handing it over his shoulder to him. He then looked to his right.

"There."

Ray pointed to a leafless, sun-dried bush where Sal's ammo bag hung from one of the branches. Sal ran over, snatched up the bag of ammo, and returned to Ray and Todd. Ray checked his watch.

"Okay, good. Less time than I thought it would take."

The three turned, taking in the city of Jerusalem for a moment as the wind picked up, rippling over their clothing, pulling the cloaks they wore across their bodies.

"Man, *it is* something to see, isn't it, Ray," Sal said, gazing over the city.

Ray gave Sal a slight nod, just enough to acknowledge him. He could sense Todd's watchful gaze and did not want Todd to see any reaction coming from him. He wanted to appear neutral and unfeeling toward Jerusalem, the city where his religion began.

But it was something to see. Something not read about in a book or seen in some movie about how the city looked over two thousand years ago; it was right here before them. It was truly magnificent from where the three stood on the small hill overlooking Jerusalem. The intricate walls surrounding the city, the homes of tan stone in the Lower City, the magnificent stone structures of white inside the Upper City, the grandeur of it all. Breathtaking.

Ray looked away from the city. He did not need his gun's technology to tell him that it would save time getting back to the mountain camp by going around the city wall ahead. He just couldn't take the logical way back—something was drawing him back inside the city.

Todd would know that going back through the city would take longer. Sal would not ask; he would just obey orders.

"You two follow me like before. We're going back through the city and then back to the camp."

"Ray—" Todd started to say as Ray held up his hand for Todd to be quiet.

"I know it's the long way back, Todd," Ray said without looking at him. "Just follow me."

Ray headed toward the city, followed by Sal. With a slight shake of his head, Todd reluctantly fell in line behind them.

# The Healed One

A man with black curly hair reaching his shoulders and a beard of the same color stood in front of the one window inside the hut, a dwelling where he was taking refuge. With his eyes closed, the man leaned his face into the light of the sun streaming in from outside.

Scattered candles behind the man lit the hut, along with the slanted sunlight. Lazarus pierced his hand into a beam of light, speaking aloud in Aramaic.

"I still feel the warmth of—" Lazarus began to say as a low tapping sound at the hut's door opened his blue eyes. Lazarus stared at the door, hoping the sound was something just imagined. Two more gentle knocks, and Lazarus knew he'd been found. The ones who hid him would tap on the door five times and then speak his name backward—Surazal. This did not happen.

He carefully walked past the door toward the only other way out of the hut—a small room at the back of the home with a crawl space leading underground to unoccupied neighboring homes. Lazarus took each step slowly and silently until he heard his name spoken by a friend.

"Lazarus, it's me, Clopas."

Close to the floor, by the side of the door, a small crack in the wall had been chiseled out for the purpose of viewing visitors from inside the hidden sanctuary.

Lazarus was sure the voice behind the door was his friend Clopas. But he had to consider that his friend may not be alone. He may have been forced at knifepoint by others.

Lazarus got on his hands and knees so he could look outside. He could see Clopas standing alone with his head lowered.

Lazarus got up to his feet, lifted the wooden beam securing the door, opened the door, and faced his friend. He quickly led Clopas inside the hut and closed the door, wedging the wooden beam back into place. Clopas leaned against the door with his arms behind his back for a few seconds. He then spread out his arms, smiling at Lazarus, a gesture saying no enemy will ever enter.

Lazarus placed his hands on his friend's shoulders and drew him close as Clopas spun him around in a friendly roughhouse way while they embraced. Lazarus pulled back from the embrace to face Clopas. He walked Clopas away from the door, bringing him deeper inside the hut.

"It is good to see you," Lazarus said.

"Lazarus, there's a powerful group of priests in the temple searching for you and Jesus, accusing both of you of staging your resurrection. Caiaphas is leading them. He has influenced most of the priests with his skilled way with words. They are planning to kill Jesus."

"How do you know this?"

"It is what I've been told by another prophet."

"Another prophet?"

"He stands behind you now."

Lazarus turned. The shadowy outline of a man stood by the door, and the door's wooden beam could be seen on the floor. Lazarus looked back at Clopas, pointing a finger toward the beam on the ground.

"You did this?"

"Yes."

"Why would you lead this man to me?"

"This is an important man, one with vision. He needs to know where Jesus is. I beg you, my friend, tell him."

"Do you know what you've done, Clopas? This man will—"

Before Lazarus could finish, Rydel closed in and stabbed S-7 into his forearm. Lazarus stood unmoving and wide-eyed, the S-7 needle sticking out of his arm. Rydel stepped in front of Lazarus and studied the man for a moment. He then pulled the needle out of his arm.

"You will take me to Jesus," Rydel ordered the man in translated Aramaic. "And never ask me what's covering my mouth or about how my voice sounds. Understand?"

Under the influence of S-7, Lazarus nodded at Rydel.

"Take me to Jesus, Laz—"

Lazarus's elongated gait had him at the door before Rydel could finish saying his name. He swung the door open and was gone. Lazarus walked at a brisk pace until Rydel caught up with him on a dirt path leading away from the hut and reached out for his arm. Lazarus pulled away from Rydel's grip and continued forward so he could do what he was told to do. Rydel stumbled a couple of steps and then ran past Lazarus, holding up a hand for the man to stop.

"Stop!" Rydel shouted at Lazarus three times before his translator repeated his words in Aramaic back to Lazarus. Lazarus stopped. Not all the kinks had been worked out with S-7. Some people needed to be explicitly told what to do step-by-step. Unlike Clopas, who always made sure he understood what he was being ordered to do, others who were tested and put under the influence of S-7 would run off right after being given an order—like Lazarus—and perform the task as quickly as they could.

"Do not run off without me telling you to do so. Do you understand?" Rydel said, inches away from the face of Lazarus.

Lazarus nodded.

"Now, Lazarus, without running, and with me by your side, take me to Jesus."

"I will take you to Him."

"Good. Go—and go slowly."

"You are here to help Him?"

Rydel stepped back, not sure of what to make of Lazarus's last response. Lazarus said it as if asking a question. Those influenced by S-7 did not ask questions with concern in their voice the way Lazarus had just done. After a while, they would become somewhat normal again. However, at first, when shot up with the drug, they were robotic.

"Yes, I'm here to help Him. How do you know that?"

Lazarus did not answer. He just stood in front of Rydel, waiting for orders.

"Lazarus, answer my question."

"What question? I do not understand. Do you still want me to take you to Jesus and not move so fast?"

Not sure if he had correctly heard the emotion in Lazarus's voice seconds before, and relieved that the man was now under total control,

Rydel pointed for Lazarus to lead the way, and he did, slowly. Behind Rydel, Clopas waited, smelling badly like the fish he sold at the market.

"You need to bathe, Clopas. You smell like a walking fish."

"I will do so now."

"I was being humorous, Clopas. Do you see any water around you?"

"No."

"Keep following me at a distance to make sure we are not followed."

"Was what you said to me now humorous? Should I laugh?"

"No. Go, Clopas!"

Clopas turned and ran off. At a slight jog, Rydel caught up with Lazarus. Side by side, the two walked down a dark path, turned down another, and faced the barren land outside the small village where Lazarus was taking refuge.

Rydel and Lazarus walked without saying a word. Lazarus stopped and turned to face Rydel, touching Rydel's face. Lazarus drew back his hand and continued walking. Rydel stood unmoving for a few seconds, then ran and caught up to Lazarus plodding across the wasteland.

"Why did you touch my face?"

Lazarus stopped. "So I could feel your soul. As much as you are controlling me now, a part of me cannot be controlled. I have been outside this world; a piece of my soul is still there."

"I don't understand, Lazarus."

"You cannot understand. You have not died yet."

# The Road Back

On a twisting dirt road leading to Jerusalem, Ray, Sal, and Todd made their way silently toward an arched stone entranceway leading into the city, with Ray out in front. As they walked, both Sal and Todd noticed—from what they could make out of the side of Ray's face, with his shemagh hiding his translator around his neck and the flapping hood of his cloak—that Ray was distant, not all there. Sal took a few quick steps and caught up to Ray, walking alongside him.

"How you doing, Ray? You're not looking so good. I'm worried about dehydration. Have some water, and let's rest a second—"

Ray turned suddenly, his face up in Sal's. "I'm not dehydrated."

Ray looked back at Todd, who was a couple of steps behind. "I need to check on something before we return to camp. You two won't be needing your translators. Leave them around your neck."

Todd walked closer and shrugged his shoulders. "What, Ray? What do you need to check on?"

"Just do what I say."

Ray turned away from Todd and continued on the road leading toward the entranceway into the city.

"Ray—" Sal started to say, but Ray cut him off.

"You two stay behind a couple of steps and just wait for my orders. No more talking."

The three walked in silence for a few minutes, then came into contact with others migrating toward the city. They stepped around the people in front of them, keeping their heads down and their legs moving. They weaved briskly through the people as Ray picked up the pace.

The three entered the city to find it still somewhat deserted. With the two trailing behind, Ray adjusted his translator into place and hid it with his tan shemagh.

At a corner tent ahead selling pottery, a man busily closed up his small business, strapping down tarps securely in place. Ray, Sal, and Todd passed by the merchant, and the man noticed the three walking with purpose. The thirty-year-old man, clothed in a grayish tunic, finished closing his shop and ran, catching up with the three, and then walked beside Ray. The man patted his forehead with a cloth, wiping the sweat from his brow, and grinned at Ray with only a dozen teeth left in his mouth.

"Are you going to see Him?" the man asked Ray.

With the hood of his cloak covering his face, Ray started distancing himself from the man until the words translated back through his translator. Ray quickly looked at the man, and as he did, he could see Sal and Todd start to make their way closer. Ray waved the two back and walked with the man, speaking to the merchant through his translator.

"How do you know that I'm looking for a man?" Ray asked the merchant.

Hearing Ray's voice, the man looked at him oddly for a few seconds. "Looking for a man?" the merchant asked, confused, while he wrapped the sweat-soaked cloth he used on his forehead around his neck.

"Yes, how did you know that?" Ray said after a moment.

"I'm going to the sermon. He's like no other, the Nazareth preacher. You must see Him."

Ray slipped his hand toward his gun hidden under his cloak. He pointed the gun at the man's side with his right hand while placing his left hand on the merchant's shoulder, gently tapping the man's shoulder. The merchant smiled.

"Yes. I'm here to see the Nazareth preacher," Ray said.

"Then let us go together."

The mini keyboard slid out from the side of Ray's weapon under his cloak, and he tapped three keys to tag the merchant. Ray glanced under his cloak to make sure he had keyed in the right command. On the small screen, he could make out: nonlethal/tag.

Finger on the trigger, Ray eased the muzzle of his Smartround gun out from under his cloak and tagged the man beside him. With his gun back under his cloak, Ray removed his KA-BAR from its sheath and held it to the merchant's throat.

"Run. The preacher is the only one who can save you if you see me again."

Ray lowered the knife from the merchant's throat, and the man took off running. Ray slid the knife back into its sheath, removed his translator, and waited for Sal and Todd to reach him.

"What the hell was that all about, Ray?" Todd asked.

"Man got too close. Keep the same distance and follow me."

Ray walked on, his back to the two.

Todd looked at Sal with concern.

"He isn't right, Sal.

"What isn't right about him?"

"The man got too close? What the hell did he mean by that? He's off. And you know it, Sal," Todd said quietly.

"Are you trying to give me an order not to follow Ray?"

"Of course we're going to follow. But there's something wrong with him. He's—"

"I'm what?"

Ray had made it back to Sal and Todd without making a sound. The two turned to see Ray standing not ten feet away—both caught way-the-fuck off guard. Sal and Todd thought they were talking amongst themselves. The two had taken their eyes off Ray for a few seconds—a bad move by both if they really wanted to converse privately.

"Is there something you need to ask me, Todd?" Ray asked, tilting his head slightly.

"Well, yeah, Ray—"

"What?" Ray quickly asked.

"What do you need to check on in the city—it can't have anything to do with Rydel, right? The others are tracking him."

Ray turned to Sal. "Sal, do you have any questions?"

"Fuck no."

Ray moved closer to Sal, quickly whispered something in his ear, and turned back to Todd. "Go ahead of us, and get yourself back to the camp. I thought your input would help in a judgment call I might have to make here, Todd. But never mind, just go."

Todd started to step closer to Ray.

"Stop. Don't get any closer."

"Okay, Ray—easy. I'll follow without another word."

"Good."

Ray continued on, putting his translator back in place, wrapping his shemagh around it. Sal and Todd obediently followed.

Sal and Todd trailed behind Ray for almost half an hour, with Ray changing his direction here and there, looking inside his cloak at his gun—clearly tracking someone. Todd scuttled closer to Sal, staring ahead at Ray while he did, and spoke to Sal in a whisper.

"Who the hell is he tracking?"

"I don't know," Sal said without looking at Todd.

As if he could somehow hear the two, Ray came to a stop ahead of Sal and Todd, turning his hooded head around. After staring at the two for a few seconds, Ray turned away and joined a passing throng of men and women in tan, brown, and black tunics visiting the city of Jerusalem. He then ran around a jagged stone-layered street corner. Sal and Todd lost sight of him. The two ran to the corner of the street, rounded it, and came upon a massive four-walled structure they had seen before. A lengthy stone staircase led up to a white edifice with several arched entranceways distanced from one another, providing entry inside the majestic carved-stone masterpiece. The two watched Ray ascend the staircase—the same stone staircase that the colonel, Ray, and the rest of the Unit hurriedly descended after their arrival.

Sal and Todd bolted after Ray and entered an area where a crowd of hundreds stood inside a large white-and-tan stone court surrounded by thick pillars. All in the crowd were silent, even the children. The people formed a circle around one man who could barely be seen through the multitude around Him. The man in the center pointed His forefinger toward the sky and stood that way for almost two minutes in silence. The man then began to speak to the crowd around Him.

Sal and Todd spotted Ray near the back of the crowd and rushed over to him.

Ray saw the two running his way and removed his translator. Sal and Todd reached Ray, tried to speak, but were silenced by Ray holding his arm up, signaling them not to say a word. "Follow me," Ray ordered and then put his translator back over his mouth.

Ray circled the crowd. Sal and Todd stayed close behind, following Ray as he searched for a better viewpoint, coming to a stop between two women wearing faded black shawls over their heads.

The woman to his right gave Ray a smile, then turned her attention back to the sermon. The woman started to walk away, carrying a small sack of food in her arms, making her way closer so she could get a better view of the preaching man.

On the move once more, Ray searched again for a better viewpoint, not quite able to get a good look at the preaching man's face, unintentionally trailing the woman holding the sack of food. And then the shouts in Aramaic came.

"Stop!" yelled a man in a deep, raspy voice.

Ray ignored it and continued walking.

"Stop!" another man ordered. Ray turned to see what the shouting was all about behind him. Two temple guards clothed in black, protected by black chest plates and helmets, passed between Sal and Todd. One of the temple guards put his hand on his sword hilt, closing in on Ray, pushing people aside.

Behind the guards, Sal and Todd raised their hooded heads, lifted their Smartround guns from under their cloaks, and took aim at the two guards making their way toward Ray.

But the two temple guards just nudged Ray aside and rushed past him. Ray turned around to see the guards approach the woman holding the small bag of provisions. The taller of the two men reached out for the woman's shoulder and spun her around; she almost tripped, falling to one knee. Rising, the woman stood upright with her head lowered.

The smaller of the two guards approached the woman and pushed the large man away from her. He gently brushed dirt off the woman's clothing, then faced her.

"Maryam."

The woman lifted her head slightly.

"Tell Jesus to leave the city," the smaller temple guard demanded. "He's caused enough trouble with His words, in and outside of the temple."

The woman stoically replied after a moment.

"He will not leave the city. How could delivering the word of God cause trouble?"

The smaller temple guard nodded for the large guard to leave them. Reluctant to do so, but clearly outranked, the larger guard walked away, brushing people aside as he did, giving his superior time to talk with the woman alone.

The temple guard returned his attention back to the woman he knew by name, satisfied the ignorant goon he had been assigned to train was far enough away not to hear what he needed to say.

"His life is in danger. I tell you this for His own good. He was a close childhood friend, helped me many times. You know that. Tell Him He must leave the city."

"He will not leave the city."

The larger guard behind the two had seen enough. Yes, the man training him was his superior. However, the bloodline of his family surpassed that of the man's.

Marcus did not like being told what to do by the small man, and why should he? He would be the man's superior in no more than a year. He was sure of it. So Marcus pointed his sword at the people around him to make a path for him, and they did, backing away as he hulked forward, joining up with his superior and the woman. Marcus smiled, ripped out a handful of grapes from the sack the woman carried, and shoved them in his mouth, a juice-trail running down each side of his grinning face.

The woman looked up at Marcus from under her shawl. She had a bronzed face that the sun had been kind to over the years, long black hair with tints of gray, and beautiful, strong hazel eyes. The purity and strength of her eyes frightened the large man.

The woman looked away from him.

Marcus could not hide being afraid of the woman for a brief moment. He then quickly returned to the way he saw the world around him. Seeing it only for what he could get out of it and what would benefit him at the expense of others. But he did not entirely come back to his senses. He did not notice James—his superior. Smaller, but extremely dangerous, James had his blade under Marcus's armor before the large man realized what was happening—the cold steel resting on his spine.

Marcus quickly became aware that it did not matter what family he came from; James seemed ready to bleed him out right here over this simple woman from the market.

"Please!" Marcus begged.

"Leave us, Marcus."

James eased the cold blade away from Marcus's skin. Marcus stepped away, stumbling at the sight of the knife in James's hand. He turned and ran, disappearing into a shadowy pillared passageway off to the far right. James turned back to face the woman.

She was gone.

Before him, three men now stood with their heads lowered. James moved past the three men, but she was nowhere to be seen. He could not go after her and abandon his route of the city he patrolled. He felt remorse and conflict but could do no more. If he were spotted helping Jesus in any way, his family and his daughters might face the same consequences that this gathering of high-powered priests intended to bestow on his boyhood friend.

James turned, took two steps forward to search for Marcus, his idiot-in-training, and stopped. He stared at the same three men with their heads lowered, standing just ahead—not moving. James rushed over and approached the man in the middle, slapping a hand on the man's right shoulder.

"You, raise your head!" James yelled.

Ray looked up and stabbed the hand on his shoulder with an S-7 needle. The hand fell from Ray's shoulder as James stood where he was, emotionless.

"The woman you were talking to—is she the mother of Jesus?" Ray asked in his translated Aramaic.

"Yes," James answered robotically.

"Walk twenty steps ahead, drop to the ground, and fall asleep until morning," Ray ordered James, pulling the S-7 needle out of the guard's hand. Ray turned away from the guard and ran after the woman. Sal and Todd followed. Behind the three, James walked twenty steps, dropped to the ground, and fell asleep on impact.

Sal and Todd caught up with Ray, running alongside him.

Ray removed his translator and shouted at the two: "Fall back and follow me like before. Now!"

—

After finding her, Ray followed the woman through the city for just over half an hour. She then suddenly entered a hidden alleyway between two closed-for-the-evening merchant stands. Ray ran ahead so fast that he lost Sal and Todd trailing behind; the two could not see where the woman in black had gone. Ray slipped between the merchant stands and into the alleyway and caught movement ahead, just a glimpse of the woman exiting at the end of the narrow passageway. He ran down to the end of the passage, craned his neck, and watched the woman walk with a handful of other people on a path leading outside the walls of Jerusalem.

Ray turned his head around at the sound of Sal and Todd running toward him, both with their slide-out screens extended on their guns, tracking Ray.

"What is it, Ray?" Sal struggled to say, slightly winded.

"Just keep following."

With Sal and Todd trailing behind, Ray followed the woman through scattered groups of people. They walked on and made their way to a small stone city just two miles away from Jerusalem.

With the woman still in sight and now alone, Ray followed her from a distance down twisting roads with humble stone homes. The woman turned down a side road that led to a small hillside with three stone huts spaced roughly fifty feet apart from one another along the rising hill. The woman made her way up to the last home on the hillside and entered. With the sun lowering, the roof of the hut glowed in deep orange.

At the bottom of the dirt road, Ray took a step and stopped, staring at the last stone home on the hillside above. Sal and Todd approached Ray from behind and flanked him as he just stood still. Ray regarded the two and then pointed toward an overhanging tree by the side of the road.

"Wait behind that tree, and *do not* move."

Sal and Todd watched as Ray walked up the hill, passing the first two homes and coming to a stop at the doorstep of the last stone home. He adjusted his translator, covered it with his tan shemagh, and slowly raised his hand to knock on the door.

—

In her stone hut, Jesus's mother prepared the meal for the ones joining her tonight. She placed the last of the vegetables into a fire-heated cauldron and wearily sat in a chair next to the fire. She gazed at the flames licking their way up from the bottom of the cauldron. Face set in stone, a tear fell from Maryam's right eye, the warning from the temple guard repeating in her mind.

A knock on the door spun Maryam's head around. She was hesitant—the ones she was expecting would not be here so soon. She stood from the chair, slowly walked over to the door, and opened it, catching a glimpse of the man's face as he quickly lowered his head, hiding under the hood of his cloak. She saw enough, though, recognizing him.

"Are you hungry? Is that why you have been following me?"

As the words translated, Ray let out a quiet sigh. Despite all his special military training, she knew. He raised his head slightly and nodded.

"Come inside."

Ray entered the stone home with a fire burning in the far corner and scattered candles surrounding the surprisingly ample space inside. From the outside, the stone hut looked small. But inside, it stretched back with many rooms ahead, all candlelit.

At a table off to the side of the fire, Maryam motioned with the palm of her open hand for him to sit. Nodding, Ray took a seat at the table. He watched as Maryam used a ladle to fill two bowls from the cauldron hanging over the fire. She walked over to him.

The mother of Jesus was in front of him. Ray could feel it, just as he felt the goodness of her Son in the alleyway.

# Hunted

With Clopas on his left and Lazarus on his right—both under the influence of S-7—Rydel scanned the land below with his binoculars from a mountain ridge. He was being followed.

"Who do we have following us down there?"

Through the binoculars, Rydel could see John Adams staring up at him through a pair of his own binoculars. John lowered his binoculars so that the scientist could see his eyes and disappointedly shook his head for a brief moment. He then pointed out Rydel to the members of Ray's Unit standing behind him.

Unable to hear what he was saying, Rydel could see by the veins bulging from John's neck that he was screaming at the members of Ray's Unit—screaming at them to hunt him down.

Rydel adjusted his translator and turned to Clopas by his side.

"You know the mountain well, Clopas?"

Clopas nodded.

"Hide us. Fast!"

Clopas ran, followed by Rydel and Lazarus.

At the bottom of the mountain, John, along with the members of the Unit he took with him to hunt Rydel down, ran up a dirt-and-stone path winding up the mountain. Out in front by a good thirty feet, Kevin communicated back to John.

"We're losing him, sir," he informed the colonel through his headset.

It took twenty minutes in their pursuit of Rydel to reach where he had stood before being spotted. John and the rest of Ray's Unit pointed their guns in all directions, trying to track Rydel. Ben, outlined in the fading sun, was the first to speak of what was obvious.

"He's gone, sir."

"He can't be."

"Sir, he's gone."

"How could he travel out of range in this time so fast?" John studied the mountain up and down. "No. He's here. He's inside this mountain. Deep inside where we can't track him, the smart bastard."

John glanced over the members of Ray's Unit.

"He's here."

## A Meal Shared with the Mother of Jesus

Ray sat at the table inside the hut of Jesus Christ's mother with his head bent forward, the hood of his cloak shadowing his face and his shemagh concealing his translator.

Maryam placed a wooden bowl in front of Ray and one at the other side of the table, taking a seat across from him. Maryam noticed the man claiming to be hungry just staring at the food in front of him.

"Please, eat." Maryam's soothing Aramaic translated back to Ray, who sat like a statue.

Maryam looked down at her plate and noticed what was missing. With what had happened in the city, the warning from the temple soldier whom Jesus had known as a boy, she was unsteady. The man told her things she had been sickly worried about concerning Jesus. Barely able to sleep for days, she felt it inside her that her Son's time was slipping away. He was in danger of losing His life if He stayed in Jerusalem. Jesus, however, would not have any of it; when they had met days before, none of her words would deter Him from visiting the city.

Breaking away from her thoughts, Maryam stood up from the table.

"The bread. I forgot the bread."

As Maryam walked back to retrieve a loaf of bread, Ray raised his head, watching her. She returned with the bread and softly smiled at him. Ray lowered his head, waiting. Maryam broke off two pieces of bread and offered them to Ray.

From under his hood, he could see Maryam offering the bread. Ray reached out with one hand over the other with his palms up, and Maryam placed the bread in his hands.

"What is your name?" Maryam asked.

His head still down, Ray waited for his translator to decipher Maryam's words so he could respond.

"Raymond."

Maryam broke off a small piece of bread for herself and sat across the table from Ray. Like Ray, she too just looked at the food in front of her. She was hungry, but her stomach twisted inside with worry about her Son. Jesus was a miracle to her and the world. She'd been blessed to give birth to Him. But now, with Jesus telling her not to worry for His well-being, Maryam wanted nothing more than to take Jesus by the hand and lead Him out of the city. Make Him listen like a little boy. She was part of God's plan to bring Him into the world; she knew this. But now, at this moment, she just wanted to do what any mother would do—protect her child.

"I know your Son's preachings well. I'm a follower."

Maryam could not place the accent of the man, a very distant traveler. An odd way of speaking she had never heard before.

"Where do you come from?" she asked.

Ray half-smiled at Maryam's words. With this translator speaking for me, I must sound as if I come from another world, he thought.

"Faraway place you most likely never heard of. A long journey."

Ray tilted his head up enough to see Maryam nod at what he had said, satisfied with the answer, as she picked at the meal in front of her. From under the hood of his cloak, Ray was also able to see the obvious—she was worried, sick with it. The woman had no appetite.

"Jesus is in danger. It's true what the soldier told you in the city today."

On each side of the wooden bowl, Maryam's hands began to tremble. She slowly pushed the bowl aside and leaned across the table, reaching a trembling hand out for Ray.

"I know," Maryam said, her voice almost desperate.

Ray could see Maryam's hand out in front of him from under his hooded cloak and did not hesitate, taking her hand in his.

"I told Him not to go back to the city, but He will not listen to me." She began to weep into her free hand. After a moment, she looked at Ray, hidden under the hood of his cloak and shemagh.

"Let me see your face."

Ray hesitated.

"Raymond, let me see."

Ray pulled back the hood of his cloak but left the shemagh in place, hoping she would not ask him to remove it or to eat the meal in front of him.

He could not come up with a plan on how to talk and understand her while eating.

He stared at the Mother of Christ, and she smiled back at him.

"Kind eyes."

The words Maryam spoke translated back, and Ray had to look away, staring down at the table in front of him. The surreal situation that he found himself in was taking a toll on his mind. He could feel the soldier inside him slipping away the longer he held onto Maryam's hand.

"Is there a way you can help my Son? Is that the real reason why you followed me, why you are here now?" Maryam asked.

The time it took for the words to translate was a moment too long for Maryam, and she pleaded with Ray.

"Please—can you help Him?"

Ray looked up at Maryam. "Yes. There's a way I can help Him. Do you know where Jesus is now?"

She shook her head. "Now? No."

Maryam stood up from the table, walked over to where Ray sat, and knelt down beside him with her hands clasped, staring up at Ray with tear-rimmed eyes.

"I beg of you…save Him."

—

The door to Maryam's hut opened, letting out the light from the burning candles inside. From behind Maryam, Ray stood in the shadows. He then stepped outside—a sky full of stars waiting for him. Hood back over his head, he stopped and turned back to Maryam standing just outside the door.

She placed a hand on the side of his face.

"Thank you," she said softly. Ray nodded and touched Maryam's hand resting on his face, turned, and walked away on weak legs, trying to calm himself before reaching Sal and Todd. He heard the door closing behind him and broke into a slow jog, feeling better, getting a second wind, taking off his shemagh and removing his translator.

By the time Ray made it past the other homes on the hillside, he was fine, focused, and ready to do what needed to be done. Ray reached the slanted tree where he had told the two to wait and walked behind it to find Sal and Todd waiting there, following orders. The two were leaning against the tree and looking in the other direction with heavy eyes as Ray approached. The journey and all that had happened had drained their military-trained minds and bodies. They should have heard him but did not.

"On your feet."

The two jumped up and pulled their Smartround guns on Ray, both stopping short of shooting and sedating him. Ray folded down the hood of his cloak and placed his headset back on, turning his head away from Sal and Todd.

"Gun and ammo found. Update if you can, Colonel Adams."

John Adams's voice answered back through Ray's headset after only a few seconds. "We had Rydel but lost his signal. He's deep inside a mountain we tracked him to. He's trying to wait us out. Return to the camp."

The colonel ended the conversation with that, and Ray turned to Sal and Todd.

"Back to the camp."

Ray began to walk away, and Sal quickly caught up with him. Todd waited where he was, looking down at the slide-out screen on his gun for any sort of message from the other Unit members, giving Sal enough time alone with Ray to ask about the woman.

"Was it really her, Ray?"

"It was really her, Sal."

—

Hours later, Ray, Sal, and Todd sat around one of the camp's fire pits, drinking coffee. From the time they had reached the camp and set up the fire, Sal and Todd could barely get a word out of Ray. With his eyes searching for something inside the fire, Ray finally spoke to Todd.

"Todd, do a sweep around the camp. I'm sure Rydel is still up in the mountains. But maybe he somehow got past John and the rest. Let's just make sure. He might try to sedate us, if given the chance out there in the dark."

Todd retrieved his rifle leaning against a rock to his left and walked away. The darkness started to swallow him up with each step he took away from the light of the fire. As the last trace of Todd faded into the night, Ray turned to Sal, put a finger to his lips for him to be quiet, and motioned for Sal to rise and follow him.

The two walked away from the fire, moving in the opposite direction from where Todd ventured, the campfire lighting a path for the two. Ray placed a hand on Sal's shoulder for him to stop. He told Sal to take a knee, and Ray took a knee as well, the two face-to-face, their skin aglow in firelight.

"I know Rydel is still up on that mountain somewhere. I just needed to talk to you alone, Sal."

"And I need to talk to you! Jesus, Ray—you whispered to me before that you spoke with the Mother of Christ. Tell me what happened—"

"He touched me."

"What?"

"Christ. He placed a hand on me in an alley where John and I saw Him heal a dead woman. Right in front of us, Sal, I swear to you! The Son of God is here in this time. That's why Rydel came back…to save Him."

"Rydel wants to save Him? Why?" Sal asked.

"I'm not sure. But I have my own reasons to save Him now. So let me ask you, are you sure you want to know what the Mother of Christ just spoke to me about?"

Sal took a few seconds and then nodded nervously at Ray.

"Positive, Sal?"

"Yeah, Ray."

"She asked me to find Jesus—and to keep Him safe, to protect Him. When He touched me, I felt the goodness inside the man. I can't turn my back on Him. Not when the Mother of Christ just asked me to protect Him…and not after I felt the miracle of His touch. There's no way I'm standing around while He gets nailed to a cross."

Ray placed a hand on Sal's shoulder.

"We are here for a reason, Sal."

"What about causing damage back in our time if we change anything here?"

"John and Will lied to us. I know it. They didn't tell us everything. I need to know right now…will you help me?"

Sal reached out, and Ray clasped hard with Sal's outreached hand. Sal glanced back toward the camp with its dying fire.

"The others, Ray?"

"We'll see."

—

John Adams searched the mountain for Rydel with his Smartround gun, staring down at the weapon's slide-out screen. Coming up with nothing, he turned to the members of Ray's Unit behind him waiting for orders. He looked away from the group and took in the mountain, planning out what he should do next.

"We're gonna split into three groups and search for a way inside this mountain."

—

Inside the mountain, a torch lit the way through the blackness. Clopas, out in front and the one providing the means to light the torch from a satchel on his waist, led Rydel and Lazarus through a narrow tunnel with protruding sharp-edged rocks—the flame from the torch he held halfway to the point of extinguishing. After two more turns on the tunnel's winding path, Clopas stopped at a black hole beside him.

"This way will lead us to the bottom of the mountain."

As the words translated back to him, Rydel pointed at the black hole. "Show me, Clopas."

Clopas pointed the torch into the black hole. The light of the torch lit a steep path that at first glance seemed almost impossible to walk down. Rydel studied the path.

"We'll be able to walk down?" Rydel asked Clopas.

Clopas shook his head. "No. We must slide down. I will show you how—"

A deep, cackling laugh filled the mountain tunnel behind the three, and they spun around. It was then quiet, just the sound of the three breathing. From the light of the torch, Rydel could make out Clopas's terrified face. Next to Clopas, Lazarus stood emotionless, calm. From the blackness in front of them, loud thumping footfalls made their way toward the three. The laughing started again, closing in.

Rydel grabbed Clopas and screamed at him.

"Get us out of here!"

"Into the hole! Slide down!" Clopas said, pointing anxiously toward the tar-black hole in the mountain rock.

Lazarus started to walk toward the laughter in the dark. Rydel reached out and grabbed onto Lazarus as the words from Clopas were translated. Rydel took hold of Lazarus, pushed him toward the black hole, and forced him down into it. He then grabbed Clopas by the shoulders.

"Go!"

Clopas entered the hole with the torch. The descending light fell over Rydel's body and flashed over the black-cloaked man standing behind him. Rydel was so close to this man that he could no longer move. The debilitating fear he felt inside him also took away his ability to breathe. Clopas's hand grabbed Rydel as he nearly passed out. Rydel felt the sensation of falling, followed by the feeling of sliding. Rydel was heading toward a sputtering light from Clopas's torch flickering inside the blackness in front of him. Able to breathe again, Rydel slid down a curving, tube-like black tunnel with Clopas and then fell onto something soft. The two landed outside on a patch of dirt mid-mountain; the torch Clopas held was now nothing more than an ember. Before Rydel and Clopas, Lazarus stood next to another hole seven feet in diameter in the side of the mountain. The moon and the star-blazing sky above lit up the patch of dirt the three found themselves on.

Rydel and Clopas ran over to Lazarus by the mountain's opening. Lazarus took Clopas by the shoulders and threw him into the tunnel-like hole. He grabbed onto the shoulders of Rydel to do the same as the laughing returned. Lazarus slipped his hands off Rydel and began walking to where the laughter was coming from.

Thin, with not much musculature to work with, Rydel found more strength than he thought possible to grab Lazarus and push him down into the hole.

Part of the mountain moved, and the shape of the black-cloaked man separated from a wall of rock and walked across the patch of dirt, closing in on Rydel. The light from the moon and stars above disappeared as if a blanket had been thrown over them.

Crystal-blue eyes seeped out from the inky darkness, illuminated in rage, outlining the full shape of a man now standing over Rydel. An alabaster hand slipped out from under the sleeve of the man's black cloak, reaching toward Rydel's face.

"I am the true light here in the darkness."

Rydel stumbled backward and felt himself falling once more.

—

Here in the darkness.

The last four words spoken to him by the black-cloaked man woke Rydel. Eyes open, Rydel turned his head and faced a dying fire. Was he in hell? Did he fail? All these thoughts ran through his head until Clopas knelt down next to him, placing a kind hand on Rydel's face.

"How are you, my friend?"

As the words translated, Rydel felt the guilt of controlling Clopas. He was no friend to this simple man.

Rydel rose from the ground and stared at the fire before answering Clopas. He was here for a reason, Rydel reminded himself. Clopas was not a poor soul being manipulated by S-7; Clopas was a warrior meant to help save the Son of God.

"Where am I, Clopas?" Rydel's translated voice asked.

Clopas lifted himself up from his knees and stood next to Rydel. "Still on the mountain. We have set up shelter here on a ridge protected by trees. No one can see us."

Rydel looked to his right and saw Lazarus sitting peacefully by the fire. As the last words spoken by Clopas translated back to him, Rydel's eyes grew wide with panic.

"We need to move! Let's go, let's go—quickly!"

Clopas and Lazarus shared a look, the two confused and concerned by Rydel's sudden outburst to leave. Rydel grabbed Clopas's right arm and then reached for Lazarus close by, both men surprised by Rydel's behavior.

"Clopas, get us off this mountain!"

Clopas led the way. The three ran down a mountain path full of jagged rocks with tips like spears—a path not meant to be taken at such a quick pace. The trail leading down the mountain curved up ahead with a blind spot approaching.

"Stop."

Clopas and Lazarus stopped running.

Rydel walked around the bend cautiously. As far as he could see to the mountain's next curve, there was no one. Luck was on their side. John and the ones with him were nowhere to be seen.

Rydel looked over his shoulder and waved a hand for the two to follow him. With Rydel out in front, the three rounded the next curve and followed the path down. From out of a crevice sliced into the mountain path, a hand reached out and brought Rydel to a stop. A black figure walked out from the mountain wall, looming over Rydel.

Unable to move past the man in front of him or run backward, Rydel relented and stood still.

He looked up at the man's face and removed his translator.

"Hello, Ben."

Ben stepped closer with his Smartround gun and pointed it at Rydel's chest, giving him a sad smile, looking at Rydel like, Man, what the hell were you thinking?

Rydel looked away from Ben and could see the black-cloaked man standing above on a narrow ridge. The dark shape stared down at Rydel with a pitch-black face—only its preternatural blue eyes under the hood of its cloak could be seen. The thinking, calculating, almost beautiful eyes dizzied Rydel's senses. Another feature came into view from under the blackness of the hood—its lips. Split black lips with pearl-white glowing cracks, forming a grin. Rydel realized that the man in the black cloak had somehow guided Ben—and the others, Rydel was sure—to find him and was satisfied that he had been caught.

The black-cloaked man laughed from above the ridge and morphed into the darkness behind him, gone. Ben heard the laugh but did not take his eyes off Rydel. From behind, John Adams placed a hand on Ben's shoulder.

"Ben, walk Rydel down the mountain with his other two friends. We'll go check out Mr. Laughing Man above."

"Yes, sir."

John met Rydel's eyes, shook his head in a way that was both sad and disappointed, and slipped past Rydel, with the rest of the Unit following as they made their way toward the overhang above.

Once there, they all took in the area and found no one on the rock ledge. Jack was the first to approach Colonel Adams.

"What the hell, sir."

"It was nothing, Jack. Just echo or the wind sounding like laughter. Let's go."

They caught up with Ben leading Rydel, Clopas, and Lazarus toward the bottom of the mountain.

"Ben, fall back with the others, and find a place to rest for a second. I need a moment with Rydel and his two friends," John ordered.

Ben joined the rest of the Unit as they walked away slowly, taking their time going back up the mountain path.

John closed in on Rydel, staring down at him. The two stood without saying a word until John yelled out to Ben—not taking his eyes off Rydel as he did so.

"Ben!"

"Yes, sir?"

"When I said fall back, I meant for you and the others to give me a fucking minute alone here."

Behind John, Ben and the rest of the Unit obeyed orders, disappearing into the dark one by one around the mountain's curving path. With his back to the other two men, John let out a deep breath and shook his head at Rydel.

"I'm going to guess Will found a way to make the backups work," Rydel said to John.

"Wow, you really are a genius, Rydel."

John looked over his shoulder at Rydel's S-7 companions. He then took in the dark land below the mountain. "How…how the hell did you figure out the exact date in time to be here? It can't be simply from history."

"I was off the first time. This is my second time here."

"You made your own Placement chip?"

Rydel looked at Clopas, then Lazarus, smiling reassuringly to the men, speaking to John as he did.

"Yes. But I ran out of resources and time to make additional ones with Will always looking over my shoulder. Destroying my work and getting to the backups…I didn't think you would be able to get to me."

John jabbed a finger in Rydel's face to shut him up, and Rydel did, frightened by John's intensity. The colonel pointed behind him at the two men Rydel recruited with S-7. "Coming into contact with these men and controlling them for as long as you have, you may have caused casualties back home in the thousands."

Uncharacteristically bold, Rydel stepped closer to John with shaking fists, clenched teeth, and wide eyes.

"No! No! I witnessed a miracle by my sister that cannot be explained away. She already knew about Placement without me telling her about it. How could she know about my work in such detail? This is what Placement is truly meant for, John. To save Him."

"We used S-7 on your sister. She said you told her about Placement. And that you came back here to save this man so He could in some way save her."

Rydel jerked his head side to side, not believing, and screamed at John. "That's—that's not what happened—you're lying! You are lying to me!"

"Let us pass!" the voice in Aramaic boomed from behind John. John continued to stare at Rydel while he adjusted his translator into place, covering it with his shemagh.

The words came from Lazarus as he made his way over and stood in front of Rydel. Lazarus waved a hand at John to move on, to walk away. Frustrated, almost using a sedation round on the man, John lowered his gun under his cloak, calmed down, and spoke to Lazarus through his translator.

"You can leave. Go. Return to the city, and no harm will come to you."

Lazarus looked at John strangely. Lazarus heard him speak to Rydel in a foreign language, but now the sound of the man's voice had suddenly changed. Lazarus quickly dismissed it, not caring at the moment.

"Harm?" Lazarus asked John as the word came through John's translator.

"Just go," John's translated response snapped back.

Ben and the others reappeared, walking closer, alarmed by the raised voices. All were wondering what could be taking the colonel so long. Ben tapped his ear for everyone to put their translators in.

Lazarus stood unwavering, as if protecting Rydel. John took a step closer to the man, placing his hand on the sheath of his knife under his cloak, but decided not to go the threatening way just yet. He spoke softly through his translator.

"Just walk away."

Lazarus held his right arm out straight with his hand palm-up at Rydel standing behind him. "This man is coming with me. He is trying to save a life that will save us all!"

Behind John, another voice in Aramaic spoke up.

"Whose life?"

John spun around to see Ben standing a few feet away with the others, all with their shemaghs covering the lower half of their faces. He could also see the unmistakable black circle of Ben's translator in his right ear. John shut off his translator, rushed over, and started to remove Ben's circular earbuds from his ears. "Fuck, Ben! No translators—I ordered!"

Ben removed his translator. "You never gave an order about using our translators, sir."

"Take them out!" John shouted at the others. Rydel walked past John, pointing at Lazarus behind him.

"A close friend of this man, Lazarus, behind me is in danger. Will any of you help me save his friend?"

John was on Rydel before he could say another word, spinning him around so that the others could not see, and gripped Rydel's throat, eliminating his ability to speak. "Please, Rydel. Don't make me do something here I do not want to do." John tightened his grip. "We are friends. Don't make me hurt you."

Panicked by the lack of air, Rydel closed his eyes in defeat and nodded. John loosened his grip on Rydel's throat and walked him away from the rest.

Colonel Adams was having a hard time with his emotions. He cared for Rydel. He was a true friend, a good man—a very good man. But Rydel had completely lost his way, speaking of this miracle he had been shown by his sister. John's loyalties rested with the American people he cherished. They were his family in his heart. That was the way he felt about the people of America; they were his only offspring. He'd never wanted a family of his own, never needed a steady companion. He lived to protect each American life as best he could.

Breathing normally now, Rydel gave John a sideways glare, sweat and tears running over his face.

"I'm here for a reason, John. You're going to have to kill me, I guess."

—

On the path down the mountain, John trailed behind Rydel and the two men Rydel had injected with S-7, while the members of Ray's Unit led the way. As they were reaching the end of the trail, John tagged Rydel's shoulder with his Smartround gun, even though they could track him by his chip, just to be safe. He was uneasy because he knew they were being followed. The unknown person laughing at them from above on the ridge, regardless of what excuse he had given to Jack and the rest of the team for the sound, was definitely close—and following them.

Ray, with Sal and Todd standing behind in the distance, waited at the bottom of the mountain, where the colonel had told the three to meet them.

The rest of the Unit walked up to Ray, then past him as he nodded for them to join Sal and Todd. Rydel walked over and stood in front of Ray with Clopas and Lazarus behind him.

"Hello, Ray."

Ray stared at the two men with Rydel. He then looked at John. "Who are they?" Ray asked John.

"Commoners from the city. But—"

John stopped what he was about to say to Ray and snapped his fingers at Todd to get his attention. "Todd, eyes on Rydel and the other two while I talk with Ray for a minute."

"Yes, sir."

John approached Ray, put a hand on his shoulder, and led him away from the rest, walking him toward an olive tree, the roots of the tree twisted and gnarled, protruding from the ground. Standing by the tree, John glanced back to make sure the others were far enough away and wouldn't overhear.

"The one standing to the left of Rydel, yeah, Rydel said his name was Lazarus. Some in your Unit had an odd reaction hearing that name. What you need to do right now is get this one simple thing through their heads: our mission here is now over. We are to stay away from the people of this time and wait to be taken back. Understand, Ray?"

Ray took it all in, standing stoically as John barked off his orders. Ray replied to John like a grunt, not like a brother-in-law.

"I understand, Colonel. And all in my Unit will understand as well once I can sit them down alone and talk to them. Can you watch over Rydel and the other two while I do that?"

Easing up on Ray, John put both hands on Ray's shoulders and changed his tone.

"Sorry, brother."

"Not a problem."

"Before you talk to your Unit, I need you to take the two men that Rydel is controlling away from here and hit them up with S-7 again so you can control them. Have the two forget this day in their lives. Then meet us back at the camp."

"Understood," Ray replied without emotion, like a good soldier.

Sweat beading on his face, John wiped it away with both hands and let out a weary breath. He loved Ray for what he was doing right now—for easing the pressure. Not being a brother-in-law, just being a soldier and not asking any more questions.

"Thanks, Ray."

—

Ray walked with the man named Clopas to his left, trailing a little behind, and the one claiming to be Lazarus walking right beside him. The overhead moon lit the small hill they traveled on. Ray walked without speaking or making eye contact, his face hidden by the hood of his cloak and shemagh.

Ray pulled out his knife and placed the edge of the blade across the throat of the man named Clopas walking behind him. The man came to an immediate stop as Lazarus continued walking ahead, not noticing. Ray removed the blade from Clopas's throat and pointed his knife in the other direction. Picking up on the gesture, Clopas ran away. Ray watched Clopas for a moment, turned, tagged Lazarus with his Smartround gun, and caught up with the man walking without a care.

Ray walked beside Lazarus, matching his every step. He turned his translator on and asked Lazarus a question.

"Is it true what they say about you, Lazarus?"

Without turning, continuing forward, Lazarus nodded.

"So you were in God's Kingdom. Describe being there."

Looking ahead, Lazarus stopped, smiled, laughed for a few seconds, and turned to Ray. "Describe it? No, I cannot. I still feel it, though, the Warmth of His Kingdom. I can still feel it inside of me."

Ray could not help grinning a little as he listened to the translated words. Ray walked ahead of Lazarus, glancing up at the illuminated night sky above. Head tilted up, eyes on the stars, and his back to Lazarus, Ray spoke through his translator to the man. "I need for you to tell me—"

Before Ray's words finished translating, Lazarus spoke. "Your way of speaking, where do you come from?"

Ray turned toward Lazarus, grabbed the man's right arm, and stabbed S-7 into Lazarus's forearm, hitting him up with the drug again so *he* could now control him. Lazarus's eyes began to take on a glazed, hypnotic look.

"Is Jesus far away from here?"

Lazarus shook his head.

"Go to Him. Tell Jesus of my ability of knowing things to come. Tell Him His life is in danger and that He needs to meet me at the top of the mountain behind us. If He will not come, force Him. Do you understand everything I have just told you, Lazarus?"

"I do," Lazarus said confidently, eager to please his new S-7 controller.

Ray pulled the needle out of Lazarus's arm.

"Go. Run."

Lazarus turned away so fast that he tripped over himself. Up on his feet quickly, he ran. Ray watched Lazarus to make sure he did not fall over himself again. He looked up at the sky once more and began the trek back to John and his Unit.

In the time it took Ray to reach the camp—taking a different route to get a different view—his mind started putting together the pieces of the puzzle for his new mission. A puzzle in his head he always had to solve on previous missions in order to be successful out in the field. If one part does not fit, use the other pieces laid out before you. That was how his mind worked in the field and would be the reason he was given the under-the-radar missions to complete. The military's gem, Ray Catlin and the Unit he had selected personally, were 22–0. All missions completed. Ray felt they were actually 21–1. The one loss a big one: Martinez had died. They had completed their mission and were able to gather up a good amount of intel after the choppers blew the mountain to shit. But Martinez was gone.

On the stomped-out path that led to the camp, Ray placed all the pieces of the puzzle together in his head to determine what had to be done in this time he had traveled back to—the pieces of the puzzle almost placing themselves together without any effort.

Ray could see his Unit seated around the camp's fire pit, with John and Todd in the distance, talking away from the group under an arched palm tree. Ray spoke to Ben through his headset.

"Ben, it's me."

"Hey, Ray."

"I need you and Sal to bring Rydel over to me on the trail leading to camp—just you two. Right now."

Ben spotted Ray on the mountain trail leading back to the camp and waved at him.

Ben stood up, gently grabbed hold of Rydel seated next to Janice at the fire pit, and motioned for Sal to follow him.

"Everyone else stay put, Ray's orders," Ben said.

Ben and Sal led Rydel away.

—

On a hillock forty yards from the fire pit, an intense conversation going on between John and Todd caused the two men to take their eyes off Rydel and the members of the Unit guarding him. The two did not notice Rydel being taken away by Ben and Sal as they continued their heated discussion.

"Some of the team, especially Adriana, haven't been right since we came across the man Lazarus. You and Ray need to get them back in line, Todd."

Todd lowered his head, agreeing with John. "Yes, sir. I know."

"I cannot emphasize how unstable this project of Rydel's is, especially if he's able to alter anything significant in the time we are in now. We got him fast, which could not have worked out better. But some of the others might want to help Rydel with what he had planned to do in this time—those that are Christian—hearing the name Lazarus and putting it together where we are now."

"Yes, sir."

John took out a slim black box and handed it to Todd. "If I'm taken down by a Smartround, use this on me—"

"Shit!" Todd interrupted.

"What?"

"Behind you, sir."

John turned his head to see what had alarmed Todd but didn't pick up on anything.

"What is it, Todd?"

"Not sure who, but two are missing along with Rydel, sir."

John spun around, taking a head count below him.

"Fuck!"

—

Ben, Sal, and Rydel met up with Ray where he waited on the trail, and Ray held up a hand for them to stop. "I need a moment alone here with Rydel. You two make your way back before John and Todd notice. I'll be there in a minute."

Ben and Sal turned and walked away without saying a word.

"You believe in what I'm doing here, don't you, Ray?"

"You came back here to save Christ?"

"Yes."

"Tell me why."

"I was shown a miracle by my sister that came straight from God. This is what Placement is for, why I discovered it, to be here right now, to save Him. Jesus never finished what He was sent on Earth to do. He needs to continue with what He was meant to do in this time. He has to be saved, Ray."

Ray picked up on movement below, keeping John, Todd, and his Unit in view from the corner of his eye while he spoke to Rydel.

John noticed that some are missing.

Ray knew it before he got the call from Ben through his headset.

"Ray—"

"Yeah, I know—Rydel and I are coming down."

Ray shut off his headset. He wanted no interruptions, having only minutes alone, if that, to talk with Rydel.

"He touched me in an alley when we arrived, Rydel. I witnessed Him perform a miracle. I can still feel His…His divinity inside of me. Coming into contact with Him in the alley was not a coincidence. I know it in my soul."

"We *are* here for a reason, Ray."

"Causing damage back in our own time, back home? I know John and Will are holding back and are flat-out lying about most of it, but I have to be sure."

Rydel almost seemed to be on the verge of tears. He began to speak, but his voice cracked and failed him. He looked down at the ground for a brief moment and then raised his head. "You think I would cause the death of thousands after all I do at the lab to save civilian lives and the lives of the military in the field? Does that make any sense to you?"

"No, Rydel, it doesn't," Ray said. And he knew Rydel was right. This was an amazingly gifted and good-hearted person in front of him. Ray was sure of it, deep in his soul.

"It is my work. I know it's safe, Ray. John just wants me back because of my knowledge of Placement. John has good intentions for my work. But it is not the reason why I was able to create it."

"If one of us dies here?"

"I believe you'll die. And everything about a person up to that point in the present will come to an end. If one of us dies here, someone from the present, when we return, would have to travel back to this exact week in time that we've breached to save the person. That's what I believe but cannot prove definitively."

Rydel stepped closer to Ray. "But you know we have to do this, Ray. Don't you?"

Ray heard the footsteps approaching and spun his head around, watching John run toward where he stood with Rydel. Ray mouthed the words say nothing to Rydel, and the two walked toward John. John reached Ray and Rydel, red-faced, breathing heavily.

"Ray, what's going on here?"

"Just wanted to get Rydel away from the others and ask him how much longer he thinks we will be here. Didn't think it would be a problem."

"Well, it is! Come on. Back to the camp. Let's go. And get your Unit back in line like we talked about. Got it, Ray?"

"I got it."

—

Two fire pits now lit up the camp. Members of the Unit stood and prepared the MREs they had packed for the trip with only a word or two spoken to one another.

The group, with the exception of Todd, started to seat themselves around the fire pit on leftover logs they had found earlier. They all ate silently in front of the fire.

At the other fire pit, about forty feet away, John and Todd sat with Rydel seated between them. From out of the dark, Ray walked over to where Rydel was being kept apart from the rest. Ray stood and stared at the fire for a moment. He then nodded for Todd to leave. Todd stood up, gave the colonel a slight look, and joined the others at the opposite fire. Now alone with Rydel, John and Ray stared at each other.

"Okay, Ray, go talk to them."

Ray stood where he was for a few seconds before following Todd back to where the others were seated around the fire. John turned to Rydel, and Rydel smiled confidently.

"Some in Ray's Unit are having second thoughts already, John. And I haven't even had a chance to talk with them. To explain why I came here."

"That's about to change. Ray is over there now, explaining that you most likely caused the death of thousands already by coming into contact with those two men."

Rydel closed his eyes and shook his head. He then raised two fingers up at John and opened his eyes.

"Two times out, John. The first two times traveling back with Placement had no effect on the climate—"

"We didn't change anything the first two times out, goddammit!"

John stood with his hands balled up into fists and stepped closer to Rydel. Rydel stared up at him, his face peaceful and warm-hearted as always. John took a step closer, and then another. A flashing thought ran through John's head to beat Rydel until he understood what he had done. Taking another step forward, he could see his right arm rising, ready to strike Rydel. His right arm seemed to be separated from himself, having its own agenda. John stopped and stared at Rydel, who still looked completely at peace.

John shook his head, put his hands in the pockets of his cloak, and sat back down by the fire.

"Sorry, Rydel. I don't know what that was. I'm tired. I told you before I do not want to hurt you. I would never strike you. You'd be dead if I did."

"You striking me? No. But the one trying to control you now is another story. It would strike me with all your training on how to kill a man if it simply could. But I don't think it's that easy for the Other to do."

John shook his head, having no idea what the hell Rydel was babbling on about. He fixed his attention on the fire, trying to calm down and rid himself of the sudden anger that had taken over him. Feeling better after only a minute, John let out a breath, shook his head again, and looked up at Rydel. "Your mind is not right. You're my friend. I care about you and the work you can produce for humanity. However, this project of yours has probably caused damage you can't even imagine back home and to the people of America."

"You are wrong about Placement, John, and what it is meant for. We are here, aren't we? Obliterating all physics as we thought we knew it. God wants us to save His Son. Us, the ones He loves most, the ones who let Jesus die."

For the first time, John took in the starlit sky, tuning out Rydel's rambling for just a minute. Rydel did stop talking for a moment as the two looked up at the sheet of blackness above, pinpricked with beautiful, white, piercing stars.

"You think it was just me finding a way to go back in time, John? It was more—it was divine intervention. God's hand was guiding me. My sister made it so clear. God was with me creating Placement all along."

"No, Rydel, it was just you. This is just your spent mind talking to you now. All that we have been through at the lab…we are true friends. But we need to get you home and make you well again."

—

Ray's Unit sat around the larger of the two fires blazing inside the camp. Ray stood over the members of the Unit for a quiet moment. He glanced over his shoulder and could see John and Rydel still seated around the other fire.

Sal reached back and placed a log beside him, and Ray sat down. Illuminated by the fire, the faces and the eyes from all in the Unit waited for Ray to speak.

"The man Lazarus all of you came across? Yeah, well, Sal, Todd, and I met up with a woman by the name of Maryam. Mary, when translated, who has a Son. Her Son's translated name—Jesus."

"So He is here, Ray?" Adriana quickly asked Ray to confirm.

"That's right. So now all of you know exactly where we are in time. Rydel came back here to save Christ. John is here to make sure that none of you, in any way, try to help Rydel do that. I'm going to help Rydel on his mission—it's something I have to do. I ask all of you to please understand."

No one in Ray's Unit moved or even blinked. They all stared at Ray, some not sure what he had just said. Their blank, fire-lit faces looking utterly confused.

"Jesus!" Carrie finally said.

"Yes, Carrie—Jesus."

"No, I mean—holy shit! I can't believe that He's really here."

Todd stood up. "We shouldn't interfere with anyone in this time, like Adams said, Ray. We can cause damage back home."

"It's bullshit," Ray snapped, glaring at Todd, silently telling him to sit back down like the rest, which he did. "I've talked with Rydel about what he created. It's safe. Nothing will happen back home. All John and the rest at the lab want is Rydel back because of his knowledge of Placement."

Janice looked around at the other members of the Unit and could see the ones who were already with Ray, the ones on the fence, and the rest thinking he'd lost it. She leaned her head forward around Ben seated beside her so she could face Ray.

"Ray…I don't think this is a life that was meant to be saved—"

"I do," Adriana quickly said to Janice from across the fire, staring Janice down.

Confused, Kevin shrugged his shoulders at Ray. "But why? Why save Him, Ray? I thought that He died for us, or something like that."

Ray placed both hands on his knees and slowly lifted himself off the log, his eyes locked on Kevin.

"John and I came across Jesus when we arrived, and the two of us witnessed a miracle—a dispute between a husband and wife ending with the woman dead. The man we are talking about now, He healed this woman, right in front of us. He's not some myth, as some of you might think He is—He's real. I can't stand around and let Him die. After three years together, and all we've been through, you are family to me. I just wanted all of you to know my intentions here. I do not want to lie to any of you."

They waited for Ray to say more, but he was finished speaking. He lowered his head and fixed his eyes on the fire in front of him. All stared at Ray mannequin-like, unmoving. And then they started to look at one another. Some dropped their heads toward the ground at Ray's revelation. Ray noticed the members of the Unit questioning what he had said.

"You don't believe me?" Ray said, sensing their surreptitious looks at each other as he stared at the fire.

"I believe you, Ray," Sal wholeheartedly said.

"You'd believe me if I said I was Jesus Christ myself, Sal."

Ray turned his attention away from the fire, waiting for the doubters—the ones who obviously did not believe what he had witnessed—to face him. Carrie let Ray know what she and some of the other Unit members were feeling.

"Ray, you haven't been the same since we got here."

Todd nodded, agreeing with Carrie. "Ray, you have never pressed your religious beliefs on any of us before. This is not the time to start. We have completed our mission here. It's time for all of us to go home."

Kevin held up the palm of his right hand to calm Ray down, or show him that he meant no disrespect before he spoke, probably a little bit of both. "Yeah, Ray, maybe the chip that sent you here is malfunctioning. I think we should leave this place as soon as we can. You need to leave this one alone."

Ray and Kevin stared at each other without saying a word for an uncomfortable ten seconds. Kevin shifted his gaze toward the fire. Ray turned his back on Kevin and the others. He stood for a few seconds with his hands on his hips before walking away.

"Ray, where are you going?" Kevin asked.

Without turning, Ray continued ahead as he answered Kevin.

"I think we should include John and Rydel in our discussion," Ray announced, saying it loud enough so that all in the Unit could hear what he said.

"Why?" Kevin asked.

Ray stopped and just stood where he was with his back to Kevin and the rest. His head dipped a little, and then he looked over his shoulder at Kevin.

"Because I can't leave this one alone, Kevin. I need Rydel's help, and John now needs to understand that."

Sal shot up from the log he'd been sitting on and held up his coffee canteen, saluting Ray with it. "That's what I'm talking about! Damn straight we're here for a reason! I'm with you on this, Ray. I'll follow you into hell."

Ray slowly looked over at Sal, meeting his eyes.

"Let's hope it doesn't come to that, Sal."

—

John stared at Rydel and was about to say something until he caught movement coming from his left. Ray seeped out of the dark and stood in the outreaching light of the fire. John quickly stood up at the sight of Ray.

"Fuck, Ray! I told you to talk with your Unit and stay with them. When I'm finished here with Rydel, we will join you—"

"John, I need you and Rydel to come join us. Need to talk about my mission here now."

John stood, nonplussed and staring at Ray, and then was finally able to speak, making sure he had heard Ray correctly. "I'm sorry, what the hell did you just say?"

"Both of you are needed by the fire with the rest of us," Ray said. Ray turned, slipping back into the blackness. Gun raised, John pointed it at Rydel to get off his ass, which he immediately did. The colonel grabbed Rydel and pushed him forward with the muzzle of his gun, pressing it against the back of Rydel's neck.

He led Rydel to the other fire pit, reaching the circle of operators around the fire. John stopped ten feet away from the group and placed a hand on Rydel's shoulder for him to stop as well. He lowered his gun and whispered into Rydel's right ear.

"I have my gun at my side. Do as I tell you to do, Rydel. Don't be stupid here."

John and Rydel stepped closer. Ray stood, waiting. The rest remained seated around the fire. Sal waved his arm in the air, motioning for Rydel to come his way. "Doc, over here. Sit next to me."

Rydel looked at John to get his permission. John nodded that it was okay, and Rydel took a seat beside Sal.

Ray pointed out a log for John. "John, sit down for a second."

"I'll stand. What is this—what's going on here?"

"You and I seem to be at odds on what we should do here."

The expression on John's face contorted into a look of one betrayed. John remained where he was, glancing over Ray's Unit before him. Half the Unit stared directly at him; the other half glanced at John for a brief second and dropped their heads, eyeing the ground. John returned his attention to Ray—and there in front of him was the barrel of Ray's gun, pointed in his direction.

"Put away your gun, John."

With Ray's weapon in his face, John slung his gun over his shoulder without hesitating.

Todd shot up from where he sat as if catching a red-hot coal from the fire burning before him. "Hey, hey, easy here, Ray. Easy, man."

"Sit back down, Todd."

"Ray—"

"Sit back down! John and I are trying to have a calm conversation here. You jumping up like that might make others in the Unit who believe what I saw nervous."

Todd glanced at the rest around the fire and could see Ray was right. Those who did not believe what Ray claimed to have seen looked at the ground or the fire; the rest glared at Todd to sit the fuck back down. Todd sat, trying not to look at the colonel. Ray then calmly spoke to John.

"John, how can I live with myself after what we witnessed? We are truly here for a reason."

"No, we are not, Ray."

John took a few steps closer toward the fire and stopped.

"All of you, listen to me—and listen carefully. The last time we used Placement, altering the past slightly for one man, thousands of lives were lost. If any of you try to save this man Jesus, I'm telling you, there will not be a world left to travel back to in our time."

Rydel stood up from his seat by the fire and pointed at John. "The tsunami had nothing to do with Placement, John."

Distance and obstacles. John's mind came up with two scenarios; he picked scenario one. John smiled a frustrated smile at Rydel and the others in the Unit, using his body language in a way so that it seemed like he was exasperated, throwing his hands up in the air. He knew the Unit was divided on what to do—all he needed was a few seconds of diversion. He took a step toward Rydel but abruptly turned away from him, then looked down at Carrie, who was staring at the fire.

"Carrie, look at me."

Carrie lifted her head and met John's eyes.

"You know we must remain where we are and do nothing until we are taken back. You know that, don't you?"

Carrie broke eye contact with John, gave a slight look toward Ray, and focused on the fire once more. John took another step closer, crouching down in front of the fire, facing Carrie. "Carrie, help me here, be a voice of reason with me and—"

John stood and sprinted the now-short distance between himself and Rydel, surprising Rydel and all in the Unit. Rydel did not notice John moving until the man had his arm around his neck.

The color drained from Rydel's face as John pulled him away from the fire—the muzzle of the colonel's gun touching the side of Rydel's head. All in Ray's Unit bolted upright. Ray stood where he was, fixed on the swaying flames in front of him, gun lowered. Without looking up at his brother-in-law, eyes still on the fire, Ray asked John a simple question.

"You sure you wanna do this, John?"

"Am I sure I want to do this? Yes, I'm sure, Ray! I'll shoot Rydel in the head if I have to and save the lives I swore to protect back home!"

"Lower your gun, John. I will not ask you again."

"You won't ask me again—is that what you just said? I'm your commanding officer. What you are doing now is mutiny! Don't fucking do this, Ray!"

"Shoot him, Sal."

To John's left, holding his rifle under his cloak, Sal had enough time to raise and fire his weapon before the colonel could react.

The colonel dropped to the ground hard as Rydel ran over to Ray. Todd rushed over to Colonel Adams, checked his vitals, and could see the Smartround Sal had fired sticking out of the colonel's neck. "Ray, what the hell did you just order Sal to do here?"

Ray pointed at Steve and Jack. "You two take the colonel and Rydel to the storage tent."

—

It was late. Each member of the Unit looked at Ray from where they sat around the fire. Ray had his head tilted upward, taking in the magnificent stars shining above them.

"I know what I saw. It was a miracle. We are all here for a reason. And that is to save Him," Ray said while staring up at the night sky.

Todd stood up and walked over to Ray, then placed a hand on his shoulder. He spoke to Ray in a supportive, comforting voice.

"Ray, did you actually see this happen up close? It could've been a stunt. I've read that many of his miracles were most likely staged, a way of bringing hope to the less fortunate people in this time. A man with an incredible ability to influence the masses. We've seen it before on our missions out. Haven't we, Ray?"

Ray took Todd's hand off his shoulder and placed it around his own throat. "Todd, the man cut the woman so deep where your hand is now. I saw the slash to her throat. It was not staged. They were alone. Why pull off this stunt in front of no one?"

Todd eased his hand away from Ray's throat, looking at him with reassuring eyes.

"All I'm saying is that maybe you saw something different because of your religious beliefs. That's all. Most of us do not believe in this man like you do. And we never will."

The statement by Todd set the tone for those in the group who felt Ray was way off on what he intended to do. Todd's words were understanding, comforting, and supportive. They hit the precise nerve of those he wanted to influence: the ones wanting to go home, knowing their mission here was now complete.

Ray glanced at the faces of the nonbelievers in his Unit staring back at him.

"Okay. We're all tired. We all need sleep. I will understand if none of you help me with what I have to do. Just don't try to stop me. That would not be a good idea."

Todd took a cautious step closer to Ray. "Ray, come on, take it easy, now. Why, why do this, how can you be so sure?"

"He touched me. I felt the goodness in Him. Felt why He was sent here."

Ray turned away from Todd and nodded at Carrie and Jack.

"Carrie, go check on the colonel and keep an eye on him. He hit his head pretty hard when he went down. Jack will stay with you and relieve you in two hours." Ray faced the rest in the Unit. "The rest of you, back to your tents. Get some sleep. This discussion is over."

—

Later, behind his lamplit, billowing tent, Todd stood alone. From around the corner of the tent, the rest of the Unit appeared from out of the dark. They all made a half circle around Todd, who had his back against the tent. The Unit waited for the man to explain why they were secretly gathered together.

"He's lost it—just like Rydel," Todd whispered in a harsh, scratchy voice.

"Bullshit," Adriana flatly said.

Todd moved closer. He stopped just inches away from Adriana, glanced back toward the fire where he could still see Ray sitting alone, then jabbed a finger up close in Adriana's face.

"Just because you two share the same beliefs doesn't make what Ray wants to do here right. It's fucking crazy! You need to be thinking about the lives of the American people, and the lives all over the world back in our time. You heard what Adams said. The consequences of—"

"You trust Adams over Ray, Todd?" Sal asked. "Are you fucking kidding me?"

"I trust my gut, Sal. And Ray has been off since we got here—don't tell me you haven't noticed too." The group started glancing at one another. Some faces were lit by the lamplight coming through the back of the fluttering tent, some faces hidden in the dark.

"We can't let him do this. We have to stop him!" Todd said.

Todd waited for each member in the Unit to nod back in agreement, and they all did. "Okay, let's get back inside our tents. Give Ray the night to think it over. If he still feels the same way in the morning, I'll take him down lightly. We'll just let him be tonight. I doubt he'll move from the fire—he's spent, probably fall asleep right there. But we need to be sure." Todd pointed Carrie out from the rest. "Carrie, keep an eye on Ray from the tent."

He then pointed to Jack. "Get in two hours' rest, take over for Carrie, and do the same, Jack."

The Unit's clandestine gathering to debate what should be done about Ray ended without another word.

Ray's Unit silently made their way back to their tents without Ray noticing, it seemed, as he sat by the fire, hunched over.

At the fire, Ray couldn't take his eyes off the flames. He also could not believe Todd would gather everyone together for some secret meeting behind the tents. He was amazed that the man gathered the whole Unit together in one place, planning to usurp him. Todd was in no way dumb, but he just did an incredibly dumb thing. Ray had heard the entire conversation through his Smartround gun, which was transmitting back from the top half of Sal's Smartround gun— he told Sal to tuck it down the side of his pant leg if something like this were to happen. Ray let out a disbelieving grunt. He had heard all that he needed to hear. The Unit was divided; however, the stronger half was with him. And Todd should have known that they would be.

—

An hour later, the only sound from the night came from the fire Ray had his eyes locked on, the sizzling sound of dead wood burning. The smell of the fire in front of Ray conjured up two different memories for him. The first was of his father setting up a teepee-style fire in the backyard on Christmas Eve while they waited for Santa. The second memory, from many years later, was of how he approached Adaumeer Badoer in front of a similar fire in the mountains of Iraq, slashing his throat before the man was able to set into motion his plan to simultaneously detonate three bombs inside Washington, DC. The Christmas Eve surprise by his father—and the takedown of the terrorist—shared the same smell of burning pine cones, the fragrance coming from the small branches he had thrown into the fire.

Peripheral vision on the tents, Ray placed another dried-out piece of wood on the fire to give it a little more life. One way or another, someone would be coming to see him soon—no way would Todd wait until morning to do what he believed must be done.

However, it was Ben and Steve stepping out of the dark ahead of Ray, the fire lighting their bodies and faces. The two walked forward with their sidearms slightly lifted in front of them and came to a stop. They took a knee in front of the fire, staring at Ray through the flames.

"Are you sure this is the right thing to do here, Ray? Are you sure?" Steve asked.

"Have I ever led you blind before, Steve? Do I seem off to you, like Todd was saying about me behind the tents?"

"You heard us?"

"Had Sal dismantle his gun, and he used the emergency comm so I could be included in any sort of conversation you all decided to have without me. He hid it down the side of his leg. So, do I come across as losing it?"

"No…no, Ray."

Ben gave a slight nod over toward the tents and spoke to Ray in a whisper. "We're with you, Ray."

"Good."

## The Gathering of the Believers

Careful.

That was the word that kept repeating in Ray's head as he knelt on the ground of the ancient past and stared up at the heavens. Taking in the starry sky, Ray waited. He put himself in this prone position to see if anyone he truly trusted in his Unit would change their opinions about him. Influenced, maybe, by a dose of S-7 that Todd may have gotten his hands on.

Todd deserved better. He unquestionably would lay his life down to protect his commanding officer—no second thoughts. If only Todd realized the importance of what has to be done here. Yet he was like John when it came to God—there was no God.

Two on the left, approaching.

Now one on the right. Coming fast. Ambush. Shit, they don't believe! Ray spun toward the two approaching from the left and raised his Smartround gun.

"Ray, it's me. Lower your gun, man."

Sal's voice.

Ray aimed his gun to his right to see Sal inching his way closer, carefully.

"You still with me?"

"Of course, Ray."

"Others are approaching!" Ray said quickly, quietly, spinning away from Sal.

"It's Steve and A in front of you. I'm gathering up the believers like you said. We're with you. Lower the gun, Ray."

Ray didn't lower his gun. He waited. Steve and Adriana appeared in front of Ray with their hands in the air—both close enough to have heard Ray and Sal's conversation.

"Okay, guys, put your hands down."

Adriana and Steve lowered their hands and slowly stepped closer to Ray. "What's the plan, Ray?" Adriana asked. Ray pointed his Smartround gun toward the tents, where the rest were sleeping. "You three follow me," Ray ordered.

They followed Ray over to the tent where Rydel and John were being watched by Jack and Carrie. Ray approached the entrance flap to the tent and gave the signal for the three behind him to surround the other tents. Ray made sure they were all in place before lifting the flap and entering the tent. The storage tent was smallish but had enough room to stand up straight. Once inside, Ray was greeted by Carrie and her gun.

Carrie lowered her sidearm at once. "Sorry, Ray. I just started nodding off a bit. You surprised the shit out of me."

Ray lifted his weapon and shot Carrie in the chest. Not propelled back by the blast, Carrie stood eerily still with her eyes wide, stunned that Ray had shot her. She looked down at a new blemish on her upper chest—a sedation Smartround. Carrie looked back up at Ray with fluttering eyes.

"The dose is being administered slowly so you can talk to her. But she's gonna fall. Catch her, Jack."

Off to the side of the tent, out of his sleeping bag, Jack hurried over and caught Carrie in his arms before she hit the ground. She stared up at Jack—terrified.

"You're okay, Carrie. You got shot with a sedation Smartround. So I know you can't move, but you can hear me for a little while longer here. You're fine."

Carrie's eyes slowly opened and closed—the drug inside her taking over. Jack dragged Carrie over and placed her beside John Adams, laid out on the floor of the tent. Turning toward Ray, Jack's eyes locked on Ray's Smartround gun—the gun aimed in his direction. Jack shook his head slightly like, You don't trust me?

"Ben said that you are with me, Jack. Kinda hard to believe, though. I thought you didn't believe in a god of any kind."

"I believe in you, Ray. The way you look out for us. The way you've always looked out for me. Maybe I am wrong about my beliefs. I know one thing, I trust you when my life is in your hands. I have for three years. If you say we are a go here—that this has to be done and we're here for a reason—how can I turn my back on you? I can't."

Ray gave Jack a handful of S-7 syringes.

"You remember everything Stevens said on how to use S-7, right?"

"I do," Jack said.

"Use S-7 on Carrie while she's still conscious, and have her forget everything here tonight. Implant in her mind that after finding Rydel, she returned to her tent and slept for the rest of the night. Be ready to do the same with the others who want to stop me. You got it?"

"I got it."

Ray waved at Rydel to follow him.

Out of the tent, the two walked for twenty minutes, reaching the mountain's precipice. Rydel stood by Ray's side while Ray scanned the land below with his binoculars.

"I told Lazarus to bring Him here."

"Lazarus may have a hard time doing that because of the Other, Ray. But it was a smart move by you, sending him after Jesus."

"The other?"

Rydel broke his gaze away from the moonlit land below and stared blankly at Ray.

"What, Ray?"

"You said the other, Rydel. What did you mean?"

"Sorry, that's not what I meant to say, I was thinking something else. A lot of thoughts going through my head with what has to be done here. I'm just tired. Lazarus will be fine. He will find Jesus and bring Him here."

# Jesus and Lazarus

The hut where Jesus and His apostles slept had nothing more than four walls and a roof. They rested on rollout mats on the ground inside the empty hut scantily lit by moonlight and starlight piercing through dime-sized holes around the edge of the roof. The hut didn't seem to have a door until one opened near the far corner. The light of the moon found its way in as a flap at the bottom of the hut opened and a shadowed man slithered inside on his belly. The flap fell, and the hut went dark. The man stood and walked directly toward one of the thirteen men sleeping on the floor. The shadowed man knelt beside Jesus Christ and shook His shoulder.

"Jesus."

Christ touched the hand on His shoulder.

"Lazarus."

"Come with me, Jesus."

Lazarus helped Jesus off the ground and led Him to the flap of fabric so the two could exit the hut.

Alone, under an oak tree with a thick trunk and wind-swaying thin boughs, Jesus and Lazarus faced each other at arm's length. Lazarus pulled Jesus's hood over His head to hide His appearance and surveyed the barren land around them, making sure the two were still alone. Confident all was well, Lazarus placed both hands on Jesus's shoulders.

"There's a man with an ability like yours—he knows of things to come. He told me your life is in danger."

Jesus touched the hands of Lazarus resting on His shoulders. "I know this, Lazarus."

At a loss for words and on how to feel about Jesus's knowledge of the danger He was in, Lazarus's mouth slowly dropped open. He was then able to utter a response.

"You know?"

"Yes."

"Leave with me—now!"

"I cannot leave."

"Why?" Lazarus pleaded.

"I must face what is to come. If I were to turn my back on all of this and walk away, the Message would be lost."

Lazarus dropped his hands from Jesus's shoulders and pulled Him closer in a desperate embrace. Lazarus stepped back, placed a hand on Jesus's face, and began to weep.

"Listen to me! Listen to me! Please! You have to come with me, Jesus! You have to—"

Jesus reached out and touched Lazarus on the side of his face. Lazarus was about to speak once more but abruptly stopped, his mouth still slightly open. His unblinking, trance-like eyes now stared back at Jesus.

"Do not go back to this man. Go home. Forget all this."

Jesus eased His hand away from Lazarus's face.

"Go, my friend. Go now."

Lazarus turned from Jesus and walked away. Jesus pulled back the hood of His cloak, revealing His face to the night, a face outlined in a patchy beard and dark skin from being in the sun. Wide nose, hair parted down the middle and reaching His shoulders, and soul-baring brown eyes.

Jesus looked up, the star-studded sky filling His line of sight. He smiled and slowly closed His eyes.

# The Other

Ray stood on a mountain peak in the darkness, scanning over the land below with his Smartround gun. He switched to his binoculars, bumping into Rydel standing right beside him. Ray lowered the binoculars and turned to Rydel.

"Shit. He's not showing up."

"What do we do?" Rydel asked.

"We can't wait any longer. He's tagged, but he's out of range. Forget him for now. Let's get back to the camp."

The two walked down from the high point and made their way back to the camp. Ahead of them, those who believed in Ray's new mission were located near and around the other burning fire pit, away from the tents. Adriana and Steve appeared as barely seen shadows at opposite sides of the fire, patrolling with their Smartround guns. Ben, Jack, and Sal sat cross-legged on the ground in front of the fire until they noticed Ray and Rydel approaching. The three rose and jogged over to meet them.

"He didn't show, Ray?" Sal quietly asked.

Ray shook his head and headed toward the fire with Rydel. Ben, Jack, and Sal followed. At the fire pit, Ray spoke into his headset for Adriana and Steve to join them. Out of the blackness, the two appeared, firelight falling over them. The popping, spark-swirling fire was all that could be heard while Rydel and the rest waited for Ray to speak.

"Lazarus is gone. Not sure if our message got to Jesus. I doubt it. So *we are* going to Him."

Ray looked over the faces of each member of his now-slimmed-down Unit and pointed toward the tents.

"Jack's going to use S-7 on the others so they will forget about our conversation before. After that, the rest of you will take them down lightly—set the rounds for thirty-six hours. I don't want them down longer than that."

They all waited for Ray to give the order to move as he paused for a few seconds.

"Go."

Jack silently moved toward the tents. The rest of the Unit believers raised and checked their Smartround guns and, as one, followed in Jack's footsteps.

After a minute, Ray pointed a finger at Rydel, wordlessly instructing him to stay by the fire. Rydel didn't move or say a word. Ray made his way toward the tents. He had taken all of six steps when Todd suddenly appeared and began walking across the camp opposite from where the tents were set up. Ray rushed toward Todd, who spun around, upon hearing Ray approach. Now at close range, Ray pointed his gun inches away from Todd's face.

"You're gonna kill me, Ray?" Todd asked—shock on his face and in his voice.

Ray all at once realized he was pointing his Beretta M9 at Todd's face, not his Smartround rifle. Taken aback by the fact he had just aimed his sidearm at one of his own, Ray lowered the gun to his side and clumsily searched for his Smartround rifle slung over his shoulder. Raising his rifle, Ray pointed it at the emptiness now before him. Todd had run off into the blackness encircling the camp.

Ray sprinted into the dark—coming to a stop after only ten seconds. He had no way of knowing which direction Todd had run off to and no way to track him through his Smartround gun; Todd was unarmed. Ray waited in the darkness for a few seconds, breaking down in his head what had just happened, and then ran back.

Ray entered the camp and stopped. The ones loyal to Ray waited outside the tents—the last order he gave minutes ago completed for the most part. Steve approached Ray, shaking his head.

"Ray, Todd isn't here."

"He got away. We can't track him. He wasn't armed, and his damn chip is not like Rydel's."

"What now?" Steve asked.

Ray waved a hand for everyone to follow him.

At the fire pit, Ray placed a couple of logs into the flames while the Unit stood and waited for orders. Finished with the fire, Ray paced back and forth a couple of times with his arms folded over his chest, coming to a stop next to Rydel.

"Tell them, Rydel."

Rydel looked over the faces in front of him glowing in firelight.

"I have the man Clopas tagged. He'll know where Jesus will be tomorrow afternoon. It would have been easier if Lazarus could've led Jesus here so we could protect Him, but it did not work out that way. So…we now have to go find Him. I'm sure all of you might be questioning what we are doing here. But by helping me, and now Ray, you'll be saving the lives of over seven billion people in our time."

Finished with what he had to say, Rydel lowered his head and stared at the fire before him. Ray took a knee by the fire pit, looking up at the four men and the one woman remaining from his Unit.

"We're gonna get a few hours' sleep, refresh. We can't go out like this. Then we leave before dawn." Ray got to his feet and tapped Jack on the shoulder. "Jack, take first watch. Everybody else to their tents."

Adriana, Ben, Sal, and Steve entered their tents. Jack started his patrol of the camp, passing the tents as Ray called out to him quietly.

"Jack."

Jack turned and walked over to Ray.

"Todd's gone. But he's probably close. Watch for him and the way he would enter a camp like the one we have set up here. Okay?"

"On it, Ray."

—

An hour into his patrol, Jack found himself back at the fire pit, close to the tents. He added wood to the fire, because Ray insisted on sleeping outside instead of in one of the tents. Right beside Ray, Rydel slept as well. Ray had told Jack he didn't want Rydel more than an arm's reach away from him. It was cold, both were in slim sleeping bags, but the fire was burning well now with the added wood. They were good.

Jack turned to check on the rest when the sound of shifting rock stopped him dead in his tracks, the sound coming from behind the tents in front of him. From the darkness between two of the tents, three small rocks rolled out and landed by Jack's feet. The rocks stopped at the same time and angled up toward Jack—as if pointing at him—then fell over. All three tents billowed from a screeching wind finding its way over and around the camp without warning.

He was all at once frightened.

The rocks just fell from above the mountain. And a sudden gust of wind drifting over the camp happens all the time in locations like this, Jack tried to convince himself. But it felt different. The wind blasting in his face felt ice-cold, and it fucking hurt. He focused on the billowing tents as another rock flew out from the darkness, passing over the tents and landing by his feet.

Is it Todd, trying to draw me out?

No, Todd was too smart for that—he would never toss rocks as a way of distracting and taking out a member of the Unit.

Jack knew this was something else.

Bullied. He was being bullied—the overwhelming feeling made Jack's face flush with anger. Images of when he was a nine-year-old boy flashed in his head. A group of kids tormenting him by throwing rocks over the fence at his new home after his mother and father divorced. The kids knew about his family somehow, calling his mother a whore, calling his mother and him by name. He was never able to see their faces but could tell by their voices that they were about the same age—nine or ten years old. He wanted a friend, or friends, from the new neighborhood—but ended up bullied and bloodied instead.

And just like that day, a small rock hit Jack on the side of his nose, and he felt the trickle of blood. Enraged, he set out to hunt his tormentors down this time.

Revenge for the two of us, Mom.

Jack slipped between the narrow space separating the tents in front of him and saw the man immediately. A hooded man in a black cloak stared down at him. The black outline of the man—it had to be a man by the broad shoulders and other distinguishable subtleties—stood on an overhanging mountain ledge above, about thirty yards away. The moon lit the man in a halo of white light, the black shape standing as still as the rock, which seemed to be a part of him, under his feet.

Jack eased his way forward. He aimed his Smartround gun at the man and shouted out to him without the use of his translator.

"Come down from there. Now."

The shadowed man pointed at Jack, his index finger slowly moving in a come-hither gesture. Jack stood motionless, near-loss-of-bladder-control frightened. The man reached down from the ledge, almost touching the ground with his hand. Impossible! Just an odd way that the light from the moon is hitting the man—a shadow, is all. Jack tried reasoning with himself of just what he was seeing until the hand slowly rose in front of him and rested on his shoulder. His whole body went numb.

"Come closer, Jack."

The voice of the man on the ledge was like nothing Jack had ever heard before. It was as if spoken from another place, not of this earth—the voice calm but menacing, soothing but evil. Jack looked down and watched himself walk closer toward the man, having no control over his body. He tried to scream but could not. He screamed in his head for his body to stop walking, which resulted in his legs running toward the man, his back arched backward trying to keep up with his legs. Back bent, running up the side of the mountain, Jack reached the man on the ledge and skidded to a stop, standing erect.

With his arm back to a normal size, the man in the black cloak reached out his hand once more.

"Take my hand, Jack."

—

Ray woke an hour before dawn. The fire in front of him still lit, but dying. His eyes searched and found Rydel still asleep in his sleeping bag. He looked for Jack around the campsite, unable to spot him. Ray glanced down, unzippered his sleeping bag, and got to his feet.

Jack was suddenly there, standing rock-still, staring at Ray from across the fire. It was as if he came out of nowhere. Having glanced away for only a few seconds so he could free himself from his sleeping bag, Ray could not fathom how Jack seemed to appear right in front of him.

Jack dropped to his knees in front of the fire as his head and body slumped forward. Ray hustled over and grabbed Jack by the shoulders before he fell into the fire, then tilted Jack's head upward so he could face him.

"Jack—you okay?"

Jack looked at Ray with a blank expression. Drool began to run down each side of his face from his open mouth. He then wept.

"I've seen him. He's gone now, but I've seen him—*I have* seen him!" Jack rambled to Ray.

"Who, Jack?"

"The One," Jack said, speaking slow and softly.

Ray reached under Jack's arms in a bear hug, lifting him to his feet, and touched the side of Jack's head with his hand to calm him down.

"I know how you feel…coming into contact with Him. You believe now. That's a good thing, Jack, a good thing. Because now it's time to save Him."

—

Ray had Rydel and the rest ready to move out in under ten minutes. Ray led the way as Rydel and the others followed him. The sky behind the group bloomed in a shade of deep purple on the horizon. The seven walked silently on their way to Jerusalem, met by a strong wind that swept over and rippled the hooded cloaks they wore.

The shadow of a man trailed the group. As the man stepped slowly closer, the black hooded cloak he wore reached back to the horizon, dragging a black shadow across the land. The man, at least a hundred yards behind Ray and the others, reached out his hand toward the group and touched Jack's back without Jack or anyone else noticing. With a hand resting on Jack's shoulder, the man in the black cloak followed the group on their journey to the Holy City.

# The Road to Jerusalem

The seven walked with their hooded heads lowered and were now joined by others traveling on the dirt road leading toward Jerusalem. Ray whispered into his rifle under his cloak. His Smartround gun recorded what he said and sent the message to the others. Each one received the message on their Smartround gun, feeling the screen slide out from under their cloak.

Keep your heads down. Do not come into contact with these people. Translators in place but off for now.

All got the message and followed Ray, keeping their heads down and distancing themselves from the people on the road. Ray was being pragmatic—if there was any truth in what John and Will were saying, the only contact they wanted was with Jesus Christ. How could that cause disaster back home?

As they closed in on the city, Ray turned and raised his arm slightly, holding out his hand for everyone to stop. He walked off the dirt road, slipping between two leaning Joshua trees, and waved for the others to join him. A good fifty yards away from the dirt road, surrounded by sun-dried bramble up to his knees, Ray pulled back the hood of his cloak, revealing his face, as the others made a circle around him.

"Okay, Rydel, where's this man Clopas?"

Rydel looked under his cloak at the Smartround rifle that he'd tagged Clopas with and then looked back up at Ray, lifting the hood of his cloak off his head.

"He's here, inside the city. I've got him."

Ray placed his hood back over his head, as did Rydel. Back on the now-deserted road, Ray led the six toward one of the city's stone entrances, where a man stood alone near the side of the arched passageway leading inside. He wore a perfectly unblemished white cloak, the hood covering his head and face. Ray walked past the man first, and Rydel and the rest followed.

The man began to laugh.

All seven turned toward the man standing by the side of the entrance. Ray and the five from his Unit stepped toward the man. Rydel spun around and ran off into the city. Not noticing Rydel fleeing, Ray and the others continued closing in on the man. The laugh—there was something about the man's laugh. Ray and his Unit believers pulled back their hoods and removed their Smartround guns, not caring if anyone saw them. They all felt it—the man was wrong.

The man's white-hooded head swung left and right, scanning over the group as the six moved his way. The man raised his head and folded back his white hood.

All six stopped at the sight of him.

The man resembled all the popular art and drawings of Jesus Christ—except for the eyes. The man's cerulean eyes seemed to glow, possessed with pure evil and hate. The man took a step forward, and the six took two steps back, instinctual fear controlling their bodies. The man smiled at them with a manic grin on the Jesus Christ–like face he was hiding behind and spoke in English.

"He dies."

The man turned his back to the six. There was not a soul near him as he made his way inside the city. Just inside the entrance, the man's head spun completely around, his neck extending down his back, slithering like a serpent, its blue eyes glaring at Ray and his believers. The man with the Jesus Christ–like face dropped to his knees—his arms unnaturally wrapping around his back—clasping both hands together in a mock prayer. Then he sprang back up to his feet and turned away. As he walked ahead, laughing, his head and neck returned to normal.

They couldn't move.

As the fear wore away, Ray looked over the members of his Unit.

"Rydel," Ray muttered.

All now noticed that Rydel was gone. Ray ran toward the city's entrance while pulling the hood of his cloak back over his head. The others did the same, following Ray through the stone entranceway and through the city.

"Over here, Ray!"

The six turned to see Rydel standing next to a street vendor's table. Heads lowered, Ray and the others rushed over. They formed a complete circle around Rydel so no one in the city could see him, all six staring down at him. Ray leaned in closer, up in Rydel's face.

"Why the hell did you run away? Did you see that man by the entrance?"

"I did, and it wasn't Jesus, Ray—"

"No shit, Rydel!"

Sal held out his hands and waved them, motioning for the conversation to slow down. "Hey, hey. Hold on. I don't know what you two saw, but he sure as hell looked a lot like the guy from religion class at first. Then I don't know what the fuck happened to him."

Rydel looked at Sal. "The week in time we're in, knowing now that Jesus is really here, then you have to understand that the Other is here as well."

Not a clue as to what Rydel was referring to, Sal threw his arms up in the air at Ray. "The hell's he talking about?"

Ignoring Sal, Ray kept his eyes on Rydel. "Clopas, Rydel! Tell me everything about how this man can help us."

"He worked with one of the disciples. He will meet this man today to supply food for him. Clopas—having no idea of its importance—will know where the Last Supper will be."

Ray grabbed Rydel by the shoulder. "Lead the way. Go."

Ray held onto Rydel's shoulder while Rydel led the way through the city streets.

—

Clopas kept moving throughout the city. They did not reach him until evening at an open-sided tent selling fish. Three men worked in the tent. Ray let Rydel loose, and Rydel turned on his translator. He walked over and stood before Clopas, who was bent over at the table in front of him. Rydel tapped Clopas's shoulder, and Clopas looked up at Rydel with eyes wide with relief. He reached over the table laid out with dried fish and hugged

Rydel tightly. After the men separated, Clopas placed his hands on Rydel's shoulders. The two then conversed in Aramaic.

"Clopas, you need to show me where the follower Simon, the fisherman you worked with, had you bring the food for his supper tonight."

"He answers to Peter now, he told me, but yes, I now know where they are, my friend!"

"I know you do, Clopas."

Rydel looked over his shoulder at Ray and the rest of the group. Face hidden under the hood of his cloak, Ray lifted his head slightly, giving Rydel a curt smile.

"Have him lead the way."

Through winding, tan, stone-layered streets lit by the light of the setting sun, Ray, Rydel, and the Unit believers followed the man Clopas. The group reached a narrow, abandoned road. Clopas turned to Rydel and the others behind him.

"This way. We are not far now."

The group followed Clopas up the road bathed in deep orange sunlight, passing alleyways left and right. From an alley on the right, a small boy stepped out in front of Clopas, the child's face sprinkled with blood. The boy took two stumbling steps and fell to the ground. Clopas picked the boy up holding the child out in front of him. The boy stared at Clopas in obvious shock—his eyes vacant, looking past Clopas at nothing. Clopas touched the boy's face with both hands, and the boy's eyes suddenly came to life. The boy began to plead with Clopas.

"Wild dogs attacked us. They're killing my mother and sister. Save them!"

Clopas turned to the group behind him.

"We must help!"

Rydel grabbed Clopas by the arm and yelled at him through his translator.

"Keep moving, Clopas."

"The boy's family needs help!" Clopas begged.

The boy abruptly sprinted back down the alleyway and was gone. Ray ran after the boy. No! Not like in the alley with the woman. I will help.

Rydel turned off his translator and screamed out to Ray. "Ray—don't!"

Ray stopped just shy of entering the alley and gave out orders:

"Adriana, Ben, wait outside the alley here. Let no one in." He shot a look over his shoulder at Sal and Steve. "You two, come with me."

Ray waved for Jack to come closer. "Jack, follow Clopas and Rydel. We'll track you—just get to where Clopas is leading us."

Ray ran into the alley after the boy. Sal and Steve followed. After only seconds of running, Ray suddenly stopped, seeing the boy up ahead, the listless child standing within a shaft of sunlight. Sal and Steve joined Ray. The three cautiously stepped closer, and as they reached the child, their eyes fixed on something resting by the boy's feet.

"What is that?" Sal asked Ray.

Before them, the boy stood over the carcass of a bloodied animal. Looking closer, the three could make out that it was a decapitated dog. The boy looked down at the dog with eyes wide open.

Ray could see that the boy was succumbing to shock and reached out to him. As he placed his hands on the boy's shoulders, they sank into the boy's body. The child melted into the ground before the three—sucked down into the earth, it seemed—and erupted back out of the ground to the left of Sal and Steve.

The boy glanced at Sal and Steve and then laid his now-hate-filled blue eyes on Ray. "He dies!" the boy screamed in English to Ray.

Eyes locked on the boy, Ray barked out an order to Sal and Steve. "Move out—now. Go!"

Not needing to be told twice, Sal and Steve took off. Ray slowly walked toward the boy. The boy darted away from him, his face caving in, growing older and menacing. Ray took another step closer to the boy-thing as it scampered away. The boy-thing dropped to the ground and started to crawl. Reaching the dead dog, it used its hands like claws to rip inside the headless animal—pulling out bloody clumps from inside the dog, throwing them at Ray. The boy-thing screamed at Ray in a man's deep voice.

"He dies! He dies! He dies!"

Ray turned and bolted from the boy. He caught up with Sal and Steve back where they had entered the alley, and the three ran out into the street. Adriana and Ben rushed up to them, noticing the horrified look in their eyes and the expression of fear on their faces.

"You guys all right?" Adriana asked.

Sal and Steve nodded unpersuasively at Adriana. Ray took a few steps away and spoke through his headset to Jack. "Jack, we're on our way."

Jack's voice came back immediately through Ray's headset. "Hurry—we have a problem."

—

Ray and the rest ran up the slanted street, spotting Jack and Rydel standing alone off to the side. Ray reached the two and abruptly came to a stop in front of Rydel.

"Where's Clopas, Rydel?"

"They took him," Rydel said, his voice desperate.

"Who?"

"Soldiers, Ray," Jack said, shaking his head, angry with himself. "We came running up the street here, and Clopas ran into a soldier, knocking him over. They took him away. I didn't know what to do. I wasn't sure if I was allowed to intervene like you said when we first got here."

"Which way did they go, Jack?"

Jack pointed at the uphill street behind him.

"Straight ahead. I lost them as they reached the top of the street. I think—"

Ray put a hand on Jack's shoulder, moving him out of the way. Eyes alert, he tracked a group of men farther ahead on the rising street. Eleven men, shadowed by the lowering sun, followed another man. Ray took two slow steps ahead, his eyes tracking the man being followed by the single-file group of men.

He looked over his shoulder at the others behind him.

"It's Him. It's Christ."

Ray took off, running up the street, as Rydel and the others rushed after him. With the group of twelve in their sights, Ray, Rydel, and the others trailed behind them. They tracked the group of men as they left the city, the sun fading away. The group of men out in front, and the pursuing group in their wake, walking in step with one another.

As night arrived outside the city, Jesus led eleven of His followers into an orchard-like area surrounded by gnarled, bent olive trees. Jesus ducked under a grouping of trees and walked on, followed by three of His apostles. The other apostles broke off in different directions, sinking into the darkness beyond the trees. Ray, Rydel, and the others followed Jesus and the three apostles, keeping them in sight, trailing them carefully.

# Todd

Todd walked back into the camp, seeping out of the darkness like an apparition, and came to a stop. He looked toward the barely lit tents in front of him and back at the blackness behind him. He knew they were gone; he had seen them leave. But Ray was good. Superior. Did he leave someone behind in the shadowed areas around the camp, maybe behind the scantly lit tents flapping in the wind?

Todd took two steps forward and stopped, almost waiting to be taken out by a Smartround. But nothing happened. He took two more steps toward the tents, five more, and still nothing. Todd ran the last twenty feet, reached the tent they'd placed John Adams in, and entered. Inside the tent, Todd took a knee next to the colonel on the ground. He removed a needle from the right pocket of his cargo pants and stuck it into a protruding vein on the colonel's right arm.

John Adams's body shot up into a sitting position, legs straight out, eyes wild. The colonel glanced at Carrie on the ground and then stared at Todd beside him. He looked down at the needle sticking out of his arm. His mind and body adjusting to such sudden consciousness after being shot with a sedation round, the colonel ripped the needle out of his arm and threw it on the tent floor.

"Guess I was right, trusting you with this…situation?"

Todd rubbed his hands over the stubble on his face, getting himself ready to brief the colonel.

"Ray, Rydel, and half of the damn Unit went to save Him. The rest have been shot, like Carrie here, with sedation rounds. Good thing I had to piss when I did, or I'd be sedated as well. Do you have any more of the drug to wake the others, sir?"

"Only two syringes."

"We should wake—"

"No. The last two syringes are for us in the event we get shot. Even the ones who disagree are probably too loyal to Ray."

Todd stood up—eyeing the colonel. "You think I'm any different—my loyalty?"

"No. I know how you feel about Ray. But I also know you're fucking sure as shit Rydel has lost it and is starting to take Ray with him."

John lifted himself up and stood in front of Todd.

"What's next, sir?" Todd asked, waiting for orders.

"We find them before they find Him."

—

Fifty yards behind a moonlit Jesus and the three men with Him, Ray, Rydel, and the others stood on rock-strewn high ground, awaiting Jesus's next move. They looked on as Jesus and the apostles with Him walked toward a dirt path. Jesus came to a stop. He placed a hand on the face of the man to His left and gently tapped the shoulders of the two men to His right. The three bowed their heads and walked away. Jesus watched them leave and then walked down the dirt path into a dense area of trees with outreaching, twisted branches. The path's overhanging branches of foliage swallowed Jesus as He vanished inside the greenery.

Taking this in from his view above, Rydel started to walk after Jesus. Ray quickly reached out and pulled Rydel back by the hood of his cloak.

"Wait, Rydel. We're looking for a way to get Him alone, if we can. Let's make sure no one else joins Him again."

Ray motioned for Ben to use his binoculars to track Jesus.

"I got Him, Ray."

Through his binoculars, Ben could see Jesus kneeling alone on a large stone in front of a cluster of bushes and trees.

"We ready, Ben?" Ray asked.

Ben nodded. "He's clear, Ray. We can…hold on…movement in the bushes around Him."

Ben jerked his head to the right with his binoculars fastened to his face and pointed a finger below. "In the bushes, Ray, coming for Him. Three teams." Ben ripped off the binoculars. "Shit—it's an ambush."

Ray snatched the binoculars away from Ben and took in what was happening below. He spotted Jesus praying alone with His head bowed. Out of the cluster of trees and bushes in front of Jesus, armed guards with swords and protective black armor surrounded Him. Jesus did not lift His head until the guards led a man in a tan cloak toward Him. The man in the tan cloak pointed a finger at Jesus, knelt down next to Him, and kissed Him on the cheek.

Ray observed all this through the binoculars. He motioned for Ben to lead the way, throwing the binoculars back to him. Ben secured the binoculars around his head and ran—zigzagging downward around bushes and through crowded trees.

Ben reached the spot where he last saw Jesus through the binoculars. And the only man left was the one who had pointed Jesus out, now kneeling on the ground, heart-wrenching sobs coming out of him. Ray caught up to Ben and brushed by him. Ray grabbed the man off the ground, lifting him up so he could meet the betrayer's eyes.

"Why did you do it?" Ray screamed at the man in English. The sobbing man stared at Ray, not understanding a word he said.

Ray glanced back at Ben. "Ben?"

Ben began searching again through his binoculars for Jesus and tracked Him down in seconds. "Got Him."

Ray slapped the man in the face, and the man fell to the ground. Behind Ray, Ben slipped through the dense trees, and Rydel and the rest followed him. Ray stood over the man for a moment, waiting for him to look up. The man finally did, trembling. Ray spat in his face, turned, and sprinted away.

Ray reached the others, with Ben leading the way. Ahead, on a dirt road, the soldiers pushed, punched, and laughed at Jesus.

They were leading Him back to the city.

—

Seated in a room inside his pillared, lamplit palace, Annas looked up at Jesus standing in front of him. Finished with his questions, angry at Jesus's curt answers, he stroked his gray beard and kept his piercing blue eyes on Jesus. Frustrated, the old man waved his hand, waving Jesus away.

"Take Him before Caiaphas," Annas ordered, speaking in raspy Aramaic to the guards around him.

Two guards spun Jesus from Annas and led Him away. Outside the room, the two guards with Jesus in their grasp were joined by more guards. The group marched Jesus down two twisting palace corridors that led to a courtyard. In the courtyard, a mob waited around small fires. The guards led Jesus through the gathering. As they did, the crowd started to ignite torches from the scattered fires and followed.

Outside the palace, the guards roughly escorted Jesus away from where Ray waited with Rydel behind a dense row of chest-high bushes. Adriana, Ben, Jack, and Steve peered over the bushes three feet to the right of Ray. Sal was nowhere to be seen. He was doing what he did best—recon.

Sal was one of the last to make his way outside. He ran over to where Ray and the others were waiting and stood before Ray. "He's being taken to another man to be charged with blasphemy, Ray."

They followed the soldiers and the mob until reaching a white stone palace not far away. The stone structure's double doors opened, pouring firelight out from within. The soldiers pushed and dragged the blasphemous man—as the others making up the angry mob were welcomed inside.

The soldiers and the angry crowd were led by another group of guards into a stone-clad court surrounded by lavish flaming lanterns. Seated at a candlelit table, Caiaphas waited. The forty-year-old man was adorned in a black turban and a flowing black robe. He had black hair, dark eyes, and a salt-and-pepper beard. The guards ordered the gathering mob to stand back as the two soldiers who held onto Jesus walked Him closer to the table where Caiaphas was seated. The guards let go of Jesus. Caiaphas shook his head in disappointment, looking up at Jesus. And then his disposition changed somewhat, knowing what he had to do and the outcome against this man, the one voicing His insane beliefs and the danger it was causing.

Caiaphas glanced at a line of priests to his right, then took in the crowd before him. He eyed Jesus once more, almost with pity. However, he knew what fate awaited the Nazarene and what must be done. Caiaphas stood up and addressed the crowd in front of him.

"In the face of God, has this man committed blasphemy?" he shouted.

The crowd roared.

Moments later, the guards pushed Jesus through the shouting mob. Ray, Rydel, and the others stood behind the crowd and could see where Jesus was heading. A group of soldiers standing by a torchlit stairway waited to take Him below.

Ray turned to Adriana. "Tag Him."

Adriana slid her Smartround gun out from under her cloak and targeted Jesus's back. Before Christ disappeared down the stairs, a blue dot appeared on His tunic as Adriana tagged her target. She slipped her rifle back under her cloak before anyone could notice.

"He's tagged, Ray."

"No more waiting to try to get Him alone. It's time."

—

Ray stood in front of a door in a torchlit corridor. He gave the door two pounding knocks with his balled-up fist, stepped back, and waited. A large soldier slammed the door open and was joined by an even larger soldier, both standing just inside the door's threshold in full black body armor. Ray stepped back and calmly spoke in English.

"Sal, Ben…"

Sal and Ben stood out of sight at opposite sides of the door with the others. The two stepped in front of Ray and shot the soldiers in the neck with sedation rounds.

"Any more, Steve?"

To the left of Ray, Steve searched the area around him with his binoculars strapped onto his face, looking for soldiers. He turned to Ray and shook his head.

"Okay, you're now the eyes leading us in, Steve. Let's move," Ray ordered. As they moved, Ray tapped Adriana on her shoulder.

"Anything, A?"

Adriana studied the slide-out screen on her Smartround gun. "Nothing yet. They must have Him in a room that's seriously walled-in or—"

Adriana cut her thought short as Jack walked in front of Ray.

"He wants me to show you something, Ray."

"What did you say, Jack?"

"The Son dies."

Jack grabbed his own head and twisted it around three times in front of Ray—the sound of bones, cartilage, and ligaments breaking and popping echoed throughout the corridor. As Jack's convulsing body fell to the ground, Ray screamed at the others.

"Move! Move!"

Ray took hold of Rydel, pushing him along with the other startled members of his Unit away from Jack's lifeless body on the ground.

"Go!" Ray shouted. They all finally did, running away. Ray stepped closer to Jack's body and reached out to check for a pulse he knew was no longer there. Jack's eyes snapped open and changed color—burning blue eyes now stared up at Ray. Head completely turned around—a foreign voice came out of Jack. A deep voice, sounding as though it was coming out of a vast canyon.

"I thought my display at the city entrance would suffice, Raymond. Apparently not. So…now you understand, because of Jack here, that you, and the ones with you, will die making any attempt to save the Son." The blue eyes vanished, turned off like a desk lamp. Ray staggered away from Jack's lifeless gaze and ran, soon catching up with Rydel and the others as they all reached the torchlit stairway that had led them down into the corridor. Ray stopped on the first step, searching above with his Smartround gun. He motioned for the others to stay where they were and slowly walked up the stairs with his gun leading the way. After a moment, Ray's footsteps echoed back down, and he wearily sat on the last step. He placed his gun across his knees.

"Everybody take a knee."

Rydel remained standing as the rest of the Unit dropped to one knee. Ray stared at the ground for what seemed like hours to his depleted Unit. He then lifted his head.

"Who wants to abort?" Ray asked.

It was quiet for almost one minute, and then Adriana spoke. "He took down one of ours—now I know we're doing the right thing here, Ray. Why would the Other do that to Jack? Maybe it's scared that we might succeed, right?"

Ray slowly looked over the faces of Ben, Sal, and Steve as the three nodded, agreeing with what Adriana had said.

"It just warned me that our lives are in danger if we do this," Ray said to Rydel and the rest staring at him.

Sal shrugged his shoulders. "Wow, like that's news to us. Name one mission where our lives haven't been in danger, Ray. Big fucking whoop-dee-doo."

Ray couldn't help but smile for a second at Sal's assessment of where they found themselves now. But then his mind flashed back to Jack, dead on the ground where they left him, and the smile was gone. "Okay then, let's do what we were sent back here to do."

Steve strapped his binoculars back on and led them away from the staircase, back through the twisting underground passageways ahead. They walked silently for ten minutes without any sign of another person—the underground passageways all deserted. Behind Steve, Adriana came to a sudden stop, looking down at her gun.

"Wait, I got Him." Looking up from her gun, she turned to Steve, his binoculars now off his face. "To the right, Steve."

"Where?"

Adriana joined Steve and, at a brisk jog with her gun pointed out, turned to her right, using the flashlight on her gun to illuminate the path. She led Steve toward, and then through, a barely lit passageway Steve had overlooked.

Ray and the others followed Steve and Adriana, walking cautiously down the dark pathway with the light from Adriana's gun leading the way. They crept into what seemed to be an even darker area with faint torchlight flickering ahead. Moving at a slow, calculated pace, they could make out two soldiers standing outside an open cell door with their heads craned inside, laughing sporadically to each other at what they saw inside the cell. Ray whispered in Steve's ear for him to watch over Rydel and then waved his gun for Adriana, Ben, and Sal to follow him. The four silently reached the soldiers and hovered inches away from their backs. Ben and Sal raised their Smartround guns, almost touching the neck of each soldier in front of them. The two looked at Ray, and he nodded for them to take the soldiers down lightly. Each soldier received a new black blemish on the back of his neck, fired from Ben's and Sal's Smartround guns. Before the soldiers fell facedown inside the cell, Adriana, Ben, and Sal reached out and dragged them away.

With the two soldiers gone, Ray moved closer to get a look inside the open cell door, joined by Adriana, Ben, and then Sal. The four looked inside and could see a temple guard in his black armor standing off to the side. In front of the temple guard, a Roman soldier stood wearing just his red tunic and baldric—no body armor. Below the Roman soldier, Jesus knelt, hunched over and facing the floor of the cell, sweat and blood-soaked wisps of hair sticking to His face. Looking at Jesus on the ground, the Roman soldier spoke to Him in Greek.

"Pilate sent me here to make sure they don't kill you yet, Messiah of the Jews." The Roman soldier hooked a look back to the temple guard behind him and smiled. "The Jew-Messiah is filthy. I will bathe him appropriately for taking me away from my evening whore."

At the cell's entrance, a red light flashed on the top of Ray's Smartround gun that he now pointed inside the cell. Ray looked over his shoulder to see Steve standing with Rydel about thirty feet away. Steve held his hand up at Ray, signaling that they were about to have company. Ray placed a hand on Adriana's shoulder, and then Ben's, drawing them away from the cell's entrance, quietly speaking to the two.

"You two get back to Steve and Rydel—soldiers are on the way." The two turned and ran back to where Rydel and Steve were standing. Ray stepped closer to Sal, who was still looking inside the cell, and tapped him on his arm. "Sal, soldiers are on the way. Take these two down lightly, and help our Lord to His feet."

Ray turned away and was gone, running fast to join up with the others so he could assist in taking down the approaching soldiers. After watching Ray run away, Sal's attention was drawn back to the cell, the sound of trickling water coming from within. Sal leaned his head further inside, watching as the Roman soldier urinated into a bowl a few feet away from Jesus, who was still on His knees. Finished, the Roman soldier stomped his way over to Jesus with the bowl and lifted it over the head of Christ. The temple guard in the cell took a step toward the Roman, looking as if he was about to say something to stop whatever the soldier intended to do. But before the guard could speak, Sal walked into the cell, making his presence known, the hood of his cloak covering his face. The two turned and faced Sal, neither of them looking surprised. The soldier barked out an order to Sal in Greek.

"Leave the wine on the floor."

"Move away from Him. Now!"

The Roman soldier and the temple guard looked at each other, confused, not understanding the words Sal had spoken in English.

"Put that bowl down!" Sal screamed at the Roman soldier, again in English. Not choosing his Smartround rifle, Sal slipped out his Beretta M9 from under his cloak—the same type of gun Ray chose for his missions—and aimed the weapon at the Roman soldier.

The soldier began to laugh, pointing at Sal's gun with his free hand. The temple guard just looked on, at a loss. Why is this man holding the small black object as if it were a threat, the temple guard thought. The Roman soldier stepped closer to Sal, removing his sword from his baldric. He pointed the tip of the blade toward Sal's face.

"And what do you intend to do with that little thing?" the Roman asked Sal in Greek.

—

The four waited, each on one knee, using a curve in the corridor for cover. It was time: Ray, Adriana, Ben, and Steve began taking out the approaching soldiers lightly and silently using their Smartround guns—the six soldiers dropping one by one. Each soldier looked at the man next to him falling to the ground.

Ray was the first to rise to his feet, but then the sound of gunfire jolted them. Ray took off, sprinting around the corner of the corridor where Rydel had been told to stay put. He grabbed Rydel and ran back toward the cell, followed by Adriana, Ben, and Steve.

At the entrance to Christ's cell, Ray abruptly stopped and motioned for the three behind him to watch over Rydel. A voice screaming in pain wailed from inside the cell. Ray stepped inside, and the first thing he saw was one of the soldiers on his knees holding his arm, screaming at the three missing fingers on his hand. The other man stared wide-eyed at the mauled Roman soldier. Ray shot the two with sedation rounds, and they dropped to the ground, falling on their sides. Sal stood awestruck at the sight of Jesus. Ray grabbed Sal by the shoulders and spun him around.

"Why the hell did you use your gun?"

"He was about to do something to Him, Ray. I—I got angry."

Ray looked down at Jesus on the ground and then at the wounded Roman, shouting out for Adriana as he did. "Adriana, get in here!" Adriana walked inside the cell and came to a stop in front of Ray.

"Wrap up the soldier's hand, A—you have two minutes. Just make sure he doesn't bleed to death."

Adriana knelt beside the Roman, a man with not much of a hand left for her to work on.

"Sal."

Sal didn't respond to Ray. He stared at the ground, shaking his head. Ray moved closer and gave Sal a gentle slap on his left cheek. "Look at me, Sal."

Sal lifted his head.

"I fucked up big time, didn't I, Ray?"

Ray shot a look over his shoulder at Adriana, busy bandaging the hand of the sedated Roman. He then slapped Sal gently on his right cheek.

"Let's get going."

"Okay, Ray."

—

John and Todd reached a gateway leading into Jerusalem and entered the dark city, scattered torches lighting the way inside. The two walked through the streets that had—in most areas—shut down for the night. As they walked deeper into the dark city, Todd turned to John Adams by his side.

"Anything, sir?"

With his head down, John focused on his Smartround gun's slide-out screen, not trying to hide the rifle anymore, pointing the gun straight ahead.

"No. Make sure the tracking is off on your gun."

"Already done. Where do we start?"

Firelight ahead outlined a cluster of men gathered outside a stone home, drinking from goblets. The colonel pointed out the group of men to Todd. "Guess it doesn't matter, coming into contact with the people of this time now. What we need to do is stop Rydel from saving this man. So let's go over there and ask if they know anything more about Jesus being arrested than the man we met on the way here knew."

John and Todd put their translators on, concealed them, and made their way over to the men.

The two reached the men, taking in the language through their translators, the men debating a passionate topic in Aramaic. John stood behind the group and spoke their language through his translator.

"Do any of you know where they are keeping the man named Jesus? He has been arrested tonight."

The men all turned their heads, their glassy eyes on John and Todd. The men started to laugh. A heavyset man with drooping eyes and a mangled tunic half-smiled at the others with him who were laughing. The heavyset man slurred out a response to John.

"Arrested! Arrested for what—preaching?"

The man's face dropped, and he sobered up quickly, looking past John and Todd. John and Todd noticed the man's sudden mood swing and looked over their shoulders. Two temple guards stood behind them. The two guards, one standing almost seven feet tall and the other a normal stature, shared a look.

"Followers of Jesus," the tall man said.

The smaller soldier pointed his sword at John and Todd and yelled, "You two, come with us!"

Todd reached for his Smartround gun under his cloak. John turned off his translator furtively while quickly gesturing that he would follow. He removed Todd's right earbud while patting him on the shoulder, speaking to Todd under his breath in English.

"Wait. Let them take us. Turn off your translator."

The two guards led John and Todd through the city, closing in on a citadel. Once inside, they passed scattered temple guard units eyeing their procession with nods and pointed fingers of curiosity. At the top of a beige stone staircase, the two soldiers pushed John and Todd forward, forcing them to walk down the stairs. As the guards followed the two, John held up two fingers at Todd. John and Todd took two more steps down, spun around with their Smartround guns drawn, and shot each man in the neck with a sedation Smartround. The guards dropped to their knees and started tumbling down the stairs until John reached out and grabbed them, supporting the two guards with his arms, pinning them against the staircase wall.

"Get the rounds out of their necks!"

Todd rushed over and removed the smartrounds from the neck of each guard. John slammed an S-7 needle into each soldier. He gripped onto the soldier he supported with his left arm and let the other soldier fall down the steps. John put his translator back in place and waited for his words to morph into Aramaic:

"Where is the Nazarene?"

—

Inside the cell with Jesus, Ray stood over Adriana bandaging the Roman's hand. When she finished, she stood up and nodded.

"Join up with the rest, A."

Adriana started to walk away. Then she stopped, staring at Jesus on the floor, fixated.

"Back in the game, Adriana. Come on."

Adriana snapped out of her fixation on Jesus and exited the cell without a word or another glance back. Now alone with Christ, Ray stepped closer and took a knee by Jesus's side. Beaten, with blood-matted hair covering His face, Jesus lifted His head, staring up at Ray with one eye open, one eye bloodied and shut. As Ray adjusted and spoke to Jesus through his cloth-covered translator, the Aramaic translation of his words began to amplify for Jesus to hear.

"We came to save you."

Jesus raised His battered face up a little more to face Ray.

"My Father in Heaven will save me." Jesus's voice was hoarse, and as the words translated back, Ray shook his head.

"No…for some reason, He will not."

Ray eased his hands under Jesus's arms, helping Him up to His feet. Jesus looked at Ray for a moment, and then His legs gave out, forcing Him back down on His knees. Ray lifted Jesus off the ground and carried Him over his shoulder and out of the cell. Rydel and the believing members of

Ray's Unit waited outside the cell. Ray removed his translator and gave an order.

"Let's roll."

Ray pointed at Steve to lead the way. Steve placed his binoculars on, adjusted the strap around his head, programmed them to find human life, and walked ahead. The group walked silently while Steve guided them away from any soldiers he could see, backtracking and moving forward through twisting passageways. At a sharp curve in the corridor, Steve lifted his arm, signaling everyone behind him to stop. He craned his head forward, staring just around the corridor bend. Steve looked back at Ray and waved him over. Ray gently handed Jesus off to Sal. Light on his feet, Ray reached Steve at the stone wall where he stood waiting. Ray took a knee by Steve's side and glanced down the corridor, not seeing anything but an empty, torchlit passage.

"What do you see, Steve?"

"Weird. Binoculars picked up two at the end of the corridor ahead. They have their backs to us and are leaning against opposite sides of the way out, taking cover behind the walls. I know we bagged all the soldiers before. It's not like one of them got away and reported they were under attack. The two ahead, however, are set to take us out. They know we're coming."

Ray took in the situation. "Okay, move out with Adriana. Maybe they came late and saw the soldiers on the ground." Ray stood and trotted back to the others, tapping Adriana on the shoulder. "A, join up with Steve. There are still two left ahead, blocking our exit."

Adriana ran ahead and took a knee next to Steve. The two whispered to each other for a few seconds and then rounded the corridor bend while Ray and the rest waited.

After three minutes, Ray spoke into his headset. "Adriana, come back…Steve?"

Not getting a response from the two, Ray motioned for the others to stay where they were. He dropped to the ground on his stomach and crawled his way through the winding corridor. On the ground in front of him, Adriana and Steve lay facedown and unmoving. Seeing them, Ray got up and rushed over without checking to see if anybody was up ahead.

At the end of the corridor, John and Todd eased their way inside, using the wall at either side of the exit as partial cover. With their Smartround guns raised, the two took aim at Ray.

Ray spotted the two and stopped so suddenly that he lost his balance and fell on his back. The smartrounds John and Todd fired followed Ray down to the ground and detonated on Ray's gun that had landed on his chest as he fell.

"Fuck!" Ray screamed, trying to get to his feet, frantically scanning his body to see if he was hit by a Smartround.

Sal came running down the corridor to aid Ray, and his head snapped back as he took a Smartround to his neck.

Up on one knee, Ray fired back with his M9, the rounds missing both concealed men and hitting off the walls. With John and Todd using the walls of the corridor exit as full cover, it bought Ray some time. With one hand on Sal's arm, Ray dragged Sal backward while pointing his weapon ahead and made it around the corridor bend behind him. Rydel and Ben rushed over, helping Ray pull Sal the rest of the way. They reached an angled half wall leading down into another corridor, and Ray ordered the two to get behind the wall. Ray dropped to his knees, searching for the Smartround in Sal's neck. He found it embedded under Sal's ear and ripped it out before the drug could take Sal deeper into unconsciousness. Ray held up the Smartround, pinched between his thumb and forefinger, showing Rydel and Ben. He then shot up to his feet.

"Where's Jesus?" Ray angrily asked.

Rydel and Ben, understanding that they had just left Jesus Christ alone and slumped against the corridor wall where Sal had placed Him, turned and ran back before Ray could speak again. He would have preferred maybe just one person staying behind to help with Sal, but that was not going to happen, as the two were now gone and out of sight. Therefore, Ray slung Sal's heavy-ass body over his shoulder and made his way back to where they had left Jesus. And miraculously, Jesus was still on the ground with His back against the wall and His head slumped forward. Ray eased Sal against the wall next to Jesus and slapped Sal across the face a couple of times. Not getting a reaction, he tried again. After several attempts, Sal reflexively blocked the fifth slap. Sal opened his eyes, and Ray patted him on the chest.

"Back in the game, Sal?"

Sal groggily answered, "I am, Ray."

"Okay—here's what's happening. A and Steve got taken down with smartrounds. We have to get the rounds out of them. Stay here and watch over Jesus. Can you do that?"

"I got it, Ray. I got it."

Ray turned to face Rydel and Ben behind him. "Come with me—you too, Rydel. Move!"

As they ran side by side, Ben asked Ray, "It's Todd shooting at us, isn't it, Ray?"

"John is with him too. Use your sidearm. Do not sedate them. There's too much at stake here now, Ben."

"Kill them?" Ben asked, hoping he hadn't heard Ray correctly.

"On my command…yes."

As they arrived at the corridor bend where the ambush began, Ray ran around the corner and reached Adriana and Steve on the ground. With a pocket flashlight in his hand, Ray searched their faces and necks for the smartrounds. Ahead, Todd appeared in front of the corridor's exit—and was met by three bullets piercing the wall he was using for cover, the bullets coming from Ben's Glock 19, missing Todd's head by only inches. Todd dropped to the ground and retreated behind the wall.

"Those are the last warning shots you get!" Ray yelled out.

Ray searched Adriana's neck, found the Smartround, and pulled it out. He frantically searched Steve's body for the Smartround that took him down. Unable to find it, he turned and motioned for Rydel to help take Adriana and Steve away. Ben stepped around the corridor bend with his sidearm drawn, targeting the opening ahead, and confirmed the path was clear.

—

Sal stood over Jesus Christ, who was leaning against the right wall of the corridor, His head slumped. Jesus began coughing, and Sal reached out to put a comforting hand on His shoulder when he saw something move to his left. Head still feeling a bit banged up, Sal's adrenaline started to kick in, reacting to what he had seen.

He pointed his Smartround gun at a shadow on the opposite wall—the dark shape of a large man. Swiveling left and right, Sal could see that there was no one in the corridor casting the shadow. He stepped toward the shadow on the wall, and it moved, rising up the wall of the corridor, making its way above Sal on the ceiling. The shape fell from the ceiling and landed in front of Sal. Sal fired a round toward the black form, but the round hit the rock wall behind it. The shadow reached out for Sal and grabbed him by the neck. It dragged Sal over to the wall, where his Smartround detonated, slamming Sal's head into the wall. Sal fell to the ground, unconscious.

The shadow glared at Jesus on the ground, tilting its head slightly. It then pointed an ink-black finger at Sal and began to walk away. Sal's unconscious body lifted to its feet and followed the shadow, walking as if he were a toy controlled by a child, his arms flailing and his legs unnaturally dangling off the ground.

—

A unit of temple guards entered the cell that had formerly held the man claiming to be the Son of God. The guards could see blood on the floor, and they followed its trail over to the Roman soldier. The guards then noticed one of their own on the ground. The commander of the temple guards—adorned in the same black armor as the rest, with a white sash around his waist being the exception—ignored the Roman and knelt beside the temple guard on the floor. The anger he felt caused his face to twitch. He screamed to the guards he commanded.

"Find Him!"

The guards ran out of the cell, followed by their commander. It did not take them long to find Jesus. They stumbled upon Him leaning against a wall—a torch above Him lighting the corridor He was in. The temple guards approached slowly, surrounding Christ. The commander stepped past his men and stared down at Jesus with angry hazel eyes, waving over two of his men.

"Take Him to the dungeon. Do not be tricked by His evil magic!" he yelled at the two. The commander lowered his head so he could face Jesus. "There's no way for Him to escape below."

—

Down the dark corridor, Ben and Rydel dragged Steve, each man with a shoulder under one of Steve's arms. Behind them, Ray followed with Adriana over his shoulder. They reached Sal, who was trying to lift himself off the ground. Ray placed Adriana against the corridor's far wall and rushed over to Sal. He lifted Sal's head carefully and noticed a bruise on his forehead. Taking a quick glance around for Jesus, Ray turned back to Sal.

"Sal, where is He?"

"I don't know. I saw something…and then hit my head somehow."

Ray walked Sal over and sat him down next to Adriana, took the binoculars from around Steve's neck, and ran down the corridor.

Ray could see the imprint left behind on the ground where Jesus had been sitting in the corridor. Two paths lay ahead of Ray. Ray searched with the binoculars, and no human movement could be seen on either path. He sprinted back to the others. Ray knelt next to Adriana, who was still unconscious against the wall, and took the Smartround gun she tagged Jesus with from off her shoulder. The screen slid out from the side of the weapon, and he studied it for a few seconds, then turned toward the others staring back at him.

"He's not showing up. We lost Him."

—

Steve opened his eyes to see Ray standing over him, staring upward. In the sky above Ray, deep purple clouds slowly swept by. Steve pushed himself up into a sitting position, realizing it was now dawn and having no recollection of how he got to where he was. He glanced toward the fire where the others slept and then turned his attention back to Ray.

"What happened, Ray?"

Ray heard Steve stir and gave him a few seconds to take in his surroundings. He had found the Smartround lodged in Steve's calf muscle after losing Jesus in the corridor. Adriana had regained consciousness but was now resting again.

Ray looked down at Steve.

"We failed, Steve. We have one more chance to save Him."

# The Storm

Alone in his office at Genesis, the sound of the door opening turned Will around in his chair to see one of the techs entering the room. Will wasn't sure if his name was Bill or Bruce—it was something like that. Whatever his name was, why the hell did he just enter without me giving the okay? Will thought.

"Sir," the tech said in a barely audible voice.

"Yes, what is it?"

"Something is heading our way."

Outside the office, Will followed the tech down the hallway to the Overlook. Will entered the Overlook and walked over to the man he did know, Robertson, who was seated in front of a monitor. With his black hair and black beard, Robertson always made Will think of a pirate in one of those Johnny Depp movies.

"What the hell's going on, Robertson?"

Robertson remained focused on the screen in front of him as he answered Will. "I sent Bob for you, sir, because I didn't want to take my eyes off of what's heading our way."

"What's heading our way?" Will asked impatiently.

Robertson looked away from the screen and stared up at Will for a few seconds before answering.

"Category five, sir. It's over the ocean now, making its way toward us."

Will leaned down to get a better look at what Robertson was tracking and then straightened up, taking a step back from Robertson's monitor.

"My God," Will said under his breath.

# Ultimatums

With the dawn in full bloom, a sky of fading purple and fire-orange blazed over John and Todd walking on a deserted road just outside the walls of Jerusalem. John stared down at his Smartround gun and picked up the pace, walking ahead of Todd, trying to get a fix on Ray and the others. Too tired to keep up, Todd walked at his own pace while John stretched the distance between them. A man in a pure-white hooded cloak—the hood covering his face—walked out from behind a palm tree and stood near the side of the dirt road, waiting for Todd to reach him. Todd saw the man at once and veered away to keep clear of the individual, walking on the far side of the road, passing the man in white.

"They returned up the mountain."

Todd spun around, slipped his Smartround gun out from under his cloak, and pointed it at the man, who had just spoken to him in English. Todd gave a quick look at John up ahead and was about to shout out to him as the white-hooded man spoke again.

"Look at me, Todd."

The kindness and the sincerity in the man's voice turned Todd around at once. Todd stepped closer, unable to control his body, and stood in front of the man. The man pulled back the hood covering his face. He resembled Jesus Christ in every way Todd had seen the man pictured and portrayed from the Christian tale. The man smiled.

"Do not second-guess yourself as you do now because of Raymond, Todd. My dying in this time is for a reason. And it will cause the death of millions in your time if Raymond or the others interfere. I will return again to save humanity."

On the dirt road ahead, John turned around so he could see how far back Todd was dragging his slow ass.

"Fuck is he doing?"

John saw Todd talking with the white-cloaked man and sprinted his way back to the two. He came to a stop in front of Todd and reached out to grab him, accidentally brushing up against the man in white. John's arms dropped to his side, and his whole body went limp. Terrified, with his lips slightly parted, he turned and faced the man in white. The man in white eyed John for a few seconds, then walked away, heading toward the city of Jerusalem. Todd took a stumbling step closer to John, watching the man in white, not believing what he saw.

"My God, sir, you were right all along! I'm sorry if I had any doubts. We have to stop them—they will kill millions!"

John watched the man in white making his way to the city and could feel it inside of him—what he had touched was the very origin of evil. The damnable images filling his mind were so overwhelming that his whole body shook with fear, and he was having a hard time not throwing up.

John gave Todd an order—one he could not perform with his shaking hands. "Call Ray. Tell him we wanna help them."

"Why, sir? We just witnessed a miracle here. He came to tell us—"

"That wasn't Him," John shouted at Todd. "That was something else—I can feel it inside of me."

"Todd, my son."

The voice came from behind Todd. He spun around to face the man in the white cloak, whose kind eyes were staring back at him. Astounded at how the man could be so close once more, Todd giddily grinned and his eyes widened. "There's no way you could've gotten behind us that fast. *You are real*," Todd said in amazement.

"I am your Savior. You must believe."

With a hand on Todd's shoulder, John turned him around.

"Fall back, Todd."

"But it's really Him!"

"It's not! I don't know what that is. Fall the fuck back with me—right now!"

John reached out with his other hand and yanked Todd by the shoulders away from the man in white. The man moved closer.

"Stop moving," the man in white demanded.

Todd dug the heels of his boots into the sand to stop John from dragging him away from the blessed man standing so close. But then Todd noticed something different in the holy man's eyes and started backing away, tripping over John and landing on his back.

A stream of black bile came out of the man's mouth, landing on the ground in front of Todd. The fluid burned a black flame for a moment and then melted into the sand. The man's glowing blue eyes fixed on Todd and then John. The man laughed—a wild, high-pitched, insane laugh.

John stepped closer toward the man in white.

"I know that laugh. I've heard it before."

A coal-black finger slipped out from under the man's white cloak, pointed at John. "Unlike the basement, you will die this time, John. That is, if you interfere in this time. Wait and do nothing until you are taken back, and I will spare your life."

Eerily slow, the man turned his head toward Todd, the eyes staring at Todd no longer peaceful and kind from the imposter Jesus. The eyes now came from hell.

"As for you, Todd…you live and return home. And when you do, your daughter will be hanging dead from the swing you set up for her before traveling here. Do not be persuaded by Raymond or John. If you help them in any way, you kill your own daughter. Do nothing, and she lives."

The man turned his back on the two and walked toward the mountains, away from the city. As he walked, he turned to John and Todd once more, blue eyes burning with hate.

Todd's body shook, and tears streamed down his face at what he saw and what he heard from the man in white. He looked up at John for answers as to what just happened, unable to speak. John moved closer and patted Todd's shoulder, trying to reassure him that it would be okay, even though he felt like he was standing on legs of Jell-O.

"Calm down, Todd. It's over."

Todd nodded at John, unable to stop the tears or his body from shaking.

"We have to go, Todd. C'mon."

—

At the highest point on the mountain, away from the camp, Ray stared down at the city of Jerusalem below. The sound of shifting gravel and heavy footfalls turned him around. A man in a black hooded cloak stood behind Ray. With the sun rising, Ray could not make out the face of the man under the hood; a shadow thrown off by the sunrise shaded the man's face.

"Your wife is eight weeks pregnant. Congratulations, Raymond. She feared to tell you because of the miscarriages before. The child in her womb will not miscarry this time. Your daughter will go on to be a doctor, healing many. However, if you go anywhere near Jesus again in this time, I will send a man to kill your wife tonight. This man will reach up inside of Kate and rip out your daughter-to-be, shoving the fetus down your wife's throat until she chokes on it."

Ray stood unmoving, staring at the black figure, and then calmly spoke. "No, you can't get to her that easy. I don't believe you."

The black-cloaked man leaned his head out of the morning shadow, the light from the sunrise touching his face, revealing hate-filled blue eyes.

"You do not believe me?" the man in the black cloak said in a deep, chasm-like voice.

"He touched me in the alley. I can still feel the miracle. He is inside of me. It is beyond just having faith now. He has to continue on with what He was meant to do in this time, and I'm going to help Him do just that."

The black-cloaked man stepped closer. With his face cast in shadow once more, he pointed a jet-black finger at Ray. "What his son came here to do will never be known in your time. Do not be so confident because he touched you and in the way you feel now. I can get to all of you." The black-cloaked man leaned his head closer, inches away from Ray. "Just ask Jack, Raymond."

Hearing footsteps again, Ray looked away from the man to see Ben running toward him with a headset in his hands.

"Ray—it's Adams. He says he wants to help."

Ray turned away from Ben, looking back to where the man in the black cloak once stood but only saw the deserted mountaintop before him. He took the headset from Ben, adjusted its fit, and cleared his throat to let John Adams know that he was listening.

"Ray, let's meet. I just met a man claiming to be Jesus."

"Not the man in the alley, was it, John?"

"No, it was not. Todd and I will be laid out, facedown in the sand with our hands behind our backs, when you reach us."

"Kevin, Janice, and Carrie aren't in their tents. Did you wake them? Are they with you?"

"No…" John answered, followed by a few seconds of silence.

"Shit—we're being taken back, Ray."

# Three Return

Will monitored the storm heading their way on one of the computers in his office with the tech Robertson seated next to him. Will had three scenarios going through his head on how to evacuate himself if the storm did not change direction. His life was paramount because of his work at Genesis—the others at the lab were secondary. If he could take a few like Robertson, he would. If taking some of the lab members endangered his life in any way, they would have to be left behind. Tough decisions must be made, and he had to make them very soon.

The door to Will's office opened, and a female tech rushed inside. Without turning his attention away from the computer in front of him, Will screamed, "Knock on the door! Don't just come in—what's wrong with you people!"

The woman stopped where she was and stared at Robertson. He motioned with his eyes and a slight tilt of his head toward Will for her to say what she came running into the office to say.

"Sir, some are back."

Will spun around in his chair and stood up.

"What?"

"Three have returned, sir. They're in the downstairs cafeteria."

Will rushed out of the room, followed by Robertson, and both men started to run. In the cafeteria, Carrie, Janice, and Kevin sat drinking bottled water at a white table surrounded by other white, gleaming tables. Through double doors at the other end of the room, Will and Robertson burst inside. The tap-tap sound of their feet hitting the linoleum floor reverberated around the cafeteria as they made their way toward the three. Will reached the returned members of Ray's Unit and stood over them. He placed his hands on his hips in a display of power—showing them that he was now in command.

"What happened?"

They shared a look of being a little out of it—tired. Kevin seemed a bit more alert than Carrie and Janice, so he answered. "Found Rydel before he could do anything. Took us three days. Went to sleep and then got taken back."

"You've been gone almost five days!"

"What…?" Kevin asked, looking and sounding confused.

"Five days!" Will shouted. "Somebody is changing something in the past—do you have any idea what's heading our way!"

"What's heading our way?" Carrie asked.

Will Stevens turned his back on the three time-travelers and walked out of the cafeteria with Robertson in tow. Outside the double doors, Will ordered Robertson to monitor the storm, and the man ran off. Will leaned against the wall outside the cafeteria, the fact dawning on him that he could not kill the time travelers. He had tried to do so hours ago with what he had added to his backup chips, and three had just returned. The situation needed to be gravely reassessed.

## The Peace Offering

Ray walked down the mountain path with Ben and Sal trailing behind—both men aiming their guns below. As they came to the end of the path, the three could see John and Todd ahead, laid out facedown on the ground with their hands behind them. Ben and Sal followed Ray as he closed in on the two men. Ray held up a hand for Ben and Sal to stay back and scanned the perimeter with his Smartround gun, making sure John was telling the truth about Carrie, Janice, and Kevin. He then aimed his gun back at John and Todd.

"Stand up with your hands on your heads," Ray ordered. The two stood up with their hands clasped on their heads.

"Ben, take their guns." Ben disarmed the two quickly and jogged away with the weapons. Ray stepped closer to John. "Come with me, John."

Ray and John walked away, and as they did, Todd aimlessly began to jog off into the barren land around him. Ben and Sal swung their Smartround guns in Todd's direction. Turning, Todd saw the two and lifted his hands in the air while shouting out to John Adams.

"I can't do this, Colonel. I'm sorry. I can't help you. If my daughter lives and I'm damned forever for not doing anything to help save Him, I can live with that…as long as my daughter is safe."

John and Ray stopped walking, looking back at Todd.

"I understand. And Ray will too. Just stay still, Todd, or they'll shoot you."

"Okay, okay. Okay, sir," Todd stammered, "I'm okay."

John and Ray walked on. Coming to a stop, satisfied that they could now have a private conversation, Ray shrugged his shoulders at John—his body language asking: Why do you want to help? Explain.

"Can't have one here without the other, right? Yeah, I just found that out. I touched the Other by accident. Felt the evil inside him, heard it in his voice, his laugh. Same laugh my sister and I heard coming out of my father as he left us to die. He'll try getting to the members of your Unit—he tried to get to Todd."

Ray's head dropped, the disgust on his face visible. "He got to Jack. He's dead."

Ray lifted his head and took in the sunrise, trying to push out the last images of Jack from his mind. John extended his hand to Ray.

"I'm with you, Ray."

—

Ten minutes later, Ray, Rydel, and John stood around the one fire pit now burning inside the camp. What was left of the members of Ray's Unit waited in the distance behind the three. John took a couple of steps closer to Rydel.

"Rydel, your sister has passed. She died the day we left to go after you. Will and I were the only ones who knew. I'm sorry."

Rydel lowered his head and tears fell from his face to the ground. He looked up and wiped his eyes and face with both hands.

"I was hoping she'd be able to hang on until I got back." Glaring at John, Rydel's face became angry, red. "Why did you lie about what my sister said to you, John? Why?"

"Because what she said sounded crazy at the time. But not now…not now, Rydel."

The three remained silent for almost a minute. Ray then slung his Smartround gun over his shoulder and turned to Rydel. "I have a plan of my own to save Him today, Rydel. But the guns and all the ammo you took from the lab—what was your plan?"

Rydel pointed at the mountains.

"From the mountains, I would follow the ones taking Jesus to be crucified and then take out everyone around Him with smartrounds. The ones I recruited with S-7 would go in, get Him, and bring Jesus up into the mountains."

Ray smiled. "Not bad, Rydel. However, you alone would never be able to take down that many targets—it's not as simple as taking a picture, like you're thinking. Put two of my best shooters up there, and they'll hit the targets you're talking about. Then what?"

"Then I would send Him away from here with another Placement chip that I was able to make on my own—a sort of one-way chip with no return."

Rydel reached under his cloak and took out a Placement chip, showing John and Ray. "Where I send Him, it will take Jesus years to travel back to Jerusalem. He'll be safe. Jerusalem will have moved on. His true message will have reached the masses before He returns."

Puzzled, John took a few steps closer to Rydel. "True message, Rydel? What do you mean?"

"When God came to my sister, He told her His Son was to prove that there is a place awaiting us after this life. Christ was meant to leave something behind in the time we are in now, proving just that."

"Leave something?" John asked, still not understanding.

"A reoccurring phenomenon that will happen each year, giving people hope. It's what Christians will worship instead of Christ on the cross."

John and Ray shared a look, taking in all Rydel had said for a few seconds, and then returned their attention back to Rydel as he continued.

"Evil and doubters there will always be; it won't change much in our time. People ignore miracles every day. But people will care more. A greater importance will be put on human life. As a result, a war will be avoided."

"A war?" John quickly asked.

"The one war is coming that will destroy the earth. The Other will kill us all. Christ's Second Coming has to be done in the time we are in now—He must continue and finish what He was sent here to do. Earth will burn if He doesn't—"

"Hey! Hey!"

The three turned to look where the shouting voice came from and could see Sal running in their direction. "Todd's been sent back," Sal said, breathing heavily.

Rydel put a hand on Ray's arm. "We need to go, Ray. It's time. They're going to lead Him to be crucified soon."

—

With their backs to the tents, Adriana, Ben, Sal, and Steve stood in front of Ray, waiting for him to speak.

"The three of us are going after Him," Ray said. "You four gather up all the smartrounds we have, and get to a high point in the mountains overlooking the city."

"What's our game plan, Ray?" Sal asked.

"Lightly take down the soldiers leading Christ to be crucified and anyone near Him. With the rounds we have, we can take down the whole damn city, if need be. After that, make a path for us to leave, take down anyone coming near Him, and take down anyone following us."

"Where do we take Him after that?" Adriana asked.

"We have a Placement chip that will take Him away from here," Ray said before pointing at Steve. "Steve, you're my first shooter." Ray looked over the faces of Adriana, Ben, and Sal. "Who's my second shooter?" Ray asked the three.

Ben and Sal glanced at each other. The two pointed at Adriana. "Adriana's next in shooting off multiple-target smartrounds after Steve. She blows the two of us away, Ray," Sal confessed.

"Okay." Ray gestured to Ben and Sal. "You two are the eyes tracking Jesus."

The four entered the tents behind them to gear up. Ray called out for Rydel, who was standing with John at the fire pit. Rydel trotted over to Ray, a concerned look on his face as he reached him.

"Need to ask you a question before we go."

"Of course, Ray."

"How is it that the Other was able to get to Jack and kill him, but not to me or you?"

Rydel waited before answering, searching for the words in his head, then shrugged his shoulders.

"I don't know, Ray. I guess it's just like it is in our time, or any time. If he could get to us all, he would. But he can't. He tried killing me but failed. Maybe the ones with faith are more difficult for him to get to. It could be as simple as that."

—

Alone, Ben prepped the area of a mountain they had all settled on to overlook the city of Jerusalem. Every way in and out of the city could be seen from this vantage point. Ben scanned the territory with his binoculars. He lowered them from his face and started to walk away.

A bloodied hind leg from a horse fell from above and landed in front of Ben. He stumbled backward, staring above at a narrow rock ledge. Standing on the ledge, a figure in a black shroud held the mouth of a small horse shut with his right hand. A large hole of torn flesh in the animal where its right leg should have been dripped blood over the rocky edge where the man stood. The man tilted his head, glaring down at Ben, and spoke to him in English.

"I want you to hear something, Benjamin."

The man removed his hand from the animal's mouth, and the horse let out a cry of terror and pain that sounded almost human. The man snapped the horse's mouth shut again in a flash of movement. The eyes of the horse and Ben connected, the horse eyeing Ben with a look of anguished pain and fear. With his free hand, the man in black pointed an elongated, pitch-black finger down at Ben.

"That will be the sort of sound your sister's boys will make as I rip out Isaac's eyes and burn off Shawn's face if you decide to interfere here. Just walk away, and I will not harm them. The only thing you are going to do in this time is wait to be taken back. I do believe we have an understanding. Am I correct, Benjamin?"

Ben stared up at the man in black, unable to talk or respond in any way. In all his times out in combat, he had never felt the fear that he felt right now—an uncontrollable fear taking over his body and mind.

The man in the black cloak lifted the horse by its face and snapped its neck with one quick motion. He threw the dead animal away, and it landed with a thud at Ben's feet. The black shape turned its back on Ben and was gone.

—

It was still early morning as Ray, Rydel, and John ran past scattered men and women on their way to the city of Jerusalem. Ahead of John and Rydel, Ray stopped so he could listen clearly to a transmission coming through his headset from Sal.

"Ray, they're leading Him through the city already. You need to make up ground!"

Ray yelled at John and Rydel trailing behind. "We need to pick it up—come on!"

The three made it to the city in less than two minutes and did not stop moving once they got there. With adrenaline on their side, they were able to keep running through the city until finally pausing as Ray got another call through his headset.

"Take the street on your left, Ray. The one with the old man sitting on the mat."

John and Rydel followed Ray down the narrow, twisting street with the old man leaning against a cracked wall of stone, sitting on a brown mat. Ray ran past the man, followed by Rydel and then John. As John passed, the old man spoke to him in English.

"If you do this, John, you will kill not thousands but millions in your time. The ones you took an oath to protect. You will kill them all."

John came to an abrupt stop, turned, and walked back toward the old man. "No. I don't believe anything you say. Nothing. Touching you, I felt the evil. I still do. I now believe in Him because of you."

The old man rose from the mat, lifting himself with the agility of a young man, and was in front of John so fast the colonel caught just a blurry glimpse of the man moving.

"If you enter into this, I will have a crowd of God-loving men and women rip off each one of your limbs and eat them in front of you before you die."

"John—come on!"

John turned away from the old man, looking over his shoulder at Ray and Rydel ahead on the twisting street. A handful of women stood on the side of the street—all looking baffled by Ray's ranting in a foreign tongue.

Ray waved for John to hurry. "Let's go, John, let's go!"

John turned to face the old man again, but the man was gone. He whispered toward the spot where the old man had stood. "Fuck you. We're saving Him."

He quickly met up with Ray and Rydel, and the three continued to run, making their way through the city.

They got a brief look ahead at Jesus being led through the city streets on His way to be crucified.

"Okay, we need to get to high ground now," Ray said.

Led by Ray, they raced through a narrow passage out of the city and to the top of a small hill with a view over the city walls. From there, they could see a twisting path leading toward a nearby hill with two suffering men nailed to crosses on the ground. A small gathering of soldiers looked down at the two men, boredom etched on their faces.

Ray glanced over his shoulder at John and Rydel. "This is it. This is our spot. When I give the order, and the people start falling to the ground, we'll go in and get Him before He even gets near that hill they're leading Him to."

Ray lifted his binoculars to his eyes and tracked Jesus being led through the narrow streets of Jerusalem.

—

With His body bent in half under the weight of the crossbeam He was dragging, Jesus crept toward His fated path to be crucified, His crown of thorns dripping blood onto His face and body. With each step He took, His body lowered, and then He finally fell, the crossbeam pinning Him facedown on the ground. Two soldiers behind Jesus reached down, one picking Him up, the other lifting the crossbeam off the ground. The two placed the crossbeam on Jesus's back and screamed at Him to continue walking, and then both men spit in Christ's face.

—

Having seen enough, Ray lowered his binoculars and gave the order to the shooters through his headset.

"Take them down—all of them."

"Ray, the woman pointing up here!" Rydel yelled.

Ray looked through his binoculars to see a woman in a black shawl pointing up at them from inside the city with two Roman soldiers by her side. The two soldiers started to run as Ray spoke into his headset once more.

"And take down the soldiers coming toward us."

The three ran toward the city.

—

At a new vantage point over Jerusalem that Ben suddenly decided was better than the one he had prepped earlier, Adriana stood by Steve's side—the two aiming their Smartround rifles below. Behind them, Sal listened to Ray's orders through his headset while moving closer to Adriana and Steve. "Now, guys. And Ray has two unfriendlies coming his way."

The compact screen slid out from the side of Steve's gun. On the screen, he could make out the two Roman soldiers heading toward Ray's location on the hill. The screen then took a snapshot of the two.

"Got 'em," Steve calmly said.

He tapped a side button on the gun, and a mini keyboard slid out from the other side of the Smartround rifle. On the small keyboard, Steve typed with fluid fingers over the small keys, entering the dosage into the rounds, and the keyboard slid back inside the gun. He pointed his Smartround gun up in the air and fired the weapon. The rounds from the gun shot straight up and then headed toward their targets below.

—

Head bent forward, limping slowly, Jesus passed sad-eyed men and women all crammed together on either side of the narrow stone street that eventually began to widen. Jesus lifted His head slightly to see the young follower John pulling back the hood of his cloak—the young man mixed in with the rest of the crowd. The eyes of the two men met, and John pushed the people in front of him out of the way so he could reach Jesus. He made it through the crowd only to be held back by three Roman soldiers, forcing him down onto the stone street. With his mouth bleeding, John turned his head to face Jesus.

Jesus stared down at him and shook His head at John, silently telling him not to interfere. John ignored the warning, broke free from the guards, got to his feet, and reached out desperately for Jesus. He then suddenly fell to the ground, unconscious, along with the soldiers trying to detain him.

Jesus slowly turned His head over the crossbeam He carried. Behind Him, the men and women lining the path to His crucifixion—and the soldiers leading Him to the cross—began to fall to the ground.

—

On the mountain overlooking the city, Steve calmly took down his targets below with Adriana by his side to clean up anything he missed. But Steve did not miss. Every multiple human target he entered into his Smartround gun—with the aid of its snapshot device—either fell on their sides or landed facedown on the street that Jesus walked. Steve then took a step back, snapped a picture of approaching soldiers, and pointed his gun in the air, shooting off the programmed rounds to take out the soldiers. The burst of pebble-sized rounds arching in the air looked much like an assault of arrows in medieval times, going up and then streaming down to find their targets.

Steve felt the presence of the Other and caught movement from the corner of his eye. He dropped his Smartround gun and instinctively reached for his Glock 19, pointing it toward a ledge above him. The black-cloaked man stood on the narrow strip of stone, staring down at Steve. Steve was only able to see the man's unnerving blue eyes glaring down at him from under the hooded cloak. Then the fear set in as he yelled out to the man without the use of his translator, sounding like a scared child.

"Come down from there!"

"No," the cloaked man flatly said in English.

Adriana heard Steve's raised voice and broke her attention away from her gun's slide-out-screen view of the targets below.

"Steve—what is it?"

Steve turned to Adriana with his mouth open—about to speak—and then disappeared in a swirling mist of the dirt he'd been standing on.

—

The only one left standing on the street was Christ.

From around the corner, John, Ray, and Rydel ran toward Jesus—the crossbeam He was forced to carry still digging into His shoulder. The three stepped over the sedated men, women, scattered children, and soldiers to get to Jesus. Ray grabbed hold of the crossbeam with two hands and heaved it away in a vertical bench-press motion. Behind Ray, Rydel noticed the people and soldiers around them.

"Ray—they're moving!"

Holding Jesus upright, Ray watched as a black mist fell over the people and soldiers on the ground—the mist lifting them up to their feet. With their eyes still closed, they moved awkwardly, trying to fight off the drug inside them, all slowly walking toward Jesus.

"Let's go!" Ray screamed at John and Rydel.

The three turned away from the ones rising around them and faced a Roman soldier standing an inch over seven feet tall. The soldier, muscular to the point of being freakish, wore Roman body armor and a steel faceplate with slits at the eyes.

Ray was unable to reach for his gun while holding up Jesus. Not taking the time to properly program the rounds to target the vulnerable areas on the man's body, John stepped forward and fired repeated smartrounds at the soldier that deflected off the huge man's armor.

"Use your sidearm! Kill him, John!" Ray screamed.

Rydel found a sword on the ground, picked up the heavy weapon, and swiped it at the Roman soldier's legs. The sword glanced off the soldier's protective greaves with a clanging sound and fell out of Rydel's hands.

The Roman soldier picked up the sword and stabbed Rydel in the chest, dropping Rydel to his knees. The sword came out of Rydel's back and pierced through his right calf into a crevice in the stone road, leaving him skewered. The top half of Rydel's body remained upright with his back slightly arched and his arms spread out at his sides, as if waiting to embrace someone. Rydel's lifeless eyes stared up at the heavens—his body displayed on the sword like some kind of offering to the gods.

The old woman in black who had pointed out the three on the hill slipped through the blind, slow-moving crowd. She reached the massive soldier and touched his shoulder. The large man crumbled to the ground. The woman then turned her head, staring at John and Ray with hateful, luminous blue eyes.

—

Seeing Steve disappear next to her, Adriana shook it off. She glanced down at the slide-out screen on her gun and could see that the soldiers, and the people who had lined the streets, were now up and walking. Adriana entered a grouping of targets into her gun and shot the smartrounds into the air. She turned her head toward Ben, who looked fucking out of it.

"Pick up Steve's gun and get into the fight!"

Ben stared at Steve's Smartround gun on the ground.

"Help me, Ben!"

"I can't, Adriana. The Other has too much on me. I—"

Ben disappeared, his Placement chip sending him back to the time he came from.

Adriana frantically entered targets into her Smartround gun, stepped back, and fired the rounds into the air. Behind Adriana, Sal looked through his binoculars, scanning the city below. "Shit! They're all back on their feet?"

Adriana set the next wave of rounds into her gun as Sal walked closer to her, still looking through his binoculars at the city below. Adriana stepped back to fire the rounds into the air and bumped into Sal.

"Fuck out of my way, Sal!"

Sal stepped back—his point of view still homed in on the reawakened crowd and soldiers. He then let the binoculars fall to the ground and screamed at Adriana.

"Save Him—!"

Sal's body and voice vanished. Out of the corner of her eye, Adriana caught Sal being sent back. She fired her rounds in the air. All targets hit, she started to acquire more with her Smartround gun.

Behind her, a man laughed.

An eight-foot-tall figure took two ground-shaking steps toward Adriana as she readied her Smartround gun. The figure leaned his head over Adriana's shoulder, laughing at her from under the black hood of his cloak.

Adriana disappeared in a swirl of dirt and dust.

—

The woman in black laughed at John and Ray. John took a step toward the woman and vanished, gone in a whirlwind of dust. Ray placed Jesus on the ground and ran over to Rydel's body, then reached into a pocket under Rydel's cloak. He ran back to Jesus, tipped back the head of Christ so he could feed Him Rydel's one-way chip, but the chip fell out of his hand. Ray eased Jesus's head back to the ground, spun left, then right, and found the chip on the ground. He reached for it and disappeared.

The old woman stopped laughing, closed her eyes, and fell down face first, crushing her nose.

Lucifer, wearing his long, black, hooded cloak, walked around those fallen on the ground and the slow-walking crowd of men, women, and soldiers now plodding aimlessly. He stood over Christ. The Devil's hooded head tilted toward the black chip on the ground, and he crushed it with his foot. Jesus stood up, and His blood-soaked hair parted away from His face. With one eye swollen shut, He watched Lucifer.

Lucifer then spoke to Jesus.

"I will never let them save you in this time. You will never finish what you were sent here to do."

Lucifer looked down at the crossbeam on the ground. He picked it up effortlessly with one hand, holding it in his palm like an offering. He folded back the hood of his cloak with his free hand, revealing his true face. No alabaster or jet-black skin, but a man in his forties with a fair complexion and simple, smooth features—the way he appeared before his descent.

Except for his eyes. The preternatural glowing blue eyes of the Beast stared at Jesus with pure hate.

Careful not to touch Christ, Lucifer placed the crossbeam back across Jesus's shoulders. He leaned his head closer, staring at Jesus curiously for a moment, and then turned his back on Christ. He raised his arm in the air, and another black mist fell over the crowd and soldiers.

Alone, Jesus stood with the crossbeam on His back and waited for what was to come, as all around him returned to their normal state of mind and being. The people no longer felt the effects of the smartrounds, the result of Lucifer's second surge of black mist seeping into each man, woman, and child.

As if nothing had happened, the Roman soldiers pushed Jesus forward. And the ones in the crowd who had gathered to watch the death of the blasphemous man started cheering once more.

Jesus looked to His right and could see Lucifer standing among the cheering people, the Devil appearing as just one more in the crowd, smiling at Jesus with his burning blue eyes from under the hood of his cloak.

# Home

The Placement chips inside John, Ray, and what remained of Ray's Unit sent them back to a room inside the lab. With the interior lights off, the room's floor-to-ceiling window let in a glow from outside lampposts. All sat on the floor, leaning against the surrounding walls at opposite sides of the room, soil by their feet. The group shared the same distant look in their eyes and forlorn faces. Ray stood and began checking on the members of his Unit.

"You okay there, Sal?"

Sal nodded at Ray. Ray approached Steve and Adriana, both looking beyond defeated.

"Adriana, Steve…you guys all right?"

The two continued staring into nowhere but slightly nodded. A few feet away, Ben held his head in his hands where he sat.

"Ben, how you doing?"

Ben lifted his head.

"I'm okay, Ray," Ben said, lying.

Ray glanced over to where John had been sitting, and his brother-in-law was gone. Ray scanned the room, but John was nowhere to be seen.

—

John ran down a white hallway, opening lab doors to his left and right, finding no one. The lab seemed to be deserted. He ran down another hallway that led to the Overlook. He caught his breath in front of the door and then slammed it open. A young lab tech and two large security guards sat around a monitoring screen. The three, having been left behind, looked over their shoulders at John.

"Where is everybody—what happened?" John asked in a voice that was both desperate and demanding.

The young tech stood up and walked over to John. "Evacuated because of a storm that was heading this way. But it stayed out to sea, passing us now. It never really came close. It's good to see you home safe, sir."

## A Meeting with the General

### *Three Weeks Later*

John and Will sat beside each other at a long mahogany table inside a spacious, sunlit conference room, the light streaming in from windows to their left. Across from the two, four high-ranking military men sat with their hands clasped together, leaning back in their chairs. General Dowling sat between the four men. The general leaned forward in his chair, his eyes on John.

"Three weeks of questioning Catlin's Unit has all but confirmed your initial report, Colonel." The general rubbed the stubble on his face. His eyes glanced back and forth from John to Will a couple of times; then he continued speaking.

"Rydel's project to save soldiers in the field had my support from the get-go. However, after it led to Placement, I've had nothing but sleepless nights because of what happened in Japan. And now this, where—"

Will abruptly stood up from his seat. "Sir, this is a project that cannot be abandoned. Colonel Adams's last time out proves it is safe. It's been weeks, and nothing has happened—"

"Who the hell told you to speak freely?" General Dowling barked at Will. He pointed at Will to sit back down, and Will quickly sat his ass back down.

The general stared at Will for a few seconds. He shifted his glaring eyes away from Will and stared at the window letting in the sun, the slanted sunlight reaching across the floor. The general looked back at Will.

"But you are right, Will. Rydel's last project cannot be abandoned. But it can be for now. From what I understand, he destroyed most of his notes on Placement's progression, so most of his work died with him. And the last two Placement chips have somehow gone missing, which no one can explain."

"That's correct, sir," Will said, and he let out a small sigh of frustration.

"All right, then. Will, you're staying at the lab, watching over the other scientists that were involved with Placement. Watch them close. You will get your orders when to start up again on Rydel's final project. Now leave the room, please."

Will stood up from his chair, gave a quick look over at John, and exited the room without looking back. General Dowling leaned forward in his chair.

"Some fucking mess, John."

"Yes, sir."

"Placement is on the back burner for now—you're needed elsewhere."

—

John walked out of the conference room to find Will waiting outside. "Something to say, Will?"

"Strange. I happen to conveniently not be at the lab, and the last two Placement chips go missing…with you being the only one with access to the chips."

John moved a little closer, and Will recoiled, keeping his distance from John. "You jumped ship like a dickless rat and left Genesis unsupervised. That's the reason the chips are now missing. And Will…if you ever insinuate something like you just did to me ever again, there will be only one of us working on Placement."

Will looked away from John, stood where he was for a few seconds, and then walked away. He reached a door with a red-lit *EXIT* sign just above it and turned back to John. "Having friends like General Dowling, I guess you're right. However, positions of power change all the time, Colonel Adams."

Will opened the door and was gone, his hurried steps making rapid thuds down the staircase, echoing away.

## Backyard Party

Three days later, John and Ray, each with a beer in their hand, stood over a fire pit in Ray's backyard. Above the two on the deck to Ray's house, Kate and gathered friends spoke and laughed loudly around candlelit tables, enjoying the crisp autumn night. John looked up at the gathering on the deck and then pointed toward the other side of the fire pit so they could face the others above while they spoke. The two sat down in wicker chairs facing the deck, making sure all from the party were together in one spot.

"After all the contact we made with the people in the past, no disaster followed us home," Ray quietly said.

"Rydel was right, Ray."

"The two chips left over?"

John shrugged his shoulders. "Gone. No surveillance of a break-in. They're just gone."

"I have to be in Afghanistan the day after tomorrow," Ray said after a moment.

"I know. I'm flying there tonight."

John reached out to Ray, and the two shook hands. An odd expression crossed over Ray's face as the two clasped hands. John leaned in closer, whispering to Ray.

"Coming into contact with the Other made me believe, Ray. Just wanted you to know that. I'll see you in Afghanistan, my brother."

John stood up and walked toward the backyard gate. The area underlit, Ray could only hear the sound of the gate opening and closing without actually seeing John leave. After a moment by the fire alone, Ray joined the others on the deck and had half-conversations with guests from the party, most picking up that Ray was distant, looking a little tired.

With the party winding down, and after saying his good-byes, Ray headed back to the fire pit and waited for Kate to join him.

Kate sat down in the wicker chair next to Ray, unhooked her bra under her T-shirt, and leaned in close, her brown eyes looking up at Ray affectionately, lovingly. "Your wife would like to take advantage of you upstairs, if you're up for it. How many beers did you and John take down out here talking alone?"

"One."

"Mmm…"

"I noticed you weren't drinking tonight either."

"No, not tonight."

"I love you, Kate. And I know I've told you I can't talk about the missions that I go out on. But my next mission is different. I'm going back to—"

"Don't! Don't you dare tell me! Never! Each time out you've never talked about anything with me, and you've always come back safe. We're gonna keep it that way. Okay?"

Ray started to speak but then stopped and nodded. Maybe she's right, he thought.

"Come to bed with me, Ray. Oh…do I have a surprise for you."

—

Twenty-three hours later, Ray sat in the back of a civilian Humvee driven by a uniformed soldier, maybe twenty-four or twenty-six years old. Ray turned his head and glanced out the window beside him at a black lake lit by a full moon. He opened his hand and looked down at one of the last two Placement chips that had disappeared from the lab, handed to him by John at the backyard party. The soldier driving the Humvee looked in the rearview mirror at Ray.

"Going back to the Middle East, sir?"

Ray met the eyes of the soldier staring back at him in the rearview mirror and answered the young man honestly.

"Yes, I am."

**THE END**

# Connect with William M. Hayes

I really appreciate you reading my book and I hope you enjoyed it!

Here are my social media coordinates. please reach out :)

Facebook: http://bit.ly/WMHayes
Twitter: http://bit.ly/2PcKoZn
Amazon Author Page: https://www.amazon.com/William-M-Hayes/e/B01MDLMS0A
My Website: https://www.williammhayes.com

If you have just a moment to spare, please consider leaving a quick review on Amazon and Goodreads. Indie Authors rely on reviews to be discovered by new readers.

Printed in the USA
CPSIA information can be obtained
at www.ICGtesting.com
CBHW071139260624
10690CB00010B/639

9 781087 986357

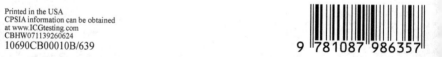